T0023157

Praise for *In a Veil of Mist*

"A moving portrait of a place and [...] brilliant novel." ANTONIA SENIOR, BOOK OF THE MONTH, *Times*

"Shows yet again how a good novel is capable of making you think and feel at the same time ... a rich and sympathetic portrayal of island life in all its diversity ... timely and compelling ... a novel to savour." ALLAN MASSIE, *Scotsman*

"Set in [Murray's] native Lewis as firmly as the stones at Callanish ... it is so credibly drawn that the book is almost a ticket to the island ... it seems an even more impressive achievement than ever." DAVID ROBINSON, *Books from Scotland*

"Human and relatable ... beautifully depicting life in the Outer Hebrides. A gripping, intelligent and often humorous read." *Scottish Field*

"A well-written and well-crafted novel from an author at the height of his powers." ERIC MACINTYRE, *Oban Times*

"A wonderfully evocative book ... brought to the page ... with consummate skill ... We'd strongly recommend [it to] anyone looking for really strong and memorable fiction about Scotland ... outstanding." *Undiscovered Scotland*

Praise for *As the Women Lay Dreaming*

WINNER: PAUL TORDAY MEMORIAL PRIZE 2020

SHORTLISTED: AUTHOR'S CLUB BEST FIRST NOVEL AWARD 2019 *and* HERALD SCOTTISH CULTURE LITERATURE AWARD 2019

LONGLISTED: HIGHLAND BOOK PRIZE 2018 *and* HISTORICAL WRITERS' ASSOCATION DEBUT CROWN 2019

WALTER SCOTT PRIZE "ACADEMY RECOMMENDS" LISTED

"A powerful novel ... A poignant exploration of love, loss and survivor's guilt." NICK RENNISON, *Sunday Times*

"A book that's big with beauty, poetry, and heart ... A wonderful achievement, a brilliant blend of fact and fiction, full of memorable images and singing lines of prose." SARAH WATERS

The Call of the Cormorant

An unreliable biography of
Karl Kjerúlf Einarsson (1897–1972),
also known as
the Count of St Kilda,
Emperor Cormorant XII of Atlantis,
Dunganon, Professor Valentinus,
Lord of Hekla

Donald S Murray

Saraband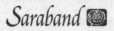

Published by Saraband,
3 Clairmont Gardens
Glasgow, G3 7LW
www.saraband.net

ISBN: 9781913393540

Printed and bound in Great Britain by Clays Ltd, Elcograf S.p.A.

1 3 5 7 9 10 8 6 4 2

Supported by
The National Lottery®
through Creative Scotland

*A note on the use of Gaelic: Some traditional song lyrics and
sayings are written with spellings that may have been superseded by today's
conventions. The author has made spelling choices to balance authenticity
to the period with current standard Gaelic.*

*This is a work of fiction, even though it is based on a true incident in history.
All characters and events are a result of the author's imagination except where
mentioned in the author's note at the end of the text.*

Maps on the following pages are derived from d-maps.com

To Maggie with love
To Craig with gratitude
To Norrie MacLennan, for his inspiration

Map of the Faroe Islands

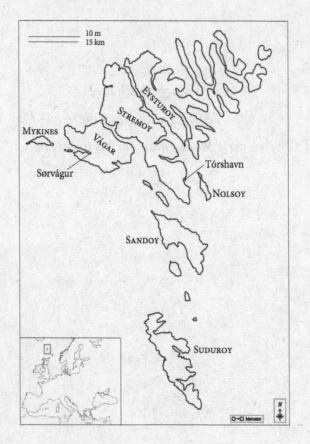

Map of Northern Scotland

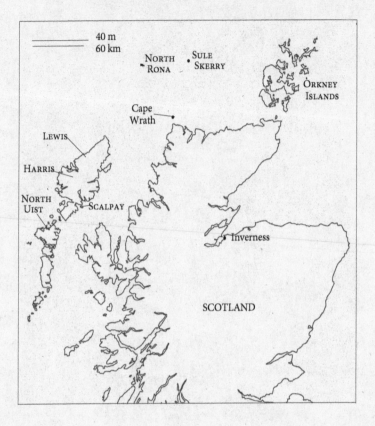

40 m
60 km

NORTH
RONA

SULE
SKERRY

ORKNEY
ISLANDS

Cape
Wrath

LEWIS

HARRIS

NORTH
UIST

SCALPAY

Inverness

SCOTLAND

Islanders on the Mainland

We mimicked swans each time we stepped on land,
flurrying wings, scurrying on the surface
as if we were unsure how to float or stand

on this new ground where – it seemed – all poise
and grace deserted us. For some time
we were muted, aware both heart and voice

did not belong in this new landscape
until we learned once more to flex our wings
and lift off to imitate the sweep

we saw in others, become part of the wedge
cutting cloud while taking flight,
no longer simple migrants that soared in from the edge

but part of this environment, now a place
where we might one day choose to settle and reside.

Prelude

Iain MacCusbic

A storm was coming.

We could see the clouds darkening over the unfamiliar shores of North Rona a short distance away, layer upon layer stacking up from the horizon they had long been stored behind, becoming dense and impenetrable, the wind, too, chilling. I shivered, regretting the decision that had taken us this far north. There had been too few fish to be caught in the narrow waters of the Minch over the last while, between the northern end of Skye and Harris. We knew this only too well. We had cast our lines there for weeks, only to lift them empty. It was this that had brought us this far away from our homes in Scalpay. Desperation. Need. Hunger.

A storm was coming.

When it arrived, it was likely to be at its most intense in the waters where we were now. Under the ocean's surface, a narrow ridge of rock stretches from Ness, at the top of Lewis, all the way to North Rona. There is a shallowness of water here, a space into which the Atlantic tumbles whenever sky and sea churn, as they seemed likely to do at that moment. When I saw the signs, the gathering of clouds, the increasing spit and fury of the wind, I turned to my fellow crewman Norman Macleod.

'Shall we head for Rona? Tie up there?'

'I don't think we need to. It'll quickly blow over.'

'What about Skigersta or Cape Wrath?' I suggested, mentioning

1

places at the northern edge of Lewis and Sutherland. There are harbours in those locations, places where we could tie up safely.

'I don't think so, Iain. It would be crazy to come all this way just to turn around again, simply for the sake of a squall. Besides, those places aren't exactly the most sheltered of harbours. As risky in their own way as being out here. Let's sit it out.'

I nodded reluctantly. There was truth in what Norman was saying. I had heard of boats going down near the Kyle of Durness or Loch Eriboll, one from Scalpay sinking near Tolsta Head. Those parts were almost as dangerous as here. Yet, despite his argument, this place was probably the riskiest of all. On a stormy day, the depths of the Atlantic could come storming like an army over that stony border between sea and land. We should really turn the boat round and head for Rona, tie up there for a day or two to allow the ocean to become still and peaceful again. I had heard accounts of boats from these parts – fishing, say, off Sule Stack and Sule Skerry – being driven towards Norway or the Faroe Islands, ending up wrecked on the coast of Europe. But I knew better than to argue with Norman about that. When the man had made up his mind, no surge of the sea could stir or shift him.

'We'll ride it out,' I heard him mutter. 'It won't be long passing.' And then, almost as an afterthought, 'Take the sail down. We don't want things to be too easy for the storm.'

It was just after that when the storm began – wind and wave combining to bludgeon the deck, washing over it with a thunderous weight of water. I gripped the side of the boat tightly, aware that the force of the sea threatened to sweep me away from my place. The thought began to occur to me that I might never see Scalpay again, the placenames of the island – Ceann a'Bhaigh, Rubha Glas, Meall Chailbost – coming from my lips like a prayer. I could see some of the sights too, streaming through my head with the suddenness of the lash of surf that crested each swell. The cattle. Sheep. Heather. Sand. As soon as they came to me, I had the thought that they were a presentiment of death, a sign that I wasn't going to come across those places anymore. I stiffened and tried to chase the thought from his head. There was no need to think like that.

No need to think like that when the boat was breached, water lapping across the deck. No need to think like that even when I saw Norman toppling into the sea a short time later. No need to think like that even when the mast was broken, shattered in half by the waves. No need to think that even when the storm continued for hours, over days and nights, till the moment I looked up to see that our vessel was a short distance away from another group of islands; when I became aware, too, that there was another boat making its way towards us from there; when I was conscious, too, that only one of the others who had gone out fishing from Scalpay a few days before with me was still on board our boat, still showing signs of life.

Karl's Early Years
in the Faroe Islands

1897–1911

Karl

IN MY MEMORY, Tórshavn was often a bitter, damp place. Even its sun was a cold star, barely gleaming through cloud, its rays carrying as much chill as heat in their glimmer. It was worse than ever that day – the morning my father took out two oilskin coats and handed one to me, heading out the door of the store and leaving Mother in charge of its stock and shelves. This was something he rarely did.

The entire place – from the dead cat in the window, cradling a violin between its paws, to the long rambling conversations that took place on either side of the counter – bore the marks of his personality. He was the one in charge of the whole enterprise, the brisk, buoyant individual with waves of thick grey hair, a long and pointed nose, who swayed from side to side like the sea. He took control of everything, even small tasks like buttoning up my oilskin coat before he headed out the door, for all that I was now in my early teens and well able to do it myself.

'There's a boat from the Hebrides arrived,' he declared. 'We must go and see it, Karl. We will not get the chance of these things very often.'

All the way down to the pier, going past the wooden houses with their turf roofs which shadowed the twisting, narrow road, my father – Magnus – was talking. He was unable to walk on the verge in his excitement, instead half-running down the centre of the road. It was a state in which I had occasionally seen him before. I'd witnessed it first when we left our old home in Seyðisfjörður, on the east coast of Iceland, a few years back. We had looked back at that settlement in its fjord – surrounded by mountains, the white trails of waterfalls cascading down from the summits of peaks and cliffs – while my father babbled endlessly about the opportunities that were going to be available on these islands to the east.

'There's far more fishing boats in the Faroe Islands than there used to be in my father's day,' he'd declared. 'More whaling too. They plan to build a new modern harbour for all the boats that are coming their way. In just a few years. Not that long. And that means there will be chances that can be taken. More money and wealth from the fishermen visiting the place from Denmark, Holland, England. The visitors will need to buy supplies for their boats. More people will settle in the town. There will be jobs. Just you wait and see.'

And all the time I was hearing this, I was aware of my mother Kristjana's eyebrows rising like question marks, a look of cold impatience shivering across her face. ('The only thing they will ever produce in this place,' she said once, 'is mist in the summer and wind in winter.') She had heard him and his ideas often enough before. Sometimes she managed to talk him out of most of them – such as a move to Gimli in Manitoba, where so many Icelanders settled at that time, signing up on a whaling ship that was bound for South Georgia in the winter months. All that had come and gone in the last few years, his enthusiasm fading as it was worn down and dissipated by her arguments.

'You're doing what you always do,' she might say. 'Dabbling in dreams.' She would sigh for a moment before speaking again. 'There are days when I'm pleased I was never taught to read or write very well. It has such a bad effect on certain people.'

Yet she could not always persuade him. It was not long after the suggestion of a move to the Faroes was raised that, with money inherited from her father, we purchased the old Royal Store in Havn – an old, ochre-red building which had stood since the days of the Danish monopoly, a dung heap not far from its front door. 'It sums up all there is to say about our colonial masters,' Árni, our neighbour, used to say. 'Dumping on us from afar.' He'd spit as if cleansing all thought or mention of Denmark from his mouth. 'For far too long, we've been under their heel. Time to move away from them.'

In my eyes, however, the dung heap had its attractions, as a location often visited by a multitude of birds. There were countless wrens and starlings, a sparrow or blackbird or two picking their way through all the dirt and debris that lay there, seeking any insects or worms to be found in its midst. There were the gulls, too, that called and screeched over the harbour, trying to scavenge from the boats that were tied up there.

'*Keow! Keow! Ka! Ka! Ka!*'

I would often imitate them as they pecked at the store window, their beaks rattling and scraping against the dirt-smeared glass as they stared at the cat on show there. It may not have been the only thing that caught their attention. Perhaps, too, they were examining the copy of Athanasius Kircher's map of Atlantis that was also on display. Its strange peaks cast their shadow on some unknown part of the Atlantic Ocean like the islet of Tindhólmur – not far from Sørvágsfjørður – with its five stone summits looming over the lash of waves. 'Here be demons,' I had heard one of the local fishermen say as he pointed towards the sketch, unsure whether the man was talking about the lost inhabitants of Atlantis or the inner workings of my father's head. I had the feeling that it might be true of both.

Rain drummed my coat as we made our way down to the harbour. I splashed through the puddles that had formed in the gravel road. There had been storms over the last few days, gusting through the township, rattling doors and windows, forcing the entire family – my father and mother, my eldest sisters Christianna and Bedda – to cower round the household stove. It was this south-westerly gale that had brought the vessel from the Hebrides, blown from around the edge of the island of North Rona, where it had been fishing towards Vágar, on the west side of our islands. It was a short distance from there that the crew of one of the Faroese fishing boats had spotted it. A rope was hurled. Someone on board caught and lashed it to the vessel, that knot enabling the wrecked boat to be tugged through waves, the haze of spume and storm. It was hauled towards Havn with the gleam of Skansin lighthouse standing on the remnants of the old fort, the low island of Nólsoy offering its harbour some shelter from the wind. When they arrived there, my father told me, the boat was wrecked, its mast and cabin smashed by the thunderous uproar of the sea. Two of the men on board had apparently been killed, washed overboard at some point in their voyage.

'There was a boat driven here from Orkneyjar a number of years ago. It had been fishing near a place called Sule Skerry, off the coast of Scotland. Only one of the crew survived. Even his body was badly smashed by the time he arrived here. This one's from farther west. Stornoway, perhaps, or Barra. Skye. Perhaps even St Kilda.' He chuckled to himself. 'I'd really like to see some of these people. All from the ocean's edge. The frontier of Atlantis. All hard rock and moorland, just like here.'

I nodded. I had heard my father speak before about these mysterious islands, a little south of the Faroes. He had spoken about how the people there, and those in places like Orkneyjar and Hjaltland, must have lives that resembled our own. Forced to have their dreams embedded in firm foundations to keep them upright. The smack of salt upon their lips. Dining on fish, mutton, seabirds, a whale or seal washed on its shores or trapped by boats near its cliffs. The narrowness of years trapped within the tight horizons of an island.

Most of this I could understand. I knew I sometimes felt cramped in Tórshavn, looking forward to my own escape, the school in Denmark I would attend when I was fifteen in a few years' time. I would visit the streets of Copenhagen, see the royal palaces in Amalienborg and Fredenborg, wander around the museums, libraries and art galleries, even view the different birds found there, so different from the guillemots, gulls and fulmars in these parts. I would be able to stretch my wings like the swans found in Denmark, not shaking off seawater like the shags and occasional cormorant found standing on rocks on the shoreline here. In the meantime, though, I had to settle for Tórshavn, the place we knew as Havn, in just the same way as our counterparts in those islands further south had to accept the limits of where they lived.

'I hope they come from St Kilda, Karl,' I heard my father repeat. 'I know it's unlikely, but I truly hope they do.'

Again, I nodded. I had known my father long enough to know that was what I had to do, listen to his monologues and give the odd reaction. A nod. A smile, perhaps. A frown. This was especially the case when he started to talk about one of his favourite subjects – St Kilda and its connection to the lost world of Atlantis.

After reading a book on the subject by an American writer called Ignatius Donnelly, he was convinced that St Kilda's cliffs had once marked the edge of Atlantis, the slopes below it on which a handful of houses stood the only remnants of that continent lost and destroyed many centuries before. I had drawn this a few times: seagulls skirling around ruined temples; oystercatchers pecking short-cropped grass in the grounds that circled palaces beside a stretch of ocean; rocks bearing the imprints of the feet of giants; the sparkle of stars on still winter nights, like roofs of ancient cathedrals.

'Very good! Very, very good!' my father had said as he looked at my drawings. 'You've a rare talent, Karl! A rare talent!'

I glowed at that time, conscious that receiving a compliment from my father was a rare event. My two sisters and I were more accustomed to his scorn than praise. However, I shook the memory from my head, aware only of his excitement as we stepped down to the pier. His mood seemed unaffected by the wreckage we saw. The broken boat was there, its mast lying smashed and cracked on a deck that had been hammered by the force and impact of the waves. I could see two men sitting on the steps that led down to their vessel, draped in the fleeces of sheep, oilskin coats which someone had provided for them. Others were hunched down next to them, faces I could recognise from Tórshavn. One was a local preacher, Pastor Anders; the other, a doctor from the town. Each was whispering to the two fishermen whose vessel was wrecked, whose friends were drowned, who faced the prospect of sailing back to the Hebrides for hundreds of miles in these hostile waters. When the fishermen spoke, the preacher and the doctor provided translations for most of what they said, reassuring them too with their own words. They found out their names: Donald MacSween and John MacCusbic – the last fact making my father dance up and down on the pierhead. ('He's probably a descendant of Uspak Hákon, one of the men who's mentioned in the Sagas. Imagine that!' he declared in a loud whisper. 'Imagine the chances of that!') The preacher and doctor ignored him, perhaps aware that there were times my father impersonated their behaviour and mannerisms. Instead, they continued with the practicalities that affected the well-being of the two men.

'We will make sure you will get home. We will make sure that will happen.'

'Our home near Harris. Little island called Scalpay,' MacCusbic – the sturdier of the two with broad shoulders and thick dark curly hair – said slowly in English, stabbing out each word with his finger. 'Long, long way away.'

'Don't worry. We will get you home. It may take some time, but we will manage.'

'Thank you. I hope so.'

And then – much to my embarrassment – there was my father bustling between them, rain dripping from the hood of his coat as he rushed in their direction.

'You know that Grímur Kamban, the one who was the first Norse settler of Faroe, may have come from your part of the world, the Outer Hebrides?'

'No.'

'They say part of his surname – "Kam" – may have come from Gaelic. The crooked one?'

'It might be … It sounds about right.'

'Good. Good. Good. And what about St Kilda?' my father stammered. 'You know St Kilda? The edge of Atlantis?'

The smaller, fair-haired fisherman nodded. Or he might just have trembled. He was shaking so much with cold and damp that it was hard to tell.

'Great! Great! Great!' my father declared. 'You will have to come up to our house in the next few days. You will have to come there!'

The two of them looked at one another, almost as shaken by the scale of his welcome as they had been by some of the waves they had encountered on their journey.

'You will have to come!' he repeated once again.

Eventually there was a nod. It did not necessarily come from understanding. It may only have been caused by the notion of bringing this whole bewildering conversation to an end.

*

They were in our home a day or two later. Father had invited MacCusbic and MacSween, visiting their lodgings and asking the two Hebrideans again and again until he had made sure they could not refuse.

'My wife and daughter Christianna are wonderful cooks.'

'I am sure you will enjoy a meal at our home.'

'My daughter Christianna speaks good English. She is also a very beautiful young lady. Very beautiful indeed.'

It all made me see my older sister in a new and different way. Her dark brown hair spilling down her shoulders. The shock of blue eyes. The dimples on her cheeks. I had never pictured her as beautiful before. Yet I saw her in a new and brilliant light that day. All dressed up, her eyes sparkling, the two young Hebridean fishermen watching her every movement as she made her way around the kitchen, bringing food to the table in order that they all could eat. She served out the mutton, kale and potatoes we had prepared for the occasion, talking to them all the time in the English she had learned from the local pastor, looking perplexed as the two young men sometimes failed to understand what she was saying.

'Perhaps they're tired,' my father explained. 'They've had an awful journey.'

'Perhaps,' she said, nodding. 'Perhaps, though, my English isn't good enough. It might be my accent that's confusing them.'

'Perhaps their first language is not English.'

'What other tongue might they have?'

'Gaelic. It's the language that mixed with the old Atlantis tongue they spoke on St Kilda.'

'Do you know any words, Father?'

'Perhaps. There's a few of them in Faroese.'

It was then my father began what was – even by his standards – one of his most extraordinary performances, lowering his head and pretending to have a set of horns, that long nose which adorned his face seeming to stretch even farther. He made a loud, lowing noise.

'*Tarvur,*' he kept saying. '*Tarvur.*'

The fishermen looked doubtful, glancing at one another.

My father made a lowing sound once again. It brought a gleam to the eyes of the fair-headed fisherman, MacSween.

'Oh, *tarbh. Tarbh!*' He grinned before making a lowing noise. 'Bull, bull!' he declared in English.

My father clapped his hands in excitement. 'Bull, bull, bull!' he yelled again. 'That's the English word.' He smacked his hands together, believing that some form of communication had been achieved.

'*Dunna, dunna!*' he shouted this time before beginning yet another impersonation. Now he quacked endlessly, flapping his arms as though they were wings.

'Oh, *tunnag! Tunnag!*' MacCusbic obtained the answer this time. 'Duck, duck, duck! In English.'

'Yes, yes!' My father laughed. 'Duck, duck, duck!'

These moments were the beginning of an extraordinary night. Long periods of silence that would be interrupted by laughter. Amid conversations dominated by our clumsy use of the English language, they would mention placenames like Mykines, Stóra and Lítla Dímun and shout out exactly what they might be if they were Gaelic words. My father would tug the locks of his hair and yell out '*Grúkur!*' to obtain an echo from the two fishermen in the word '*Gruaig!*' And then there was the moment he took out a jug of buttermilk, that liquid which I have always especially detested and shouted '*Blak!*' and '*Blaðak!*' Again, the call would be met by a loud enthusiastic response.

'*Blathach, blathach, blathach!*'

And then my mother and sisters sang one of these interminable Faroese ballads which used to plague my schooldays, the teacher Mr Dahl compelling us to sing verse after verse of these songs that belonged to our past, knowing he was breaking Danish law by doing this in a classroom. ('Why are you wearying us with this?' I remember asking this teacher once. 'We should be spending our time learning French, English, German.' His face turned the same shade as the waters of the inlets in these islands after the *grindadràp*, the beaching and killing of whales, had taken place. 'Because it's who we are,' he declared. 'We are certainly not Germans. Nor French. Nor English. Nor even Danish.' I kept quiet after that, reminding myself that there had been a time when he had kept to the law, insisting only Danish was spoken in his class. The change had only occurred a few years before.) The women in our family showed much more pride than me in their Faroese roots. Their voices rang out as they stood in front of our entire household and guests, giving a message of comfort to the Scottish islanders, if they only knew the words.

Hvør, ið hesa vísuna syngur,
tá ið hann fer til sjó,
óræddur skal hann tann sama dag
bæði sigla og ró.

Whoever sings this verse,
Whenever he goes to sea,
Fearless he shall that same day
Both sail and row.

MacCusbic responded with his own song, a slow and maudlin number that was likely to be about the delights of his own island (like many of its Faroese equivalents, it also probably never mentioned the wind, rain or mist that was ever present there). I watched Christianna's eyes well up as she listened to this, moved by the voice of a fisherman who looked more Spanish than Celtic, as if some previous boat had washed up on the rocks there, bringing his ancestors to these shores. When he finished, she walked across to the dresser to pick up a handkerchief from a drawer. As she dabbed her eyes, she also picked up a sheet of paper and a pencil, scribbling a note which she folded away in her fingers.

'That was wonderful,' my mother declared.

'Astonishing,' my sister Bedda said.

'I wonder if there were any Atlantean words within the song,' Father mused before bowing down low once again to make lowing noises. '*Tarvur!* Moo, Moo. Moo!'

They all laughed once again – the fair-headed fisherman performing a duck impersonation.

'*Tunnag, tunnag, tunnag!* Duck, duck, duck!'

And then just as the evening was coming to an end, I watched

Christianna slip the note into the fingers of the Spanish-looking figure.

'Good luck. Good luck,' she said as he took it without speaking, clenching it in his hand.

They walked out of the door then, our cries and cheers echoing in their ears as they walked down the road to their lodgings. During our time with us, they had lifted the clouds that so often cramp and tighten round the horizon of Havn, making us forget the peaks of Húsareyn and Kirkjubøreyn, which loomed over our lives. Instead, we had experienced visions of a wider, more exciting world. I know, for me, it was one of those moments that made me decide I must escape the confinement of Faroe, to obtain a sense of other countries, their strange and different tongues.

I would imagine it did much the same for Christianna. She disappeared the next few evenings, slipping from the household to visit a 'friend'. Her absence alarmed my mother. I can still recall her face as she fretted over where her daughter might have gone on these occasions. The lines that life with Father had furrowed on her features grew deeper. Her blue eyes were tearful once again.

'Is it MacCusbic? Do you think she might have gone to see him?'

'Perhaps,' my father said, not lifting his eyes from the *Dimmal-etting*, the local newspaper he was reading.

My mother reached for one of those same handkerchiefs her daughter had employed on the night the fishermen visited. 'Oh, no. No. No,' she repeated. 'What if she gives into him? What if she allows him to have his way with her?'

My father shrugged, as he often did when my mother became her most hysterical.

'Magnus, what if something happens?' she said.

Finally, he prised his eyes away from some detail of Danish national politics, a subject in which he was never particularly interested, seeing the way some people in both the Faroes and Iceland saw their world through the perspective of those in Copenhagen as being something to regret and deplore. 'It happens,' he declared.

'What?'

'It might even be for our good. The good of this place. There's always the danger of interbreeding here. Cousins marrying cousins. A Harrisman or two might widen the choice. Especially one who could be a descendant of Uspak Hákon, the chieftain. Improve the lot of our children. Expand the choices of future generations.'

'Magnus ...'

'Well, whether you like it or not, it could happen.'

'I know. And in a small place, no one gets over something like that.'

'There are worse things. Some children even flourish after a start like that. There are benefits to being an outsider sometime.'

'Not many.'

She turned away at that point, unable to tolerate him and his attitudes. Yet for all his response to her words, my father was the one who waited up for Christianna that night, steeling himself to put a stop to her ways, aware that if anything happened to his daughter, life with my mother – difficult enough most of the time – would be near impossible.

Christianna was shaking when she arrived, her pale face streaked with tears, a handkerchief once again clutched within her fingers. It seemed to be a constant companion with her those last few days, since the men from the tiny isle of Scalpay had arrived in Havn. She would wash one out each morning to have it dry again in her hands by the afternoon. This time, it was wringing wet, twisted time and time again in her hands.

'You'll have to let him go,' my father said.

'I know.'

'He is not from here. He does not know a word of Danish or Faroese.'

'I know,' she repeated.

'So, he'll find it impossible to settle down here.'

'I ...' she began before she faltered, her body trembling, her eyes bubbling over with loss once again. 'I know,' she continued. 'He's going on a boat to Copenhagen tomorrow morning. After that, Edinburgh. He's leaving, Father. Leaving.'

'Oh.' He looked relieved. 'That's good. I thought the waters you were stepping into were far too deep, the channel too wide to cross. It would have been impossible for the two of you to manage.'

She laughed scornfully, shaking her head. 'You don't understand me,' she said.

'What do you mean?'

She smiled. 'That's what I want from life,' she said. 'Deep waters. Wide channels. Can't you see that? Can't you see that I don't want to settle for Havn? Can't you see I'm just like you?'

THERE WAS MORE THAN A LITTLE TRUTH in Christianna's accusation. Our father's restlessness and desire to travel was evident in the companions he met down at the harbour, fishermen from Orkneyjar, Hjaltland, Rotterdam, the occasional visitor from

Bergen or Trondheim. He even gave his attention to a few of those who visited the island from Denmark, giving a pale smile when they dispensed their usual insults and told jokes about the seabirds many people ate within the archipelago.

'It gives us the ability to fly up and down the hills that are around here,' he would say. 'Unlike the Danes, who can only stand or move fast on flat land.'

It was when he spoke to foreigners that he was at his most exuberant, his hands waving, his feet restless enough to patrol a continent, no longer confined by the narrow borders of the islands on which he lived. In contrast, when locals came into the store, he would sometimes demonstrate a different kind of briskness, hurrying them along to purchase whatever item they required from the shelves.

'Yes. Yes. We have dried cod. A leg of mutton. Anything else? I haven't got all day.'

They put up with this, and the way he sometimes mocked them, because they had little alternative. The other store in Havn was owned by a man called Jacobsen. His prices were higher, and credit rarely given. He also did not have my father's powerful sense of smell, that ability to sense when food was turning rotten by dipping his giant nostrils towards the goods in question. As a result, what was found on our shelves was mostly fresh and high quality. Nevertheless quite a few of the customers would mutter when they were served by him, groan or swear when they left the building.

'I can't stand that man.'

'What a bloody clown.'

'He's got a sense of himself that's as huge as his nose.'

It was perhaps this that had led to our leaving Seyðisfjörður. This impatience with the locals, his dislike of the tight and narrow limits of their minds, imposed – he often said – by the cramped and narrow geography of Denmark, the country to which Iceland and the Faroes belonged. He would mutter about this often, how the people both in Faroe and back in Iceland talked mainly about the weather, the deaths and illnesses of people in the community, the occasional birth or fishing catch, the ordinary, dull and mundane details of Danish politics. This was not true of him. Each evening was a journey, one on which we often embarked with him. He would read books to us; our neighbours, too, coming to our home to listen. Barely literate, they loved the music and rhythm of his voice when he chose not to mock their ways, the strange and alien subject matter with which he was acquainted.

Sometimes it was the Sagas or books about his other great passion, the thousand stories that exist about the lost continent of Atlantis. On other occasions it was novels, such as ones written by Alexandre Dumas – *The Three Musketeers*, *The Man in The Iron Mask*, *The Count of Monte Cristo*. It was the last of these that appealed to me most; the host of identities taken on by the central character, Edmond Dantès, whirling through my imagination. The way the character altered – giving me the chance, too, to think of myself in different ways. One moment I was the Englishman, Lord Wilmore; the next I was the Italian priest, Abbé Busoni. Later I became the Count of Monte Cristo himself; Sinbad the Sailor, saviour of the Morrel family; the Maltese Sailor, too, rescued by smugglers, transformed in my mind into a Faroese version, paler and more insubstantial than the original standing beside Skansin lighthouse. Each figure, fresh and distinctive, took on flesh and reality in my mind.

I began to draw them, basing my characters on one or two who walked into the store, perhaps to order lines or hooks for their boats. The Maltese Sailor was a sullen man called Tristan.

I learned to read the set of his shoulders, the pace and stride of his boots, even the slight changes of expression in his unsmiling face, as if, like Edmond Dantès, he was set on revenge against those who betrayed him, sharpening his knife and hook as though he were prepared to stab their blades in the backs of others. The moment would come. My version of Abbé Busoni, one of Dantès' disguises, was based on Pastor Anders, the preacher we had seen that day with the Hebridean fisherman, continually rubbing his fingers together, his eyes welling over with sorrow and concern.

'For all evils, there are two remedies – time and silence.'

The book sparked other thoughts – the chance of escaping both Havn and my own flesh and bones and becoming someone else living in a different place, taking on a new reality. I drew myself as the Count of St Kilda, swaggering around in robes on that far island's cliffs. Or Lord of Hekla, the volcano in Iceland that my father and mother sometimes talked about. It was believed to be the entrance to hell. The fire and smoke that puffed out of its crest or slopes revealing the doorway to the underworld where Satan and his legions ruled. ('Some Icelanders,' my father said, 'had even heard the sound of Danish voices echoing from its summit – proof that the Devil lived within its depths.' And then he would imitate one of the men from the east coast of Denmark, mimicking the sounds they made.) I drew my own face at its most tormented and demonic above the volcano's fumes, my eyebrows raised like my mother's when she had to deal with her husband's eccentricities, my grin mimicking my father's when he was at his most enthusiastic and energetic.

'It's excellent,' he told me when he saw it. 'Truly wonderful.'

My mother raised her eyebrows in a mix of confusion and despair.

I took both responses as encouragement – my mother's bewilderment always a sign that the two men with whom she shared her life had surprised her yet again. I began other work, seeing myself as Jonah emerging from the entrails of a whale some of my fellow islanders had succeeded in driving into a bay, its waters flushed with blood as they culled it. I was Emperor Cormorant XII of Atlantis or – my other name – the Count of St Kilda, wearing a black cloak and golden crown and perched on a dark rock surrounded by shags and cormorants, where waves pitched and rolled, each layer of stone thrashed with water. Out of this, I fashioned a pair of family crests and two sets of calling cards – both written in my version of the Atlantean tongue – to give to people I met. I even possessed a voice to go with this, imagining I was a Danish aristocrat talking about those I met each day in Havn.

'They're so backward and uncivilised, you know. They reek of fish and sour milk. One can smell them before one sees them.'

And then there was the other writer my father used to read a great deal – the words of another French writer, Jules Verne. The first works of his we encountered as a household were *Five Weeks in a Balloon*, *Around the World in Eighty Days* and *Journey to the Centre of the Earth*.

The last of these appealed to us most. We would sit down at my father's feet at the fireside, listening to the book's opening words – 'On the 24th of May, 1863, my uncle, Professor Liedenbrock, rushed into his little house ...' – and know that we were returning to a strange, surreal version of our former homeland, travelling towards Snæfellsjökull, on another other side of Iceland than that to which we were familiar. We heard the strangeness of the words that my father read aloud, pronouncing them differently each time.

In Sneffels Yokulis craterem kem delibat umbra Scartaris Julii intra calendas descende, audas viator, et terrestre centrum attinges. Quod feci. Arne Saknussemm.

Descend, bold traveller, into the crater of the Jökull of Snaefells, which the shadow of Scartaris touches just before the kalends of July, and you will reach the centre of the earth, as I have done. Arne Saknussemm.

And then there was the familiar. The descriptions of the country we had left a few years before. The bare rocks in the landscape. The range and variety of seabirds I had seen. The houses made of earth and turf, their walls sloping as if they were almost embedded in the ground. The people working, drying and salting fish, carrying them aboard vessels for export. Their unsmiling faces, thoughtful eyes. The notion that they were condemned to live only a short distance outside the Arctic Circle. The men with their coarse dark jackets. The single women wearing knitted brown caps. The married ones with something resembling a coloured handkerchief on their heads. It all recalled the smells I had been used to, and which were still sometimes found around my home. The tang of dried fish, hung meat and sour milk that still made me choke and gag in later life. The familiar stink of the dung heap that stayed with me all the years I spent in Havn, haunting me all my days and nights. Even my father's voice would become dull and quiet when he read these sections, as if he were trudging across its barren spaces with Professor Liedenbrock and his colleagues, labouring over each step, resenting the chill and whip of rain.

'It doesn't sound so different from here,' Hørður, one of our neighbours, said. 'Bogs and streams. The pale green grass. Crags and rocks. Mud. Bog.'

'It doesn't.'

But then even the familiar became strange. My father read of entering the abyss that lay just below the peak of Snæfell, its perpendicular walls, the pattern of its stones, outlandish geology, that sense the men in the party had of entering a cavity in which there was no known destination.

'Munkastova,' Árni, another of the neighbours, declared.

'Sorry?'

'It's one of the biggest sea caves around here. Out near Sørvágar in Vágar,' he continued. 'I went out there once in a small boat. Kept listening to the way each sound echoed while I was in there.'

'Yes,' my father nodded. 'It'll be a little like that, except each sound will spiral downwards. Not forward or back. A deep abyss. Stones and lava fragments scattered throughout, jutting from the walls.'

He continued to read. But then even the familiar became strange. My father read of the group entering the abyss that lay just below the peak of Snæfell, that long cavern with its perpendicular walls, the pattern of its stones, outlandish geology, that sense the men in the party had of entering a domain in which all was unfamiliar and strange. With each step of that downward journey, that sense of the weird and extraordinary increased. The men encountered a clump of mushrooms that grew like a huge forest, their stems similar to tree trunks, thirty to forty feet high, their caps almost the same size as outstretching branches or domed buildings, with gills below as foliage, gigantic and inexplicable leaves.

'That's astonishing,' Árni declared. 'I've never heard of anything like that before.'

My father and I looked at each other, conscious that Árni was taking every word seriously, believing each word that had been read.

'Well, it's rare anyway,' my father said, smiling. 'I've certainly never come across it.'

'No,' Árni agreed. 'Not even in my fishing days.'

Father read on, telling of the strange beasts encountered by the men on their journey to the centre of the earth. The mastodons with their trunks and giant tusks, ancestors of the present-day elephant. The ichthyosaurus with its lizard's head, a snout like a porpoise and crocodile teeth. The plesiosaurus, like a snake but one with the shell of a turtle, paddles for feet. Hørður and Árni listened as these two creatures battled, their mouths falling open as they heard how the tails of the animals thrashed water, how their teeth sank into one another, cutting into their exposed flesh, making red gashes and open wounds.

'Oh, wow!' one said. 'I never knew there were such beasts.'

'Neither did I,' the other declared.

'What sheltered lives we have led, not knowing these things.'

My father looked at me once again and grinned. 'We know nothing about the world, living here at the edge, our view limited by the perspectives of our masters, the Danes,' he said. 'It is only those at the centre who are aware of all the mysteries that can occur here on Earth. And yet, we people in remote parts have advantages. There's decent people living there. Pure and Honest. Isolated. No danger of contamination.'

I remember smiling to myself when he said this, aware for the first time how gullible and innocent people could be, how easily they could be tricked and fooled.

It was a lesson that stayed with me for the rest of my life.

Christianna

That evening changed my mind about the way I saw both my father and the world. At first, I only saw how innocent and naïve Hörður and Árni were, and I laughed at them with Karl, bleating like a sheep, making fun of their reactiôns. Then I poked fun at how they were unable to tell the difference between fiction and fact, believing every word of Jules Verne's novel despite how my father had told them it was a made-up tale about an underground world.

'Ha! Ha! Ha! Hee! Hee! I can't believe how stupid they were. They thought the story was true!'

Well, these were words which my sister Bedda challenged me about. The poor soul had inherited my mother's eyebrows, often sharp and quizzical, focusing on each questionable remark made by my father. Broad shoulders would stretch, eyes stare, jawline jut. Even her curly dark hair bristled like nettles when she would express her point of view, as if she were prepared to sting those who quarrelled with her. With the sharpness of her tongue, she possessed the skill to do it, too.

'What makes you think our father isn't naïve too?' my sister asked.

'Sorry?'

'What makes you think our father isn't – in his own way – as daft as the two of them?'

'Well, he reads. He studies books. Those two haven't.'

'He may have read books. But what has he seen? What has he done? Where has he gone in his life? The eastern edge of Iceland and here. How does he know what is false or true in these books he has come across?'

And even as she spoke, I knew immediately that she was right. So, how did my father have a clue about whether his stories were true or not? All he was doing was talking, finding some satisfaction even in hearing his voice echo in the room, loud against the relentless rapping of the rain or the fury of the wind. Occasionally he would find someone with whom he could quarrel, an activity that seemed to give him even more satisfaction that listening to his own words endlessly repeated. There was, for instance, the time a few days later Pastor Anders came to our house and mentioned the name of Jonah.

'You've seen many men coming out of the belly of the whale any time?' my father said. 'Just wondering. There's been plenty of opportunities around these parts with the number being cut open and killed.'

He also reacted when the pastor spoke about Noah and the flood, how 'in the six hundredth year of Noah's life, in the second month, the seventeenth day of the month, the same day were all the fountains of the great deep broken up, and the windows of heaven were opened. And the rain was on the earth forty days and forty nights.'

'Was that when the whole of Atlantis sank?'

Pastor Anders looked at him doubtfully.

'Is there anything in the Bible about that?' my father asked.

'No. I don't think so.'

'It's mentioned in the Jules Verne book *Twenty Thousand Leagues under the Sea*.'

Well, then my father began to speak about this, how the story of Atlantis had been first found in Plato's work – an island which once was in the Atlantic Ocean, larger than Libya and Asia together; how it was the home to 'a confederation of kings, of great and marvellous power, which held sway over all the island, and over many other islands also and parts of the continent'.

'You know where some men believe the edge of Atlantis was?'

'No.'

'The cliffs of the island of St Kilda in the Hebrides. You know where that is?'

The poor pastor swallowed and looked away, his face turning pale. 'No.'

'Well, well, well! And you call yourself learned!'

And so I began to feel sorry for Pastor Anders. Really! Why did Father believe he had the right to act that way? The poor man was even trembling.

'I have never called myself learned. I am only a poor humble servant of the Lord.'

For once I noticed my father's confidence dwindling. He gulped and shivered, as if he were aware he had gone too far.

'Perhaps you need to be more learned,' he declared. 'Perhaps people expect that when a man steps into a pulpit. But then what do you expect from a group of holy men who've brought prohibition to these islands, draining away all the enjoyment in life for some?' His long nose fumed and blustered when he said this, returning to one of his occasional obsessions. 'No sense of what people need for their survival in a part of the world like this. No idea that they might sometimes need their spirits raised.'

But his voice drained away as he said this, conscious of the looks Bedda and my mother were casting in his direction, aware too of my rare disapproval. Only Karl seemed not to be conscious of the way in which his father had behaved. His eyes still shimmered with his own bright vision of the man.

And in the silence that followed, Pastor Anders turned to all of us, his Bible in his hands.

'Shall I say a word of prayer?' he said.

Us three women nodded, my mother murmuring her agreement. My father muttered and grumped.

'Would it be all right?' Pastor Anders said, staring at my father once again.

My father nodded after a few moments. 'Yes. Yes. Yes.'

'I shall begin then,' the pastor declared. 'Our Father, our Lord, there are some whose views of the world are limited. They are walled and encircled by the world they live in, led astray by the words of others, the false knowledge they obtain from the people they come across, the books they have read. Let them see there are greater mysteries for them to investigate and uncover; those found within the human heart; those, too, that are concealed from their vision – the affairs and concerns of the Holy Spirit and the grace of Your gift to us of Your only Son. There are some who are blind to Your kindness and generosity, who prefer not to see all that You have given and provided for us ...'

My father coughed and mumbled.

'... Remove the mist that covers their eyes. Cure and heal their blindness. Let them see how they have been led astray. Let them discard the falsehoods and fantasies in which they seem to believe and find greater and more rewarding truths for themselves, including the sacrifices that You have made for the sake of all our souls. Do this for us all and we shall be eternally grateful. Amen.'

As his words washed over me, I felt a change begin within. It was as if a cut had opened in me, one that was as sharp, deep and jagged as some of the chasms that waves have carved and hewn in the cliffs found around the coastline of these islands. Boulders giving way; layers of basalt toppling into depths of water; the shore's defences surrendering to the strength and force of the sea. The entire familiar landscape being shifted and transformed in an instant.

For a moment, I stopped dreaming of foreign places – even those occupied by men like MacCusbic, the fisherman from the little island of Scalpay I had met several months before. I began to realise, too, what had caused me to feel that way about him. Back when I was staying in Seyðisfjörður, one of my friends had given me a book as a gift just before we left the place. It was a little too old for me – a romance about a tartan-clad prince from Suðereyar who had sailed north to Iceland, winning the heart of Vilborg, a young woman who lived there. I turned its pages again and again, conscious that I was entering a more grown-up world than the one I normally visited when I read. I asked my father where Suðereyar was, its reality as fantastic to me as the Atlantis of which he often spoke.

'It's the Outer Hebrides of Scotland – Lewis, Harris, North Uist.' My father pointed out a string of islands in a book of maps on the shelves – more stretched out than the Faroes on which we now lived. 'Not that different from here. Fine people living there. Pure and isolated. Little danger of contamination.'

The magic of that place remained with me for years. I learned to recite the names of those islands almost as well as those that surrounded me in the Faroes. 'Lewis, Harris, North Uist, Benbecula, South Uist, Barra …'

It was only with the words of Pastor Anders that this began – in any way – to dissipate and disappear, for all that it still existed at the edge of my consciousness, coming back into my thoughts again and again over the years.

'WE KNOW NOTHING ABOUT THE WORLD, living here at the edge,' he said. 'It is only those at the centre, the capital cities of Europe, who are aware of all the mysteries that can occur here on Earth.'

There was another legacy of the night we listened to *Journey to the Centre of the Earth*, one that my father could never have predicted when he spoke those words. They made me restless, all too aware that there were few of the truths of existence that could be discerned or discovered if I spent the remainder of my life in Havn. It was during this time I began to read incessantly – anything that came into my reach, the fairy stories of Hans Christian Andersen and the Brothers Grimm, the novels of Robert Louis Stevenson, Balzac and Sir Walter Scott, the tales of Hoffman in which a boy called Konrad gets his thumb cut off by a giant scissor man.

Snip! Snap! Snip! The scissors go;
And Konrad cries out 'Oh! Oh! Oh!'
Snip! Snap! Snip! They go so fast,
That both his thumbs are off at last.

I turned through the pages of all these works and any phrase book that would be useful in teaching me a foreign language. Guides to English, French and Spanish. An introduction to German or Italian. It seemed to me that, as I turned the pages of these works, walls began to breathe, the seas around my home started to narrow. I could feel myself step over the width of waters and arrive in Hjaltland, Orkneyjar, even Paris or Rome. No longer was I confined to the islands where I stayed. Instead, I could travel anywhere, walk foreign streets, come alive in different times if I was offered an invitation by the pages of a book.

My restlessness was spotted by my teacher, Jacob Dahl. He could see that while I occupied a desk, I was rarely in his classroom, dreaming instead of the world I found within my books. It was because of this he came to our house one afternoon, diverting my father from the task that occupied him a few times a year – sorting and storing the many fleeces the local shepherds sold to him for sending on a boat to Denmark. A plump, rounded man with thinning dark hair and a thick black moustache, Dahl nodded in his direction.

'Can I have a word with you?'

'Of course.'

The two sat down by the kitchen fire. Dahl spoke to my father, doing so in a blunt and definite voice.

'Karl cannot stay here in Tórshavn,' he said.

'Why?' my father asked, aware that this was a different Dahl from the one that was normally on view. The teacher usually encouraged his pupils to stay in the islands – rather than going to Denmark, as so many of the brighter individuals had done for years – believing it was the only way to transform the place. He thought that the people of the Faroes had to improve and develop their own resources, even taking the time to translate much of the Bible into the native language of these parts. 'It will be easier for the people here to reach the Kingdom of Heaven if they can read the Good Book in their own tongue rather than become confused and head in the opposite direction by reading Danish.'

But with me, it was apparently the opposite.

'He will be stifled in this place,' Dahl declared. 'He has great natural ability as an artist. Real talent. He needs to mix with others with his mindset. Otherwise, his creativity will be lost. Life here will destroy them.'

'Oh.' My father gave his customary sly look, one I recognised from dealing with some of his customers. 'But I need him to work in the store. He will inherit this after me.'

'The store?' Dahl's face coloured. 'But he has such a different way of seeing the world from others here – that would be the end of him.'

'What do you mean?'

Dahl shuffled awkwardly. 'His attitudes are odd among the boys here. When he sees a bird, he thinks about drawing it or imitating its sounds. Some of the others look at it and think right away about eating it.'

My father laughed. 'There's a kindness and gentleness about him then. That should be encouraged.'

'Perhaps. But it's out of place in these parts. We must eat the seabirds here. Otherwise, we would not be able to survive.'

'That's true.' My father nodded. 'But staying here in Havn might be a way of rooting him. He needs to do that. He lives too much in his own head most of the time.'

Dahl's shoulders rose. His jaw clenched. 'If he stays, he will only waste his talents by dreaming of being somewhere else.'

'And why is that?'

'Lots of reasons. It's partly all these books he reads. He never stops. They make him curious about other times and places. Big cities and other countries. They make him restless continually. Most of them have nothing to do with our existence here in Faroe. Nothing to do with island life.'

'Oh, I don't know,' my father said, grinning. 'Some of them are set on islands. Books like *Robinson Crusoe*, *Treasure Island*, *Coral*–'

'They're not reality, Magnus. They're just dreams.'

'Sometimes it's hard to tell the difference.'

'It's not that hard.' Dahl sighed, shaking his head. 'We both know there's no future for him here. He doesn't fit in. Not with the others. Not with the boys in his class. Nor with the girls either. If we want him not to be lonely and isolated for the remainder of his days, he needs to go from here. Stretch his wings. Spend a few seasons, at least, away from these shores.'

'Like the *tjaldur*? The oystercatcher?' my father said, referring to the bird whose arrival on the 12th of March was celebrated by the Faroese, who call that day Grækarismessa, or St Gregory's Day. The coming of the oystercatchers means the end of winter, their orange beaks a small reminder of the sun that occasionally will light our skies over the next few months, before those black-and-white wings flutter once again in their search for perpetual light.

'Yes. He might once again settle here after a while. But he's not going to do that if he doesn't have some time away first.'

For once, my father nodded, his customary jocular air disappearing. 'So, where do you think he should go to?'

'There are a number of possible schools which might assist him. Some good at teaching languages. Others specialising in art. And, of course, it's almost as important that he should spend time visiting art galleries and museums. There is no prospect of that here, of course.'

'No, that's true enough.'

My father paused for a moment, thinking, perhaps, of walking down to the old houses in Reyn or to the harbour to greet strange fishing boats from Norwegian islands like Hitra or Karmøy, perhaps those from Orkneyjar or Hjaltland at the northern tip of Scotland, but doing so without my company; of making his way through the buildings in Tinganes, the peninsula at the edge of the town, without having my presence to inform and educate. ('Remember that time we had a descendant of the Norse chieftain Uspak Hákon in our house?' he might say. 'You know, he is described as a kind-hearted, loyal man who behaved leniently to his brothers in one of the Sagas?') But he also knew I would soon be approaching the age of fourteen and decisions would have to be made about what kind of existence I would have on this Earth. He could not dream or dither forever.

'Have you any suggestions where he should go?' he asked the schoolteacher.

'A number of thoughts.' Dahl smiled, aware that his attempt at persuasion had been successful. 'I have a friend, Christian Johansen, whose mother comes from here. He works in Sorø Academy in Sjælland, in eastern Denmark. As you know, Sjælland is an island, so that should help him adjust over the next while.'

My father nodded.

'It's a school that many people who are talented in art, music and story-telling have gone to throughout the years. Yet it is not solely for them. Engineers and mathematicians have also stepped through its doors. Great talents have been sharpened there.'

'I have heard of it,' my father said.

'I thought you might have,' Dahl declared. 'Well, will I write my friend a letter and find out? He may, of course, come up with other suggestions.'

My father nodded his head reluctantly.

And that was it – the beginning of my journey from the edge to the centre, my transformation and attempt to discover all the mysteries that beforehand had been hidden from me. It would all take longer than the eighty days it took for the characters in Jules Verne's novel to make their way around the world.

Much, much longer than that.

Christianna

Let me be honest. My young brother, Karl, became unbearable the day he was told he was going to school in Sorø. He no longer made even the slightest pretence at being part of the family, far less a member of the Faroese community. He put on airs and graces, displayed that long nose of his more prominently than ever, strutted and spoke in a strange, pompous manner that was novel and outlandish even for him. The mere act of cleaning out the store became a performance. He would lean on a broomstick, then twirl it between his fingers, making loud and odd pronouncements. 'Never fear quarrels,' he would declare after arguing with a classmate, 'but seek hazardous adventures.' Or else he would quote some verse he had learned from some book or other.

Sound, sound the clarion, fill the fife!
To all the sensual world proclaim,
One crowded hour of glorious life
Is worth an age without a name.

So, one time, Bedda humiliated him by telling him to clear out the household ash and bring it to the dung heap a short distance from our door.

'I think I will call myself Dunganon,' he announced. 'It will sum up all I think about the Faroe Islands.'

'What do you mean?' Bedda asked.

'Dunga *non*!' he said, as if he were French. 'The entire place is a veritable dung heap.'

'Perhaps,' Bedda responded. 'But there's no doubt you're going to end up headfirst in one in the near future. And that doesn't depend on your destination.'

'Ohhh' – Karl shook his head in her direction – 'what did I do to deserve such a sister?'

At first, his behaviour didn't trouble me so much. I had long been aware that fourteen-year-old boys are among the least pleasant creatures in existence. Karl conformed to that description, for all that his horridness was somewhat unique. Besides, I had more serious matters of my own to consider. For some time, a young, fair-haired man from Sørvágar in the island of Vágar had been visiting the store at every opportunity, whenever his fishing boat arrived in the harbour. There was a red mark on his face, as if his cheek had been scalded by a heated poker or spoon, and this seemed exaggerated by his blush in my presence, turning his entire features crimson. He would buy a few items, mumble and look away, unable to look too long in my direction. All this was the opposite way of behaving from the one which I had noticed sometimes among other men who visited the shop. Some would step within the doors and spend a considerable amount of time staring at me, taking in my every move and gesture, the sweep of my body, the tangle of my hair. It was an experience which, particularly when I witnessed it in older men, made me shiver and recoil. But the shyness of the man from the other island created an opposite reaction in me. I felt drawn to the way he fumbled and muttered, the awkwardness of his manner.

'Think someone's interested in you,' Bedda declared.

'No. He's not.'

'Are you being deliberately blind? Saving yourself for the ghost of a fisherman from Suðereyar? You know that living there would be much the same as staying here? Except you wouldn't be able to speak the language.'

'I know that,' I said, grinning. 'I worked that out a while ago. It's no longer such a temptation for me.'

'Well? Are you interested?'

But I didn't answer. Largely because he had attracted my notice. He would say nothing to me when he walked around the store, but his eyes kept flicking in my direction all the time. This quietness was such a contrast with the men who had occupied my life till this time – my father with his stories, my brother with his posturing – that I began to see something refreshing in it. Quietness and blushes, as opposed to an endless rush of words. A life linked to the solid earth and rock of a location like Vágar, rather than one filled with the restless exploration of dreams and other locations. Rootedness, rather than the restlessness with which my poor mother lived each day of her existence, continually listening to my father's obsession with books and words. Perhaps, I told myself, an existence in Vágar would cure me of my faults, end the restlessness that had for too long been part of my being.

So, then came the day the young man sidled up to me in the store.

'Would you like to come out for a walk?'

Karl

I FELT GLAD to be leaving Faroe shortly after my sister Christianna got married. Unlike Bedda with her stern demeanour, she was the one with whom I always felt the greatest kinship. Throughout our years together, it was clear there were similar stirrings of adventure in her soul. We would speak to each other about a life among city streets, exploring alleyways and thoroughfares, shops and stores, coming to know them in a similar manner to how our local fishermen became aware of the channels and currents around our own islands, or the shepherds in these parts were familiar with the streams and summits found within our cramped and narrow shores.

'How wonderful it would be to go to Paris or London,' she might say. 'It would be great to discover what its streets were like.'

And then she would pause, as if testing out the reality of these words on her tongue. 'What people we could meet there! What places we could come across!'

And then she goes and chooses Heðin for a husband, a quiet, shy and pious fisherman from a small stretch of land near Sørvágar, the edge of these islands, the far periphery. I recall asking her why she had chosen that place, the coldest in the archipelago with snow and frost for more days than anywhere else in the vicinity. She smiled once and declared, 'Perhaps he and I can bring a little warmth to it.'

I blushed as only a boy barely into his teens can. And then I asked why she had picked him, instead of travelling to far locations as she and I had planned to do for years. She gave me one of the most intense looks I had ever seen on her face, her words coming slowly, as if there was a weight and a burden attached to each one.

'Perhaps it's more important to spend your life exploring yourself rather than travelling to other places. Perhaps journeying to other countries only gets in the way of all that.'

I shook my head. 'Surely you can do both.'

'I'm not sure you can,' she said. 'To really discover yourself you need stillness and calm. If you're travelling, you have to plan your movements before you undertake them, walk along unfamiliar places, deal with the strange situations you come across. You can't do both – explore strange cities *and* find out about yourself. The two can't be done together.'

I said nothing, aware that, in my father's view at least, travel extended the reach of a man's soul. Even the possibility of it occurring was having that effect on me. During the last few months in which I lived in Havn, I began to become aware of how on these dark, still nights that occurred in Faroe, the Milky

Way seeped into my spirit; how in the chill of winter, the huge expanse of the Northern Lights became part of my essence, their arrival extending the reach of my imagination over sea and sky, as if I were the one that was dancing miles above the land. Even the dizzy heights of cliffs left me reeling with the power and wonder of the natural world of these islands. It was as if the multitude of seabirds that clustered there had entered me – the sweep of gulls and gannets, the shades and colours of puffin, even the black and white plumage of guillemots as they flapped towards the shore. There was something magical within me, a power that had been granted by the possibility of leaving home. It brought me, day after day, down to the eastern harbour, spending each dry and windless hour there sketching the seabirds that could be seen, the fish that boats carried to shore. With my pencil, I transformed them, giving them human expressions, chiselling jawlines, sketching eyes, providing arms and legs where they once possessed wings or fins. I remember my father looking at me with amazement when he saw these sketches, amazed at what his son had fashioned on a simple sheet of paper.

'I wonder if it's wise to let you go away from here. Who knows where you might end up?'

'Atlantis?' I muttered. 'Hy-Brasil? Avalon? St Kilda?'

'Oh, further even than that. The moon or the planets?' He grinned.

But he didn't have much time to consider me. Christianna occupied too many of his thoughts. He tried to persuade her not to marry Heðin from Sørvágar, speaking to her one afternoon at the kitchen table.

'He's a nice man,' he said, 'but he's not what I had in mind for you.'

'And what would that have been instead?'

His face flushed before he answered. 'A doctor. A lawyer. An accountant. Someone who stayed in Copenhagen. Aarhus. Odense. Perhaps even further afield than that. Paris. Rome. Berlin.'

'Oh? And what made you think these people would have been interested in a storekeeper's daughter from Tórshavn?'

'You're much more than that,' my father muttered. 'My knowledge and teaching have made you much more than that.'

Christianna raised an eyebrow. 'It might have done at one time. It might have made me a person with some deluded notions about herself. Fortunately, I managed to put an end to all that, to look at myself with more realistic eyes.'

'Not necessarily more realistic. Just more limited. Like most people in these parts.'

'There are different kind of limits,' my sister declared, returning to similar arguments to the ones she had explored with me a short time before. 'Some people think the only answers come from looking outwards. It's a way of stopping them looking deep into themselves.'

I noticed Bedda nodding as she said this, aware that her sister had come to the same conclusions as she had done. My mother looked on, as impassive as she often was these days, as if even to be aware of disagreement was somehow to be aware of the turmoil it might bring.

'People have the right to make up their own minds,' she said once to my father. 'And that includes your daughters.'

'Even if what they're doing looks like folly.'

'Yes. Even so. You just ignore it and hope for the best. It's not the first time in my family history when that has been done.'

My father looked at her intensely for a long time, as if he was puzzled by her words, wondering what she meant by them. 'Yes.

I suppose that's true,' he said finally.

'Well, take a lesson from that. Sometimes it's the only thing that can be done.'

'All right then.'

And so the wedding occurred a month or so later, Heðin's relatives arriving from Vágar, filling up our home with their talk of sheep and fish, even the coal which they mined upon the island, bringing it in sacks to our house. In all the celebration, there were two individuals who sat on their own throughout much of the proceedings. One was my father, brooding, perhaps, as he contemplated how he had presumed his daughter's marriage to be very different from this. He had dreamed that his guests might bring fine wine and champagne, speak of other matters apart from their flocks and boats, talk of the far-off cities they had visited during lifetimes of travelling. He watched it all from a distance, his lips only imitating movement when others joined in a chorus, became immersed in the fervent songs of faith that some enjoyed.

Hvør, ið hesa vísuna syngur,
tá ið hann leggur seg at sova,
hann verður ei í svøvni svikin,
tað hevur sjálvur Jesus lovað.

Whoever sings this verse,
Whenever he lays himself to sleep,
He will not be betrayed in sleep,
That has Jesus Himself promised.

And then there was me, thinking of the journey I was about to take, every bit as overwhelming as the one being undertaken by my sister, the trip to Esbjerg in a few days' time, onwards then to my new school in Sorø, the existence that was waiting there.

AND SO MY LIFE ROLLED OUT in a circle – as my sister Christianna might have said. Another stroll down to the eastern harbour, but now there was a boat waiting to take me to Denmark and another, different life; to give me a last look at Skansin lighthouse and the old fort at its base; to sail out beyond the island of Nólsoy, which had sheltered me most of my existence. My father had booked me on a cheap voyage to Esbjerg with men who brought supplies to his store on a cargo vessel, rather than waste money on a boat heading for the capital, Copenhagen. 'It's only a few extra hours on the train,' he had explained. 'It'll give you the chance to see the place.'

Once again the rain was hammering down, wisps of cloud trailing over Húsareyn and Kirkjubøreyn, the houses of the town weighed down by the constant burden of the weather. My father had dressed me in an oilskin coat, for all that I was fourteen years old and well capable of buttoning one up for myself. This time, however, he was carrying a case for me, and we were accompanied by my mother and Bedda – my sister Christianna having gone to her new home in Vágar.

'To live among the peasants there,' my father would declare in the moments when he mourned her choice. 'Talk about throwing away your existence. I only hope she doesn't regret it.'

'Even if she does, it's her choice,' my mother said.

'Yes. I suppose you're right. However …'

He had prepared me for my new existence in a quite different way, readying me for the jokes he was convinced some of the Danish boys and even teachers would make when I arrived in school in Sorø. He had heard so many in various encounters in Havn and his former life in Seyðisfjörður – the snide remarks of the colonial masters, the jibes and jests they made when they were doing business with them.

'I could tell you were from the Faroes. You were born walking at a slant. You'll have problems walking on the flat ground in these parts.'

'Oh, I knew there was one of you around. There was the stink of rotten fish everywhere.'

'Or was it the smell of *skerpikjøt*? I would recognise the whiff of that dried mutton anywhere!'

'What shines and reeks in the darkness? A man from Tórshavn eating mackerel in the moonlight.'

He told me, too, how I should defend myself: 'Make the place out to be a lot more backward than it is. Tell them you live in a cave. Tell them you use lava from the nearest volcano to do your cooking. Tell them every time you want to dry yourself you have to stand naked outside in the wind. They won't know the difference. Not until the day comes when they work out that you're winding them up. They'll stop it then. When they realise you're making an idiot of them and not the other way round!'

And then he paused, becoming a little more serious.

'Remember. Some of these people see these islands as part of their empire. We were part of Norway till nearly a hundred years ago. Then, with the likes of Iceland and Greenland, we were switched to Denmark. They even had a trading monopoly here. None of the people living in these parts were allowed to trade. And some of these attitudes remain. For all that they live in a low-lying part of the world, they look down on the people both here and in Iceland. Never forget about that. You'll have to work twice as hard to stand level with them. At least in their eyes anyway.'

I nodded. 'I knew some of that. Jansen told us it in school.'

'Well, never forget it. People in bigger places love to look down on those from smaller ones. It makes them feel a little taller.'

'I'll try and remember,' I said, smiling.

There were other ways in which I was also prepared to leave. On the way to the harbour, there was the sight of several of the young lads with whom I had been in school. A few were already involved in the fishing lives they would follow for the rest of their time on this part of the Earth, mending their lines while they sat along the pier. Another was carrying a spade, with which he hoped to dig soil or plant seeds. There was a girl among them – Ásla – who had also been with me in school. She looked like Aslaug, the woman in the Sagas from whom her name had been derived; fair-headed and remote, she had a fishing line draped around her shoulders which she was carrying for her uncle, who worked on one of the boats. She had been a strange girl, distant from the rest of us – a legacy, perhaps, of the fact that unlike most children in her class, she had no idea who her father was; a legacy of a night her mother had spent with a Norwegian or Dutch fisherman. Yet even she nodded in my direction as I went past, before grunting something like the rest of them, aware that I was cut out for a lifestyle different from the one they would be following.

'Come back and see us sometime,' one of them, Arno, yelled. 'You can give us some money then.'

'I will,' I responded – perhaps a shade unconvincingly, conscious that I had never been firmly rooted in these islands. I was on their edge, like the island of Nólsoy to the east of the town, its whale-like shape occupying its horizon rather than the centre of its existence. I remember one occasion Arno mocked the way I had sketched my notion of the Emperor Cormorant enthroned upon a rock. He had looked at the crown and jewels that decorated the bird, the robe that fluttered above its wings.

'I hope none of those jewels get stuck in my teeth when I'm eating it,' he said.

The only time they seemed to react to me in a favourable way was when we occasionally played out a scene from something I had read during my childhood. We might lift up broomsticks in our hands and clash them against one another.

'All for one – and one for all!' they would shout, as if they belonged to some Faroese equivalent of the Three Musketeers.

Mostly, though, through the books I had read throughout my childhood, I belonged somewhere else, far distant from this shoreline, a constant gap between my lives as theirs. They had come to the same conclusion as another man who was waiting for me at the harbour, my teacher Jacob Dahl. He thrust out his hand to me as I stood there, wishing me good luck.

'And don't forget us here. The people of these parts need their exiles as much as those who stay here. You are our voices abroad. Sometimes those in Copenhagen hear them much more loudly than ours.'

'I'll do my best,' I assured him.

'I'm sure you will,' he said, nodding.

And then there was my family. My mother brought advice and the knitted Faroese jumper she packed away with the rest of my belongings. 'If you're ever cold or hungry, make sure you wear it. It will bring you good fortune then,' she declared. My sister Bedda gave me a quick kiss on the cheek. 'Make sure you come back here as often as you can. You don't want us all to forget about you.'

My father handed me a book he had wrapped up and kept dry below his coat. 'It's another Jules Verne one. One I have never read to you,' he announced. '*Twenty Thousand Leagues under the Sea*. You might enjoy reading it on the boat.'

I glanced in the sea's direction – its white peaks and grey depths, how sometimes its waves seemed starker and steeper than the dark cliffs that surrounded me here in these islands. Its savagery and desolation were such that I decided that this was the last book I wanted to read now, in case I ended up twenty thousand leagues below its surface, the fantasy of the French writer's words becoming a damp and hideous reality as I plunged downwards into its depths. But I said nothing, conscious that I would not be seeing him for a while, aware too of the tears streaming down his face like the waterfalls that sometimes flooded over the slopes and chasms of the islands I was just about to leave.

Karl's School Years

1911–1912

Karl

THERE WERE A FEW HEADIER SIGHTS and smells greeting me in Esbjerg than I had ever encountered in Havn. In waters close to the port, there was a flock of barnacle geese, a bird that – according to my father – some believed hatched from eggs that formed on tree branches. Sour milk, rotten fish and smoked eel – the scents that I have hated for much of my life – percolated the harbour when I arrived there, a concoction that made my stomach swirl and throat gag. I had only taken my first few steps on the shore of Denmark when sickness overwhelmed me in much the same way as it had done on the boat that had brought me to its shores. On the vessel it was the stink of mutton that had affected me, hanging in the ship's hold, together with the peaks and troughs of waves. There were times when I thought its bow was plunging down gullies and canyons before being raised over ridges and crests again. It was like I was still clambering across Faroe, where the flanks of hills are lined with strips of basalt the people call *hammars*, where surges of lava once halted many centuries before, up and down, high and low. Whether I liked it or not, I was not going to escape the hold of those islands. They still had a deep grip on my mind and heart.

I felt that, too, on the train. Outside the window were miles and miles of flat, rolling landscape, haystacks and fields, horses with farmers tugging them along by the reins, occasional villages and towns, the almost complete absence of the seabirds that were familiar to me in Havn, that sense I had that most of my neighbours there would go hungry in these parts, deprived of their usual diet. Instead, there were pigs and cattle, the rise and sweep of both small birds and loud, cackling geese, small reminders that while more and more people in Denmark were moving to the country's cities, most still lived in farms and on the outskirts of towns.

Inside the compartment, there were all sorts of voices. The speech of the people of Copenhagen was, of course, familiar; but in Faroe their voices, and those of others from other parts of Denmark, were only occasionally heard. Now they seemed to surround me everywhere, jabbering away, talking about the everyday routines of their lives, something they rarely did when they visited us. And then, too, there were the Germans, their voices swirling between confidence and uncertainty as they travelled among a people with whom they had been at war only a few decades before, a bloody squabble over who was in charge of the length and breadth of Schleswig-Holstein. Their speech hushed when there were soldiers in the carriage, all too aware that these men were part of a force which their countrymen had humiliated and destroyed. As soon as they left, their voices increased in volume again, untroubled by the presence of a young boy – who might well have been Danish – in their carriage.

'These Danes, they're nothing but losers. Grim, humourless losers.'

And then there were the English people, their boat having arrived in Esbjerg from Harwich a few hours before. They spoke in whispers, talking about the Grand Tour of Scandinavia they had planned for themselves.

'It is wonderful to step on the Continent,' one said, imitating my own thoughts. 'It means we can escape from our narrow little island for a while.'

I learned to imitate them even on that short journey to Copenhagen, mimicking their every word and gesture, the flourish of their hands, the rise and fall of every moment of talk or conversation. It was a performance that my friends Karl, Bjørn and Kasper all enjoyed and appreciated when I met them at the school. I followed the voices of the people I encountered both that day and many afterwards, staying in character for hours on end, until I became tired of being another person and wanted to be myself once again.

'Well done.'

'That's fantastic.'

'You're great fun to be around,' Kasper, a pupil whose mother came from the Faroes, said. 'I get so much pleasure out of your company. It's as if your time at your home gave you the means to pick up the rhythms of the way people speak.'

'You should hear me imitate seabirds,' I said, grinning. 'I've a real skill at that.'

'No doubt,' he laughed, 'but that's normal for a Faroe man. You should hear the way my mother sometimes squawks.'

And then he walked away giggling to himself, sounding like a crowd of gulls crying out near the edge of cliffs.

There was something in all this that, in some strange way, stayed with me for my adult life. It prepared me in the learning of all the languages with which I grew familiar over the years, studying German, French, Spanish, Italian, English, as well as the three – Danish, Icelandic and Faroese – I had already acquired in my early years. Not only did I have a gift for language and drawing, but also for impersonation. I practised this again and again with the schoolteachers I encountered in Sorø, noting their mannerisms and peculiarities. The mathematics teacher who would spend hours looking for his glasses when they were perched on top of his head. 'Did any of you boys steal them?' he would ask, staring at us with an inquisitorial gaze. There was another – a teacher of biological science – who could be diverted at any time into talking about how the clubs AB Copenhagen and BK Frem worked together to arrange the so-called 'English matches' between Danish teams and professional foreign clubs to create football tournaments in the capital city. His arms would wave and lips slaver as he stammered in excitement about the matches.

'We are learning how to play the game from their examples. Someday we will be able to take them on and beat them.' He would whirl round and gaze at me. 'After all, we have advantages here in this part of the world. We have flat ground here on which we can train. Not like the Faroese, eh, young Einarsson? If they played football there, they would have to run squint and sideways all the time. You wouldn't score many goals that way,' he would say, giggling at me.

He would not have laughed quite so loudly if he had known what I got up to a short time later. I would draw his bald head and beetle-black eyebrows, the shirt that so often slipped from the waist of his trousers, the braces that so often fell off his shoulders, the shoes that stamped so loudly they could trample on any beetle, spider or other insect that came near his tread. And then there was the flood of spit that gushed from his mouth, accompanying the nonsense which he spoke.

'In young Einarsson's homeland, they are more used to the flavour of gulls and gannets than they are to the taste of chickens and ducks,' he would say before going onto explain how domestic hens descended from the red junglefowl, birds that could only fly vertically in short bursts. 'Our chickens have less ability to fly even than that, due to the way farmers have chosen to breed them, increasing the size of the bird's breast meat, as that is what man likes to eat. This is the reason why they fall and topple each time they take off from the ground.' He would snort and giggle before making his next remark. 'Unlike Einarsson's kin, who grab the nearest puffin or guillemot that's flapping around. Such is their appetite.'

I would impersonate him when he made remarks like these, emphasising each slurp and dribble, the sweep and sway of his arms. My audience would laugh as they watched me act like this, especially the youngsters who came from places like Iceland or the western coast of Jylland.

'All that wind has blown your common sense away,' he'd declare to the latter.

'Come on, we know your mind is as slow as the average glacier,' he would say to the former.

And then there would be those who idealised islands like Faroe, Iceland, Greenland. One was Johansen, the art teacher who came from Odense and was friends with my old teacher, Jacob Dahl. Johansen spoke about Odense often, talking about the cathedral and the statue of Hans Christian Andersen nearby. Sometimes he would speak about the stories the latter had told, tales like *The Steadfast Tin Soldier*, *The Little Mermaid*, *Thumbelina*, *The Wild Swans*. Once I created an image based partly on one of his creations, *The Emperor's New Clothes*. Instead of using a person as its centre, I drew instead my friend Emperor Cormorant XII of Atlantis, this time standing on the cliffs at Mykines, kitted out not in his customary dark plumage but clad in the white feathers of the gannets found there. Johansen clapped his hands when he saw this, his mouth bubbling in excitement.

'That's wonderful, Einarsson! Wonderful. You must have a thousand stories like that, Karl. You come from such a distinctive, different and magical part of the world.'

He talked about it for days, mentioning my work to any teacher who came near his room.

'An amazing young man. Blessed with an abundance of gifts.'

I would mimic men like him, their sanctimonious words, how they thought people from my part of the world somehow could keep ordinary human wickedness at a distance, possessing a sense of virtue that those who lived in larger communities or continents lacked.

'Oh,' they would say, clasping their fingers, 'they're all honest people where you come from.'

'You can leave your doors open and belongings outside and know that nothing will be disturbed.'

'Decent people. Pious people. Prayerful people.'

There were times, though, when mockery and impersonation wasn't quite enough to fend off the behaviour of teachers like these. I would escape into the school's large library or sit back and read the books I had stacked in a corner of the dormitory. They included Danish translations of Dickens, Balzac, Robert Louis Stevenson's *Kidnapped* and *Treasure Island*, the works of the Russian masters, Chekhov, Tolstoy, Gogol. And then there was that book my father had given me on that day I left Tórshavn, *Twenty Thousand Leagues under the Sea*. I read it often, identifying with the figure of Ned Land with his harpoon, chest swelling behind his striped shirt as – like so many of those I had seen growing up – he killed a whale, shark or dolphin.

I found in its pages a way of escaping Sorø and its academy, with its grey walls, library, the long walls of its church, acres of forestland – all alien and sometimes forbidding to me back then after leaving behind my homeplace, with its bare heights and dips, its many stretches of land without a building in sight. As I read, I could see a sea, wider by far than the one that swept around Sjælland where the school and Denmark's capital city Copenhagen had been built; one that smacked against the tall rocks of cliff and skerry, stretching into the distance like the scale and sweep of my imagination back then. There seemed to be no limits to it, no point at which it could end. Even my immediate surroundings were transformed by my reading, the roofs of the academy open to the sky, its walls fallen, arches and ceilings dislocated, its rooms and tracks empty. I was in a place where Captain Nemo had taken me, where there was a rock of black basalt on which the word 'Atlantis' could be traced:

> *What a light shot through my mind! Atlantis! The Atlantis of Plato, that continent denied by Origen and Humboldt who placed its disappearance amongst the legendary tales.*

Verne's words inspired my drawing, the sketches I etched out on the page:

> *Beyond Europe, Asia and Lybia, the columns of Hercules, where those powerful people, the Atlantides, against whom the first wars of ancient Greeks were raged.*

Christianna

So, LET ME BE CLEAR. I never expected to hear from my prince from Suðereyar again. Instead, I worked in my new home on the edge of the township of Sørvágar in Vágar, preparing food, cleaning clothes and house for my husband, Heðin, and our first daughter, Dagrún.

I rarely lifted my eyes to look beyond my immediate surroundings, occasionally walking a short distance on an island that Pastor Lukas said resembled a dog's head barking in the direction of the Atlantic Ocean, growling at storms; going to visit, perhaps, the shores of Lake Leitisvatn, the longest and deepest stretch of water in these shores. In winter, its features would – like the ground beneath me – often be white and grizzled with snow, this being the coldest part of the Faroe Islands. Aware how the land's surface would creak and groan each time I stepped upon it, I would mainly stay close to our home. Only on warmer days would I venture farther outdoors. And even then, it was the silence that struck me. There were few raised voices of the kind I would sometimes hear in Havn, the bang of a hammer as someone tried to repair the walls of their home, the rumble of a cart as it made its way down to the harbour. All sounds – apart from those of nature – were muted in my new location. The cry of a gull. The bleat of a sheep.

Raising my head, I would glance at the five peaks of Tindhólmur, the lighthouse flashing on the nearby island of Gáshólmur, perhaps catching a short glimpse of Mykines with its countless seabirds on days when fog or storms didn't shroud and conceal its outline. There were times, too, when I would carry our child and a couple of pails to a nearby well, or the short distance to where Heðin's relatives stayed. They were quiet, pious people, as muted in their own way as the natural world around them. If ever they raised their voices, it was to mention the birth of a child in the district or to discuss what this one passage or another from the Bible meant. Sometimes they might even go to the church and ask the likes of young Pastor Lukas what he thought its purpose was. For all his youth, his forehead would become like one of the few fields they furrowed with a plough – a mark, perhaps, of the grief he had experienced when his young wife had died a year or two before.

After that, a gleam might come into his eyes.

'Let me tell you ...' he would announce, before embarking on some theological lesson he had learned at the Lutheran college he'd attended in Denmark. It might be about Jesus calming the waters, a common theme in the sermons he delivered inside his church, appealing to many of the congregation within its walls. He would talk about how Christ was on a boat on the Sea of Galilee with his disciples when waves washed over the vessel, threatening to overwhelm it with their fury and force: '"You of little faith, why are you so afraid?" He had said, bringing stillness to the waters a moment or two later. "What kind of man is this?" the others asked. "Even the wind and waves obey him."'

That sermon unleashed its own storm within me. In my mind, I visualised that day MacCusbic sailed on his boat through the Minch – close to islands like North Rona and Sula Sgeir, which my father had pointed out to me on my map – and how the seas and wind had overpowered them, driving them eastwards, north, too, of Orkneyjar and Hjaltland, until they eventually arrived in my home. I recalled, too, the turmoil that moment had unleashed within me, the longing and need I had experienced for the touch of his skin, the brush of his lips, something I had rarely felt for my own husband. And then it was almost as if Pastor Lukas was aware of what was going on in my head. He seemed to look directly at me from his pulpit.

'Remember, too, these kinds of storms are not something we only experience on a boat. They can come at us at any time, even when we walk and step on dry land. They can be caused by moments in which we feel tormented and mistreated by others, when we feel dissatisfied in some aspect of our lives, when we experience temptations or longings of various kinds. Jesus asks us to have faith in order that these instances can be calmed and made peaceful, put to one side in order that we can be at ease with ourselves.'

I bit my lip, trembling under the pastor's gaze. He was right. It was time to put that man from the Outer Hebrides out of my head and be content with what I had. Heðin might be a distant and remote individual, as far away sometimes when he lay beside me in our bed as he was when he was out on his fishing boat. Besides, I would never be in touch with MacCusbic again. He was probably now back in Scalpay, fishing in the narrow waters of the Minch, his life lit up by that lighthouse he had told me about, one that was among the oldest in Scotland.

But hear from the man from Suðereyar I did. It happened on a day that Heðin was out fishing on his boat. The letter was delivered a year or so after I arrived in Vágar, sent from MacCusbic's home island of Scalpay many months before. My old address in Havn had been scrawled out by my mother, though I think it had lain with her for quite some time before, unsure whether in passing this on she was encouraging her daughter in some adulterous relationship with a stranger. Finally, she must have decided that the chances of this happening were non-existent. The distance was too great. I opened the envelope with trembling fingers as Dagrún slept nearby, glad that she wasn't awake to see me reading what was inside.

Dear Christianna,

I am writing you this letter to thank both you and your family for all the help you gave me and Donald when we were washed up in the Faroe Islands. I'm back home now and sending you this from the port of Stornoway, where we're tied up at the moment. It's been on my mind to do this for a long time but somehow when I am back in Scalpay I never have the chance. I am out fishing at Rubha Glas or making sure the cattle or sheep are fine and grazing near

Meall Chailbost or Ceann a Bhaigh. These names mean nothing to you but to me, they are beautiful, wonderful places. I could never imagine spending a lifetime away from them. It took long enough to reach these shores on the way back from the far north. By the time we voyaged all the way from Copenhagen to Leith I was desperate to see them, the hunger in me increasing mile by mile as we travelled most of the rest of the way by rail and sea.

I also have other news. A few months ago, I married the widow of one of those lost on our voyage, Christina Macleod. Our families are neighbours – our houses are near the North Harbour where I have always lived – and I have known her all my life. For the last few years, she was married to Angus and had two children by him. I know she'll make a good wife for me. She's strong, kind and hard-working, the kind of woman any man would want in my life. We're also expecting a baby. The strange thing is that the night I was told this, your face appeared to me in my sleep. You were smiling as you told me one day our families will meet once more. I do not know how that will be possible, but it would be good to see it.

Anyway, give my best wishes to your parents, brother and sister. It was good to meet them. Even in the hardest time I have ever known. I still am not sure how we lived through it, but somehow we did, even when two other men died. It was thanks partly to your kindness but also that of your pastor, doctor and all the other people we met in Tórshavn during those times. Someday we may return the favour.

Best wishes,

Iain

I sat for a long time crumpling the letter, remembering that fisherman and the intensity with which he looked at me during the time his boat had been washed up in Havn– that blue-eyed gaze, the ghost of a smile within them. He had put his arms around me once and I felt traces of his touch for days afterwards, remaining there – the Lord forgive me – in ways my husband's fingers had never done. We even had a different way of communicating. I would list the names of the Faroe Islands.

'Streynoy, Vágar, Esturoy, Sandoy, Mykines, Suðuroy, Borðoy, Viðoy …'

And he would respond by naming some of the islands in the Hebrides and beyond.

'Scalpay, Skye, Harris, Lewis, Raasay, Rona, Berneray, Scarp, North Uist, Benbecula, Barra …'

And then I would mention the names of some of the highest points in these islands, the words on my tongue becoming as jumbled as my sense of geography.

'Slættaratindur, Kopsenni, Vestmannabjørgini, Árnafjall, Eysturtindur, Beinisvørð …'

He came back at me with another set of words, the names of hills and heights that were in his own home islands.

'Clisham, Roinneabhal, Ceapabhal, Quiraing, Duntulm, Lingerbay …'

I was just about to start on lakes and stretches of water in the Faroe Islands when he interrupted me. He leaned over to kiss me, the words stalling on my lips.

As I sat there thinking of that moment, Dagrún stirred, shifting in her sleep. Her movement brought me back to the present, my life with Heðin here on the edge of Sørvágar. He was a kind, decent man, hard-working and thoughtful, his days mainly bound up with the sea and the church. I often compared him with my own father, much more predictable and steadfast than he had ever been. I could never imagine him liking the works of Ignatius Donnelly and his ideas about Atlantis, or the novels of Jules Verne. His only aspiration was to feed those of his own household and to be a better, more godly man. His fingers clasped together in prayer, he would mention his own dreams and ambitions.

'Oh, Father, we depend on you for so much, the shelter of our homes, the warmth of the fire, the food that fills our bellies. Let us never forget to be grateful for the mercies You provide until the day You reward us with an eternity in both Your proximity and that of Your Son.'

So, a modest, decent man. One who possessed faith and decency. And yet I could not stop thinking of this other man, so far from these shores. It was as if there was more of my father within me than I had ever realised. His desire to be different. His love of unusual ideas and drama. His wildness and eccentricity.

I would write him a letter some time, the next occasion I was in Havn. They would not notice who it was from, or addressed to, if I wandered into the post office there.

Karl

KASPER WAS WITH ME the first time we returned to Havn the following summer. For all that the parents of his mother, Nita, stayed not far from our home, he looked very much like a Dane as we walked together near the harbour – tall, sinewy, fair-headed, upright, a confidence in his stride which I could mimic but never quite match. Most of those with whom I had been to school – like Arno – recoiled from him, regarding him as one of the colonisers who had ruled these islands for centuries, not even allowing us to open local businesses for years but insisting that we buy all our merchandise at the Royal Store which my father now owned. Arno's nose would curl in disdain every time he saw Kasper near the fishing boats, as if he carried from Copenhagen something a lot more powerful in its stench than anything ever brought to these shores in the holds of those vessels.

'I hate him,' his every look appeared to say. 'I just have to look at him to know the reasons why.'

And then there were others who seemed to be more moderate in their opinions of those who lived in Denmark.

'They're not as bad as they used to be. 1864. The Second Schleswig-Holstein War. The loss of the Danevirke. That took them down a notch or two. They don't think of themselves as that superior anymore.'

They would follow up these words with a quick history lesson, mentioning how Danish forces had been defeated by Bismarck's Prussian forces and the Austrian army, how the fortified walls of the Danevirke that protected the country from attack had been overwhelmed, invading troops sneaking round its edges in a cold, hard winter, one that froze both water and marshes at either end. After that, the whole of Denmark had been overwhelmed.

'That was a great shock to our masters. Cut them right down to size. Denmark lost its heart and soul then. Never been the same since. Heads a little more bowed than before.'

These people would look at Kasper with a mixture of sympathy and self-righteousness, half-believing he and his kind needed the fall they had experienced some half-century before, that they required to have the long legs that provided them with such a giant stride cut from under them.

And then there was the way others treated him. They would regard him with a respect and reverence they never gave to a youngster who had been part of their tiny world in Havn. The women spoke to him about the latest fashions in Copenhagen and thereabouts; the men questioned him about politicians like Carl Theodore Zahle and Klaus Berntsen, wondering what they were really like as men. 'We don't really know anything here,' one said. 'All we ever get are gales and rumours.' Above all, they would interrogate him about the death of Frederick VIII a few months before, how it had occurred when he had taken on a false identity, adopting the name 'Count Kronsberg' and staying in a hotel in Hamburg. He had been found by a police officer lying on a park bench and died soon afterwards. Those working around the harbour would crowd round Kasper, asking him questions which had been on my lips and thoughts often before.

'What on earth was he doing there?'

'Had he been with prostitutes? I've heard there was a brothel nearby.'

'Did he take on a false name often? Or was this the very first time?'

Through all this, Ásla, the strange girl from my Faroe school-days, looked at him. Her blue-eyed gaze was as piercing as his own, taking in every move and gesture he made, every slight flourish of his hands, his lopsided grin. I noticed her quiver when we walked away from her. It was as if she had been transformed into the mermaid that was the symbol of Copenhagen by his very presence, the one who was turned into sea foam when she lost her true love.

'Who is he?' she asked me the first time she saw him.

'Kasper,' I answered and mentioned his mother's people, well known upon the island.

'He's beautiful,' she said.

I must admit I was a little jealous at this reaction. All the time I had lived there I had been viewed as a halfwit and a scholar, the

mad storekeeper's son. One of my classmates had even impersonated a cat holding a fiddle every time he saw me, reciting an
English nursery rhyme which a visiting fisherman from either
Hull or Grimsby had taught him to recite after seeing it in the
store window.

Hey diddle, diddle, the cat and the fiddle,
the cow jumped over the moon ...

He would mew after saying this, licking imaginary whiskers
with his tongue and fingers.

For all that he was unconscious of it, there were some ways in
which Kasper returned the idolisation, spending much of his time
praising the people that were around him.

'They're fine people. Amazing people. Brave, courageous,
quick-witted, adapting to all that's going on. Those in Denmark
are soft compared to them. They endure harsh weather, hunger,
the failure of both the sea and crops from time to time. Most men
and women in Copenhagen would crumble if they had lives like
that, but they keep going. Remarkable. Remarkable.'

I laughed. 'You're only saying that because some of them are
your kin.'

'Perhaps,' he laughed. 'But I think there's more to it than that.
People on islands must become a little like the rocks and soil
on which they stand. Independent. Self-reliant. No matter what
winds or waters wash against them, they must remain straight.
That's not like in cities. There's always people on hand to keep
them on their feet.'

'That's true here too, I suppose. Most people have plenty of
cousins.'

'But that's different. If people in cities need help in one thing or another, there's always someone there for them to turn to. Experts. Those who have unusual or special skills. There's no one like that here. They all have to adapt here, turn their hands to something they know little about. Repair. Make do and mend. Fix everything that's possible to fix.'

I nodded, knowing what he was talking about. They never burned wood here, the way they did sometimes in Copenhagen, even when it was damp and rotten. Instead, they would scrape clean every post or plank that showed signs of decay, finding some way of making use of it inside or outside their homes. Little was ever thrown away – from a torn line to a whalebone. Most was stored and put aside for the possibility it could be used again one day. It was something my father would bristle about from time to time.

'They're all so mean and so shoddy here. Hard to have a store in a place where they never want to buy anything new.'

Peculiarly, my time in Sorø had made him more restless than before. He would question me about how much of Copenhagen I'd seen during my time there. Had I come across Rosenborg Castle, the Tivoli Gardens, the National Museum, Christiansborg Slotsplads, the Rundetaarn, even the place where the now lost statue of Leda and the Swan once stood? I would either nod or shake my head when he mentioned these places, waiting for the description of each location after I mentioned it. There were times when I would delay giving this information, pausing for a moment to see the look of anticipation on his face.

'What did it look like? What did it feel like being there?'

And I would give a short description of the stonework of each establishment, the plants, trees or even exhibits to be found there, the sights that drew my attention.

'It was all right,' was how I'd sum up the experience.

He fulminated when I made a remark like that. 'It was all right!' he'd yell. 'You have these opportunities, and all you can say is that. I thought you were a young lad with a rare eloquence, a gift for words, and you limit yourself to these few. Remarkable! Remarkable!'

I grinned before I spoke again. 'You know what the oddest thing of all is?'

'No. Tell me.'

'The way my soles click along on cobblestones as I walk along the street.'

'What do you mean?'

'It's like I'm dancing when I'm walking.'

'Oh.'

'I never really experienced that before I walked around Copenhagen. Here the ground is always soft, mud, grass, snow, heather. I found it hard to get used to. And then there's the gas-lighting in the streets …'

'What is that like?'

'It's as if the Milky Way has fallen down from the heavens and is glistening in every building.'

'Oh,' my father gasped, 'I've never thought of that. Never occurred to me at all. Mind you, I've never had the chance to be aware of it.'

Even my sister Bedda used to suppress a giggle at the end of these conversations. It all fitted in with one of her private theories she shared with me once.

'Your father doesn't know that much about the world, Karl. All he knows is what he's found out about in books.'

Despite her mockery, there was a part of me that still loved my father very much. I enjoyed the way he imitated the customers that came through his store, copying their every eccentricity. The woman who used to unleash a frenzy of strange noises, the chattering of teeth, the trumpeting of her lips every time, regardless of weather, she stepped through the door. The man who would stamp his feet and dance as he stood at the counter, celebrating his purchase of tobacco. 'There's nothing like it. Nothing quite like it,' he'd declare, clutching a small container of Amphora Virginia in his hand.

My father would imitate, too, the mannerisms of Pastor Anders each time he climbed into the pulpit, the way he drew his fingers down the bridge of his nose, the shuffle of his shoulders, his repetition of certain expressions and phrases. ('Even after the fierceness of a storm, the Lord provides us with His mercies. They are washed upon the shore, seaweed that fertilises our land, driftwood for the roofs of our homes. And so it with the storms that afflict our lives.')

He could perform these impersonations to perfection, even those of acquaintances he had left behind in Iceland many years ago. 'Remember Adalsteinn?' my mother would ask him and, moments later, his arms would whirl like a blizzard, words stammering from his lips as he recalled one of the men he had known there. My mother would laugh at all this. 'Believe it or not,' she declared when his performance died away, 'that's one of the men who asked me to marry him before your father came along. Can you imagine the honour of that?'

And then there were the books my father read. There was one that particularly held my attention that summer, one that was among my father's most treasured books: Ignatius Donnelly's *Atlantis: The Antediluvian World*. It contained stories and arguments that enthralled me for years, outlining the evidence that a lost continent, which once stretched from beyond the British Isles to the mouth of the Mediterranean, had been destroyed in a cataclysm like the Great Flood in the Bible, the survivors taking to the waters like Noah and his family in their Ark. Many arrived in Ireland. Even today, according to the writer, much of its population were the red-haired, blue-eyed descendants of the Aryan race that once occupied Atlantis. They were the first people who became truly civilised, living in a world that included within its borders the Garden of Eden, the Gardens of the Hesperides, the Elysian Fields, the Gardens of Alcinous, the Mesomphalos, the Olympos ...

'All washed away, apart from a few stacks and islands like St Kilda, the Blasket islands off Ireland, the Hebrides, Hjaltland, Orkneyjar. Amazing, really,' my father said, shaking his head at the scale of the tragedy. 'Superb people. Strong and intelligent. Their legacy is still with us, if we only looked around us. Who were those who brought the tools of the Bronze Age to Europe? Who were the first to manufacture iron?'

When I had a little spare time, I used to draw the figures I imagined from the book. Strong, broad-shouldered, stern-faced men who bore swords and spears in gardens that glowed with sunlight, in pyramids, temples and massive stone structures that provided their own testimony to the skills and intelligence of those who built them. In the distance, I would sketch creatures I imagined were in existence back then, sea-dragons slithering through the depths of waves, trolls like those that were said to haunt places like Trøllanes on Kalsoy on the twelfth night of Christmas, tormenting the inhabitants of that island.

Sometimes, too, I would draw them around the lake and cliffs at Sørvágsvatn on the island of Vágar where my sister Christianna now lived, imagining this location as St Kilda, where the survivors of the Great Flood had gathered – strong, broad-shouldered individuals among buildings hewn and shaped from stone. There were similar stacks and summits there, dark chasms and ridges found among clefts in rocks, seabirds weaving above the heads of the survivors of the cataclysm that had occurred all those centuries ago, wiping away all signs of that great Aryan civilisation.

'Very good! Very, very good!' my father said as he looked at these sketches. 'You've a rare talent, Karl! A rare talent.'

Kasper

THAT IDIOT KARL NEVER REALISED how much his fellow islanders disliked him. He seemed unaware of their glances and mutterings, how they occasionally swore when they saw him near the harbour.

'Here's Lord Seyðisfjörður,' one might say, mentioning that part of Iceland from which the family had originally come.

'Count Sorø,' another would add, taking the name of the school we both attended in vain. 'The Duke of Tórshavn.'

They would snigger then behind the runt's back, mocking the way he'd sometimes carry a stick in his hand, twirling it within his fingers.

'If he only knew how much of a clown he looks,' Arno muttered, shaking his head.

The fact that he was originally an Icelander explained none of this. There were many of them in the community, adopted as children by Faroese fishermen as an act of charity when Iceland's economy was going through hard times. Cared for like their own, they grew up in Havn and other places in the islands, their origins in that distant territory barely recognised or noticed.

Part of it was inspired by resentment against his father. Some of the islanders used to overhear him mimic and imitate those who came to his store, his voice echoing outside the walls of the building. 'Are you sure you've nothing cheaper than that?' he would say, repeating a favourite question whenever a customer left, imitating their every turn and twist of speech. 'They're nothing but skinflints,' he would add. 'Even the smallest coin is imprinted on their fingertips. It's pinched so firmly in their hands.' The only reason they continued going to his store is that it was by some stretch the cheapest in Havn; the other storekeeper, old Jacobsen, being a lot less generous in giving his customers credit. They paid a great deal, however, in other ways. Their feelings were hurt each time they stepped within the door, humiliation part of the cost of every purchase they made there.

But Karl wounded them in quite a different way. Sometimes, the clown would set up his easel at the edge of the harbour and watch the men and women working there. He would stand behind it, shifting from foot to foot as though he were performing a dancing move, shifting with an easy grace as he tightened his grip on his pencil, beginning to draw – the shades of rock and stone, the tangle of lines, the expressions on the faces of the people he saw labouring before him. Some, like Arno and Ásla, had even been in his class in school. That didn't matter. The pretentious fool saw them purely as models for his art, the basis for sketches. He would draw them rigorously and exactly on a large piece of cream-coloured card that was fixed securely against the wind. At times, the wind would blow too fiercely for the card to stay in place. At other times, the paper would turn soft and damp in the rain or mist, preventing him from continuing his artwork, blurring the lines of paint, ink or pencil. He would shake his head and fold away all he had done, heading back to his father's store for shelter.

'It's the only time I welcome a downpour, when it chases that clown away,' Ásla would say, grinning. 'So glad to see the back of him.'

'You don't like him?'

'What woman likes any man to watch them when there's fish-stains on their clothes, far less stand there and draw them? No. I can't stand the likes of him, peering at me all the time.'

I laughed when I heard this, aware that these people disliked the fool for the same reasons my fellow students enjoyed his company so much at school. His ability to imitate others. The deftness of his fingers as he drew. Even his gift for foreign languages – the mastery he had gained of English, French, German, Spanish. When he was in Sorø, there was something of the chameleon about him, taking on whatever shade or colour happened to be around him. But this skill seemed to desert him when he was on the island where he had spent most of his childhood.

He stood out like a flamingo upon the moorland there, a parrot among peat.

Christianna

MY REASON FOR GOING TO HAVN was to see my brother, Karl. He was back at home from his time in school and was – undoubtedly – irritating the people of Havn with all his jumped-up, pretentious ways; that long, protruding nose he possessed, his sense of his own self-importance. Despite all these undoubted failings, I loved him. There was a tenderness in him, one that I had observed at a young age. He would go out to the dung heap, which he claimed to hate and despise, and leave a small trail of seeds or crumbs on its summit.

After that, he would sit and sketch the small birds that landed there, sometimes even stretching out his fingers to see if a wren or starling would eat from his palm. Even when he looked at the seals, shags and guillemots on the coastline, he would watch them in a different way from others on the island, noting the flinch of feathers, the ripples in the water into which they plunged and dived.

As well as this, there was his undoubted love for me. I had told him a few years before how much I loved the splendid sight of swans during these rare times when they arrived in the islands, and he would send me drawings of them from Denmark – the arc of their necks, fluffed-out white feathers, uplifted tails, their grace and posture when they flew.

Each time I see them touchdown on a lake or at the harbour in Copenhagen, they remind me of myself when I first came here, he wrote. *They scurry and skid on the water, taking ages to find their balance and poise. Nowadays I try to imitate them when they take to the air, pretending I have been here for a lifetime, moving with as much swagger and grace as I walk down the street as they can muster in the sky.*

I smiled when I read this, remembering the things I loved about him. But there were other reasons for travelling to Havn too. I wanted to show my daughter Dagrún off to my father and mother, sister Bedda, even the neighbours for whom I had time and understanding. I also wanted to send the letter to the fisherman from Suðereyar, the one I had written some time before. I scribbled the words down when Heðin was out fishing, feeling as if each line was an act of infidelity, a betrayal of the man I had married.

Dear Iain,

Thank you for the letter which I got a little time ago. It was so good to hear of what is happening in your life and your marriage.

Much the same is happening to me. I have a new husband called Heðin and a little daughter called Dagrún. I think my life here cannot be all that different from yours in Scalpay. Heðin spends much of the time fishing. We also go to church quite a lot. My husband has a very strong faith and gets on well with the pastor here. We cut peat, too, for the fire and look after sheep and a few cows.

It reminds me so much of the place you mentioned in your letter and spoke about when we were together. Sometimes I feel as if I've moved to Scalpay instead of Sørvágar, a little south of Tórshavn and north of the Outer Hebrides where, according to my father, Grímur Kamban, the founder of these islanders, might have come from. Who knows if that's true or just a fancy tale found in the Sagas?

But you're right on one thing. I sometimes think about you and believe that either one day we or our kin will meet again. Who knows when that time will come?

Yours, Christianna

I slipped off the morning after we arrived to go to the post office and send the letter. There was other news waiting for me at home when I returned. My sister Bedda had news. She wanted to marry Hjarnar Jacobsen, the eldest son of old Jacobsen, who owned the other store in Havn. And this made our father whistle and groan, reacting in a much more furious way than he had done when I came up with the suggestion of Heðin. At that time, he had only objected to the location where we planned to live. ('Why on earth are you going there? Why not go to Spitzbergen? Trondheim? Murmansk? Scalpay? Can't you think of some place more awkward you can go and stay?') With young Jacobsen, however, it was much more personal.

'That dull old miser ... Why would you want to get yourself tied up with a family like that? They've no interest in anything apart from the jingle in their pockets. They count every øre five times or more each and every night.'

He fulminated and muttered, growled and whistled, expressing his discontent over his daughter's desire to marry this man. However, she just looked at him in response, her dark eyes full of disdain. Her broad shoulders were hunched in a way that might have been designed to stave off his attacks.

'It's a good choice,' she declared. 'Both of our families will benefit from the match. The two stores can come together and dominate the place.'

And then she spoke more fully than I had ever seen her do before, casting aside any reticence and restraint.

'Besides, who can I marry around here? A fisherman like my sister?' She glanced in my direction as she said this before shaking her head. 'A farmer?' Again, there was the same movement. 'Some Dane or Norwegian who might swagger his way to these parts? There's little chance of that. Prince Charming only appears in ridiculous fairy tales. He rides a white horse. Precious few of them in these parts. No. Hjarnar Jacobsen is a good match. An excellent choice. We will do well for one another.'

I pretended not to hear her words about the prince, recalling my own one swathed in tartan from Suðereyar. 'Is he the one who used to be sent to our shop?' I said instead, recalling how one of old Jacobsen's sons – a tall, fair-headed, sullen individual – used to come into our store and note the price of every item for sale. There we used to watch him mouthing numbers – the cost of rope and butter, a dangling leg of lamb. When he was on the premises, Father used to ask Karl to pretend he was studying arithmetic as part of his homework for school. He would yell out mathematical equations and questions in order to confuse our visitor, trying to ensure there was a jumble of numbers rolling around his head.

'Yes. That's the one,' Bedda said.

'Oh,' Karl said.

'But what if he's like his father?' my father asked. 'I've heard that of all his three sons, he's most like the old man.'

'If he is, I'll put up with it,' Bedda declared. 'There's profit in it for both of us. If he's truly like his father, he'll completely understand the likes of that.'

Karl

IT WASN'T JUST BEDDA'S DECLARATION that darkened the atmosphere when both Christianna and I were at home. There was the time shortly afterwards that my father took the two of us aside, wanting to talk to us alone in the kitchen. We sat there beside the stove while he took a seat beside the table, drumming his fingers on its surface for a long time before he spoke.

'You know what's behind Bedda's plan?' he asked.

'The marriage?' Christianna said. 'I hope there's some method in it, that it isn't just madness.'

'Oh, there's method in it all right,' Father responded. 'Possibly too much. And it's all about me.'

'What do you mean?'

He drew his seat closer towards us, edging towards the stove. 'I haven't been well the last while. Pains in my chest. Sweating. Unable to sleep. The doctor says it might be to do with my heart. After all, it's how my father died. And he was only a few years older than me at the time.'

'Oh, Father,' Christianna said.

'That's awful news,' I added, seeing for the first time that my father was mortal, not fixed behind the counter of his store for ever.

'Oh, shhh … It might be a few years yet before it happens. No need to worry. Mind you, Bedda doesn't think that. The morning after my first sleepless night, when I'd wrestled for hours with the pain, she started panicking, asking the same question again and again.' It was at this stage he began to imitate her, the sulky turn of her lips, the deepness of her voice. '"What is going to happen to Mother and me if something happens to you? We can't cope on our own. Not without Father." She talked about that for hours on end, going on for ages. "We have to make plans. Changes."'

'And marrying Hjarnar was the plan?' I muttered.

'Aye. That was it. Apparently, old Jacobsen's son had asked her to go out him one time he had seen her walking out in the direction of Tinganes, standing there on the peninsula and looking out towards her. He slid over towards her and asked if the two of them could go out on a date. She blushed and said no, stepping away as quickly as she could. The second time he had seen her outside the store. Again, the same question and the same answer. It was a night or two after that I had my first attack. I remember how alarmed and worried she looked, as if she could already foresee my funeral taking place. Two days after that, she walked down to Jacobsen's store to ask him the same question.'

'And he said yes?'

'No doubt about it. I can see him rubbing his huge, greasy hands together as he did so. He's his father's son, that one. No doubt about it.'

'Poor Bedda.' Christianna shook her head. 'What does Mother think of all this?'

'Bedda's not that poor. She's rich in lots of ways. She can see ways of making profit that the rest of us don't even notice. It's how she's thought this through. As for Mother' – my father shrugged – 'she does what she's always done. Says very little. That's part of the price she's paid for being married to a man like me.'

Christianna raised an eyebrow. 'Some would say that it's part of a price we all pay.'

'Aye. Well, Bedda will have to pay it more than most.' He drew his shoulders up, wrinkled his face and spoke in a voice that we instantly recognised as belonging to Hjarnar, his words interrupted by a continual cough and splutter, a clearing of the throat. '"Are you sure you had to spend as much as that on a skirt, Bedda? Couldn't you have saved an øre or two by spending it somewhere else?"'

'I can imagine there's going to be countless conversations like that,' I said.

'No doubt,' my father said, nodding. 'But I can see what's going on in her head. If anything did happen to me, there's the danger there wouldn't be a place for either her or your mother here in Havn. The store might have to close. It would certainly be too big for them to run on their own. Marry Hjarnar, and they still have a business and a roof over their heads. Life would be a little easier for her, even if she did have to put up with a mean-spirited object like that in her bed. It's small comfort, but better than none.'

'Yes. I can see that,' Christianna said.

'But it also might have implications for you, son.' My father's gaze turned in my direction. 'If anything happens to me over the next few years, who's going to pay for your schooling? Who will see you through your early years in work? I doubt very much it's going to be Bedda and her husband. Can you imagine the way he's going to react to that?' Again, he adopted Hjarnar's voice and gestures, his shoulders hefting up. "'Do you seriously expect me to pay for that boy's learning? All his daft drawing and silly languages, tongues that no one around here can speak? How's that going to profit the likes of me.'" He shook his head. 'No. It's all too easy imagining Hjarnar getting his way out of that one. Even if I do leave a trust-fund to see you through. "Why are you putting a rope like that around my neck? Don't you think running a business in these parts is hard enough without that kind of burden?"' He kept silent for a moment before he spoke again. 'No. I'll do what I can to protect you. But I'm afraid you're going to have to find ways of helping yourself. Just in case anything happens to me.'

Despite the proximity of the fire, I froze. 'Such as? What can I do?' I asked.

'There's foreign visitors all the time in Copenhagen, isn't there? French, English, Germans, Swedes, Norwegians, Austrians, even an American or two. All going to see the mermaid and whatever else can be found. And you can speak their languages.' He brushed the edge of his nose with a finger. 'And where there's travellers, there's money. Enough to bring in a krone or two for your pockets.' He paused before undertaking his Hjarnar impersonation again. "'*Comprendre? Verstehe? Forstå?* Understand? *Bheil thu tuigsinn?* as the Scalpay fisherman might say.'"

He winked in the direction of Christianna as he said this, his daughter blushing as he spoke. And then he tapped my shoulder, ignoring the tears that were flecking my cheeks at the prospect of losing him, the only man I loved on Earth.

'No point in crying,' he declared. 'We've just got to act the part. Put on a mask when it's the last thing we feel like doing. You remember that, Karl.'

I nodded. For all my loss, I was determined not to let my feelings show.

The Great War Years
1914–1919

Karl

I NEVER SAW MY FATHER AGAIN. It was years later I heard how he had passed away. A month or two before he had read a translation of Shakespeare's *Hamlet*, some words from the play fled his mouth as he sat at the kitchen table, feeling a burst of pain sear his chest. He tried to ward off the agony by quoting the words of the ghost of Hamlet's father, as he patted and squeezed his woollen jumper, declaring:

> *I am thy father's spirit,*
> *Doom'd for a certain term to walk the night,*
> *And for the day confined to fast in fires,*
> *Till the foul crimes done in my days of nature*
> *Are burnt and purged away.*

Eventually, however, both the pretence and the performance came to an end. He stood up, brushing against my mother's shoulder as he stumbled out of the room.

'I'll have to go to bed,' he declared.

He never reached there, stumbling to the floor almost as he said the words. My mother rushed towards him, calling out my oldest sister's name, forgetting in her panic that she no longer lived there.

'Christianna!'

Needless to say, no one answered. Not even Bedda, who now lived in the Jacobsen's store a short distance away.

I did not attend his funeral. Like many things that occurred during that time, my attendance at the cemetery near Argir was prevented by the war that had broken out two years before. I heard about what happened in two letters. One was scribbled by my mother and made little sense. Each sentence rambled and meandered across the page. Shaken and unsettled by the extent of her grief, it was easy to imagine her pen wavering as she tried her best to write: *We have known for ages now it was coming but it was still a shock when the time arrived. I find it hard to accept he is gone and the house is quiet without him.*

The other was composed by Christianna a day or so after the funeral. She said that with the wildness of the weather she had only just managed to reach it in time herself, her husband Heðin taking her and their daughter to Havn by boat. In the whip of rain and wind, they had lain his body at the cemetery, the older men coming up to her afterwards and offering sympathy on the loss of our father.

'He was quite a character, the Icelander,' one of them said.

'As unpredictable as Thordarhyrna,' another declared, referring to a volcano in that island from which he had come so many years before. 'And just as fiery.'

In her letter, Christianna told me there was no point in my returning to Faroe.

By the time you receive this, the funeral will be long gone. For all that we loved our father, the time for tears will be past. We will need to get on with our lives. Besides, your journey will cost a lot of money which you and the family can ill afford.

This dreadful war is not only causing many people to lose their lives. It is also taking away their jobs and money. Neither of the stores are doing well these days. No one living in these islands has any cash to spend. Not even for the essentials, far less anything else. There is hardly any grain to make bread.

And the other reason for not travelling is that these journeys are dangerous. Too many innocent people have already been killed by accident in this conflict. A bomb or a bullet isn't able to tell the difference whether someone is English, German or Faroese. Or if they are a scholar or a soldier.

I bit back tears as I read this, knowing it was true. For all that Denmark was neutral in the conflict, quite a few Danes had been killed. Some of the fishing boats out of both Havn and Esbjerg had been sunk, the Danish Navy having laid down mines at the request of Germany in the straits between Sjælland and the isle of Fyn, and in the stretch of water between Sjælland and Sweden, to control the Baltic Sea. There was always the chance that the worst might happen. I looked once again at the letter.

I know how much you might want to come back here, Christianna continued, *but it's safer to stay in Sjælland for the moment, for all that I know it will be hard to deal with your grief on your own.*

To be truthful, I wasn't entirely on my own. I journeyed to Kasper's home after I read the letter, a place I often went to visit during these early years in Denmark. There were reasons for that. His mother had been asked to keep an eye on me, something that the people of Faroe often requested of those who had moved to Denmark when their offspring were away from home the first few years. Kasper's mother, Nita, had taken it upon herself to do that. 'I remember what it was like when I first came here,' she had said. 'The shock of being surrounded by so many people. Life was so much easier when it was just sheep, waves and birds.' More than her son, she was the one I spoke to. She knew what life in Havn was like. To her offspring, it was just a holiday. And so I passed the note to Nita after I smoothed out the sheet with my hand, removing all the creases I had made when I first read it, crumpling each word with my fingers.

'The old man's gone,' I said. 'I thought he was immortal.'

'Aye. We all think that,' Nita said. 'And I suppose he is in a way. You'll never forget him. Everywhere you go, you'll feel his shadow upon you all your days.'

'It'll be a larger shadow than most.'

'That's true. He was quite a character.' Kasper's father, Verner, nodded, the tight grey curls that were knitted together on his head trembling as he did so. 'You know your sister's right in suggesting that you don't go home just now.'

I said nothing in response.

'It's far too dangerous,' Nita said. 'The world's at war everywhere around us. And you don't want to get caught in the crossfire. That's all too easy to do when the Germans are at one side of us waving their guns and the British are at the other. Best to stay where you are. The time will come when you'll be safe to return to Havn once again.'

'But it'll be hard.'

'No doubt about that.' Kasper's father spoke once more. 'I've heard others speak of it, how hard it is to deal with death when there's an absence. People whose brothers, sisters, sons and daughters have gone to the States or Canada and died there; how difficult it is to mourn those who have travelled to foreign parts. It'll be the same for you. I've no doubt about that.'

'But you've no choice,' Nita added. 'No choice whatsoever.'

'I'm afraid not,' Verner said. He stretched out a hand to pat me on the back and comfort me, giving me the lopsided smile that his son had inherited. Knowing the remoteness and coldness that Kasper often complained about in his father, it was a gesture I appreciated. He was an architect and seemed to have the same distant air in dealing with his fellow human as he possessed when planning the construction of new houses for a city that was expanding year upon year. 'Sometimes we just have to get on with whatever life throws at us.'

I placed my head in my hands when I thought of all that had been said, conscious they were probably right but aware it would take time even to admit this to myself. I knew that until I saw the mound of earth in the cemetery in Havn, perhaps even the headstone above his freshly dug cave, I would not be convinced that he was gone from us. My father's spirit would be just like the ghost of Hamlet's father at Elsinore, 'doomed for a certain time to walk the night', waking me in the darkness, reminding me again and again that 'the time is out of joint.'

And there is no doubt it was. Circumstances – and my father's death – had forced me to abandon my whole educational existence sooner than I would have liked. Money stopped coming from home. Bedda wrote to me about this in one of the few letters that actually reached me during these years of war: *You'll have to go out and find a job. We cannot afford to put you through university now. The money just isn't there. It probably never was. Not even when father was alive.*

It was the art teacher, Johansen, who gave me the chance to escape the mess I was in. The man from Odense turned to me when I told him the news that I would have to leave school with nowhere to go. 'I can help you out,' he declared. 'A friend of mine has a studio in Copenhagen where you can stay for a few months at least. He's away in New York and can't get home because of the war. I'm sure I can also find you a job. One that you've got more of your share of talent to do.'

The man did precisely as he promised, no longer mentioning the kinds of stories that he so often spoke about in class. No mermaid. No tin soldier. No wild swans. Instead, short, blunt sentences.

'I've got you work in Kronprinsessegade. The large lithographers who occupy the offices there. I'm sure you'll do well for them.'

'Thanks,' I muttered.

'I know it's not what you would have chosen, but sometimes people have no alternative.'

'I'm very grateful,' I said.

'It's either that or starving.'

I nodded, aware that he had done me a great kindness, for all that I slightly resented it. I had pictured myself studying either art or languages at university, going on, perhaps, to teach young people, stepping in front of them in large lecture theatres wearing the same long, flowing robes which I envisaged putting on while pretending to be the Count of St Kilda. It was a deep disappointment to me that I would never have the opportunity to take on the part.

'I know you'll make the best of this,' Johansen declared. 'You have the talent for it.'

In some ways, for all my resentment, he was right in saying this. I worked in Kronprinsessegade for several years. It was a job that helped me develop many of my talents. This was not only in terms of artwork – the illustrations and calligraphy needed for my employment, the ability to create catchphrases and slogans that might capture people's attention. The other workers would come to me, too, for help with languages when there was material to translate.

'What does that German word mean?'

'What about that English sentence?'

'That French expression?'

And I'd work out the meanings for them, drawing on my understanding of each tongue.

'You're a very valuable young man,' Brandes, the manager, used to tell me, his eyes sparkling behind his thick-rimmed glasses. 'There's a bright future for you here.'

My head reeled at the compliment, aware the words came from the member of a prominent family in Danish society. A distant relative of his, called Carl, was one of the founders of *Politiken* newspaper and sat in the Landsting for the Social Liberal Party. He was a friend, too, of the Prime Minister, Carl Theodore Zahle. He had power and influence, and a way of charming and enticing people when necessary. He was also regarded as one of the most unpleasant men in the workplace. The office used to echo with his insults at some of the men who were employed there.

'You bloody lazy idiot! How did you make a mess like that?'

I would entertain my colleagues with my impersonation of him – the whirl of arms, stamp of feet, even the sudden snort from his nostrils that often accompanied his rages, mimicking too the clockwork noises of the machine where the compositors worked. *Clickety-click! Clickety-click! Clickety-click!* – the roar and vibration of the great rotating machines like an echo underlying his words. They would laugh and snigger at my performance, their anger at his antics defused for a time by their amusement.

'You've got him! You've got him!' they declared.

And then there were the letters and documents I sometimes forged for my colleagues and friends. The statement from a doctor that might prevent a younger brother being called up for the army. The degree certificate for a university somewhere in Denmark or Sweden. A school prize being awarded. A letter-of-discharge that would permit some German deserter to remain in the country for the rest of his existence. All of this would be rewarded with a few extra kroner being crammed into one of my pockets, nothing being said except a few words of praise.

'Remarkable! Remarkable!'

I also hand-set leaflets and news-sheets for both private firms and public organisations, working on the lettering and illustrations, trying to ensure they would catch the attention of those who came across them, whether pinned against a wall or on a newsvendor's board. I helped design theatre and concert posters, those advertising new Danish films like August Blom's *Pro Patria* and Holger-Madsen's *Pax Aeterna*. I learned, too, to impersonate some of the actors in them, such as Valdemar Psilander as Lieutenant Erich von Wimpfen in *Pro Patria*, Frederik Jacobsen playing King Elin XII in the latter film, copying their every gesture, mimicking each lift of their eyebrows, downturn of their mouths. And then, too, there was August Blom's *Atlantis*, the film which I mistakenly thought was about that lost world in the North Atlantic. Instead, Olaf Fønss starred as a doctor who was on a ship of that name which sank while crossing that same ocean to the States. I imitated each expression, each look of distress that crossed the faces of those who appeared on screen, much to the amusement of my colleagues.

'Well done!' they would say, 'There's a career waiting for you in the movies.'

I thought of my father at moments like these, aware how much he would have enjoyed all of this, relishing the stories that were being told in a fresh and inspiring way.

And then there were the Rosenborg Castle Gardens that my work looked out upon. I could occasionally glimpse the members of the aristocracy through the wrought iron grill that surrounded the grounds, aware of all – the Boy on the Swan, the Horse and the Lion – that was within. I would note the way they held themselves – how the men twirled sticks or how the women carried umbrellas resting on their shoulders – taking note of each distinctive mannerism. Sometimes, too, I could hear their cries as they summoned servants or praised and criticised the efforts of others. When that happened, I echoed their phrases, letting the sound of their words pass my lips once more.

'That was simply splendid, Louise.'

'Frederick … Alexandrine … Francis.'

Someday, I would be like them.

Someday, even if I never had the opportunity to go to university, I would learn to be a duke or a count, a member of the privileged and entitled ones who governed much of the Earth.

Someday, that chance would come.

Christianna

LIFE GREW DULL WITHOUT FATHER.

So, even if I no longer saw him anymore, I thought about him constantly. Glimpsing a bull, I'd picture him as he was on that day MacCusbic came to our house – head down, shoulders hunched, pretending there were horns sticking out from his skull and lowing as he shouted, '*Tarbh, tarbh!*'

Or imitating too the sound of a duck as he flapped his arms.

'*Dunna, dunna! Tunnag, tunnag!*'

There would be so many moments when he came to mind – the countless readings of Jules Verne's books, words that took me either to the depths of the Earth or towards the sway and sparkle of the stars. Then I thought of him on those nights when the Northern Lights burned bright above my head. In the surge of colour that lit up the darkness, there seemed to be somehow the possibility that these tales were true. Man could voyage towards the moon and the planets, stretch out his fingers to brush the Milky Way.

It wasn't quite the way I saw my existence now. Heðin was a quiet man. There were hours that the only way I knew he was in my room was the faint smell of fish he trailed around him. Words rarely slipped from his mouth, all hooked and snarled inside his head. Sometimes Dagrún might squeeze a word or two out of him, if she clambered on his lap and tousled his curly hair. A smile might appear. A laugh.

'I'm going to tickle you,' he might say.

Otherwise, there was little. A few words when he was heading out on his boat. A few words some ten or twelve weeks later when he returned. As I looked at my life, I began to recall another story her father once read aloud to the household, *In the Cart*, by Anton Chekhov. When he had finished the tale, he shook his head.

'What on earth was that all about?'

'I've no idea,' I laughed.

The answer was clearer now. It was about a young teacher who had been working in a village school for years. Her life seemed trapped by its walls, forced to think most of the time of the children she taught, the four girls and a boy she was preparing for examinations, the arithmetic problems they would have to master. She had declared 'she felt as though she had been living in these parts for a hundred years, and it seemed to her that she knew every stone, every tree on the road from the town to her school.' For all that there were no trees anywhere in the vicinity, I felt much the same as Chekhov's character. I knew every *hjallur* – the drying sheds where fish and *skerpikjøt*, dried shanks of mutton, hung for months on end – and the streams or stretches of ocean they stood alongside, built in these places to ensure the meat would be free of flies. I could even identify every single chicken and duck that I fed outside the house, recognising them by their clucks and cackles. There were times when I could shut my eyes and guess exactly where I stood, knowing the spot from the rush or ripple of water I could hear.

And then I would dream, perhaps of Scalpay, knowing exactly where it was now from the book of maps I had bought, able to trace the quickest route there past North Rona, the Butt of Lewis, Cape Wrath, Stornoway, each Hebridean loch and headland. MacCusbic would be there, the fisherman from Suðereyar, trapped in his marriage of convenience, forced to wed the widow of the man whose life had been lost on the boat that had been blown from the north end of the Minch all the way to Faroe. I would travel to see him, win him over, settling on that shore or, maybe, persuading him to move, together with me, to somewhere on the mainland of Scotland – Glasgow, Greenock, Edinburgh, Dundee, all places I had come to know from my familiarity with that book of maps.

Or there might be Pastor Lukas, that bright, broad-shouldered widower whom I had seen so often in the church at Sandvágar. I felt a strong attraction towards him, his dapper clothing, thin fair hair and grey eyes. He looked as trim and neat as a new boat, one that had not been cracked or damaged by the waves, as so many had in these parts. His fingers were unblemished, his face unmarked and unscarred. The only thing that marred his appearance were his teeth. They crossed back and forth within his mouth, like wooden bollards which had once been circled with ropes tying boats to the shore, twisted this way and that by the surge of waves. I would watch him often as he stood in the pulpit, preaching about that other great sweep and rise of water, the Flood that had destroyed the world thousands of years before.

'The Lord said to Noah, "Come into the Ark, you and all your household, because I have seen *that* you *are* righteous before Me in this generation. You shall take with you seven each of every clean animal, a male and his female; two each of animals that *are* unclean, a male and his female; also seven each of birds of the air, male and female, to keep the species alive on the face of all the earth. For after seven more days I will cause it to rain on the earth forty days and forty nights, and I will destroy from the face of the earth all living things that I have made."'

I followed the movement of his lips, recalling how my father had often spoken about these matters, how that same surge of water had swept over Atlantis, drowning most of its people, hammering and pounding the pillars and columns those who lived in that great civilisation had built for themselves. There was no doubt that – for all their differences in terms of faith – the pastor and my father had much in common. They had a wider vision than most of those around them. They could create their own spells, one based on all they had read in the books they had studied – with one provoking restlessness, the other seeking to prevent it, allowing the people of Sørvágar to feel content in the place where they resided. Pastor Lukas even had that effect on me. I could hear it in the magic of his words, how they lifted the mood and spirits of his congregation.

'In some ways, God has already provided us with an Ark. At a time when most of the countries nearby us are in conflict, when men throughout the continent are being killed and slaughtered by one another, He has given a safe haven, a place where we are protected from all the wickedness which man's sinfulness has let loose upon the Earth. There is not a day when we should not be grateful for His kindness and mercy towards those of us for being here, especially when there is so much risk and danger elsewhere.'

And I sensed him looking at me once again, as if he was somehow aware of the thoughts that sometimes ran rampant in my mercy.

'God is aware that everywhere around us, there are temptations, lures and enticements that appeal to us. He knows, too, that if we succumb to them, we are putting our own safety and salvation at risk.'

Karl

MY HEAD WAS STILL FILLED with images from the film *The Birth of a Nation* that morning. The scene where Abraham Lincoln was shot. Where a black man had tried to rape a white woman. How she had finally escaped from his attentions by diving from the top of a cliff. How a young white man had fought a crowd of black men inside a wooden hut, until he was shot and killed. And then, too, wearing the white uniform of the Ku Klux Klan, each face and body obscured by sheets and pillowcases. The burning cross. The call to arms.

And the words, too, printed in white on a dark screen:

The bringing of the African to America planted the first seed of disunion.

The former enemies of North and South are united again in common defence of their Aryan birthright.

The white men were roused by a mere instinct of self-preservation – until at last there had sprung into existence a great Ku Klux Klan, a veritable empire of the South, to protect the Southern country.

The last sentence the words of US President Woodrow Wilson.

I remember speaking about the film to some of the young men in my workplace about the techniques D.W. Griffith employed, the use of close-ups to capture the expressions on the actors' faces, flashbacks, music that underscored the events that were happening, how hundreds of extras were employed in battle scenes, the night-time photography, even how quotations like those above were part of the way authenticity was added to the film.

'It was marvellous. Never seen anything like it in my life. There was so much about it that was new and exciting. So much from which we could learn.'

Brandes interrupted. Seeing me from his office door, he beckoned me over. There was no mistaking the grim look on his face.

'I've got bad news for you,' he declared.

'Yes?'

'We're going to have to pay you off. It's not something we want to do. We recognise how valuable you are. But you know yourself that times are tough. We may not be involved in the war that's going all around us, but we're just like everyone else. We're having to pay a price for it. So' – he paused, looking down at his desk to try to hide his embarrassment – 'we've discussed it with the union. They've decided that the younger ones should go first, those without a family depending on them. Last in, first out.'

I said nothing, my head reeling as I wondered how I was going to survive over the next while. I hadn't received any money from my family for over a year. They, too, were finding it hard to get by, something that my mother had told me about in her occasional letter. *Things are hard here and people are finding it difficult to survive – the only way they can do so is getting credit from the store, as if we is making any money out of it all.* I was finding it difficult enough to pay for my one room in Vesterbro at the moment, especially after the landlord raised the rent a few months before, seeking, like so many others at this time, to profit from the crisis in the country. My arms and legs shook and trembled at the thought of all I was going to face.

'Don't worry,' Brandes said, smiling. 'It's happening all over. Unfortunately. I've heard Carlsberg are paying more people off. So are Riedel & Lindegaard, the iron foundry. Not good times.' Again, he paused, brushing his fingers through his dark hair. 'Yet I want to give you a little reassurance. If it were left to me alone, I wouldn't pay you off. With all your skills in art and language, you're a very valuable person to have around these parts. I'll make sure you're the first person to be taken on when things turn right again. You have my word on that.'

'Thanks,' I said, nodding. 'I'd be really grateful if you did that.'

'Good … Good.' He grinned. 'I promise to keep my word on that.'

He stretched out a hand towards me. I looked at it for a moment, aware it looked so unlike the fingers of the men in Havn. There were no bruises on the skin, no cuts on fingers. Every digit was in place. None had ever been gashed or wounded by hard physical endeavour. The hand belonged to a man who never – like my father – had to bend his back to carry a box or barrel into a store. Or one who was compelled by his need to eat to tug a line full of fish on board a boat. His palms and knuckles had never been ravaged by harsh weather. He had never known want or hunger or even that weariness which comes from physical tiredness. None of that had been part of his experience.

'I'm not like the others,' I heard myself say, 'not the rest of the young ones that have been paid off. Most of them have family close to hand. They might even still be staying in their family homes. That's not like me. I'm here with no one I can ask for help from. Except for a few who might have come from Faroe some years ago. They do their little bit in looking after their own. But, even then, they might not have much to give. Besides, I'm not really one of them. Both my parents don't come from these parts, as some of them have reminded me over the years.'

'Oh.' Brandes looked embarrassed. It was clear from his dark looks and demeanour he had not expected this. 'I'm sorry.'

'So, I'd be grateful to return to work as soon as possible. Very grateful for that.'

'Of course. Of course,' he mumbled, trying to avoid my gaze as he did so. 'We'll do our best about that. But remember there's no guarantee. Not for me, you or anyone.'

I did my best to ignore what he was saying, pretending not to hear him. 'Good. Good. Good,' I declared. 'The sooner I'm back the better.'

I still felt dizzy and sick as I went back to my apartment that evening. One I had signed up for a month or two before, it was in the middle of Istedgade, a long, endless street which in some sections seemed to be filled with the unemployed. Some sat near doorways or beside cafés, smoking and whistling through their fingers at the women walking past, clutching the hands of their children or going to buy groceries from the local shops. A few of the men were drunk, seeking, perhaps to numb themselves to the reality of their existence – without hope or comfort. There was one that bellowed every night, mourning the loss of his childhood home in Mors.

'I wish I were back on the island,' he would yell. 'I wish I were back at home!'

There were moments when this echoed my own thoughts, though his home island lay in the Limfjord, a shallow inlet of water that cuts across the north of Jylland, not distant, deep and stormy like the one I came from.

Downstairs from my home, a woman called Miss Jensen lived. Men came to visit her at all times of the day and night, a small reminder of how syphilis plagued the nation at that time, how some of the women visited Danish soldiers just to have enough cash to feed their households. Many of their husbands pretended not to see this, though occasionally there were shouts from nearby rooms or alleyways.

'You bloody slut! You damn whore!'

There were, too, German deserters who had slipped off trains filled with troops heading in the direction of France from the eastern front. Everything about them seemed broken by the war. Clothed in whatever they could find or steal, they waved false papers when they were questioned by policemen, yelling and cursing at them whenever they were stopped or questioned.

'Who the hell do you think I am? A bloody Hun!'

I felt uncomfortable with all of this. I had been brought up in a household where both airs and graces were nurtured and encouraged, bad language condemned. Instead, we took on the voices of the Count of Monte Cristo and his kind, Earl or Lord Dunganon with his huge Scottish estates, the Prince of Suðereyar in that book I had discovered my sister reading, all wrapped up in tartan as he braved Icelandic winds. We were like the landowners and aristocrats of Russia that revolution had so recently swept away. We spoke of ourselves in the plural, believing that this was how nobility always addressed the world.

'We think it is time our dinner was served.'

'We require our stomachs to be filled.'

'We endured too many sleepless hours last night, our bodies tossing and turning.'

When my father read, it was as if he were pretending to be a tsar or king, his words resounding in what he imagined to be their accents. Even the poorest of the customers that came to our door – and there were many of that number – had grace and manners when compared to those surrounding me in Copenhagen. Give or take the odd enmity, they were restrained both in their behaviour towards each other and their language. I could not imagine them involved in some of the antics I was seeing in Vesterbro.

For the first time since I had left, I was missing Havn.

For the first time since I had left, I was starting to drink heavily.

Every night of my life.

Kasper

I DIDN'T WANT TO GO and see the runt. I'd heard so many tales of the way the idiot was behaving from our mutual friends, how he had allowed himself to go to rack-and-ruin, his clothes and entire appearance being affected by want and need, sleeping often outdoors or on the floor of a dirty apartment. It had altered his way of dealing with others, becoming coarse and crude on occasions. There was the girl Kirsten who told me that when they met, he had spoken about how repelled he was by dairy milk.

'It's bad for you,' he'd said. 'Not natural. Every time I drink it, I feel sick. Humans should only take human milk. When did a horse ever suckle a calf?'

'But what's your alternative?'

'Oh, that's easy. We should get a crowd of large-breasted women. Like yourself, Kirsten. Place them on a farm and get the milk from them. A much healthier option.'

There were the ways, too, the clown had managed to survive. He became friends with one of the zookeepers at Copenhagen zoo. Walking out to Frederiksberg in the morning, he would obtain some of the left-over meat for the tigers and lions, bringing that to an open fire he created from wood he'd gathered to boil and cook. He would steal saltshakers from the city's cafés and restaurants. An hour or so later, he would go to a park bench and, within view of the police, sprinkle this on the wood. He would then use the last note he had crumpled in his pocket to sniff and snort it, knowing that some eager officer would come his way.

'Is that cocaine you're sniffing?'

The idiot would never deny it. Tugged away, he knew he had achieved his ambition. Together with obtaining free bed and board for the night, he had become the Count of Monte Cristo he had read about in his childhood. The feeling would intensify when he arrived at the police station. There would be the surrender of a few possessions, such as his threadbare clothing, empty wallet, a watch. He would then be provided with a prison uniform, taken by guards down an endless corridor, before being locked behind a heavy metal gate that creaked as it is closed behind him. Delighted at all that had occurred, he would shake his head and quote some of the words written by Dumas in that book.

Happiness is like one of those palaces on an enchanted island, its gates guarded by dragons.

It wasn't the only thing that was unpleasant about him. He would sometimes talk obsessively about Brandes, the man in the lithographer's office whom he considered responsible for his sacking.

'A two-faced Jew, that man. One minute he's praising me and saying I'm the most talented man in the place. The next he's giving me my books.' He shook his head. 'Just goes to show you can't trust the word of anyone from that race.'

And then he would impersonate the man, a whirl of limbs, an endless shower of insults.

He would use similar words about the Dansk Litografisk Forbund, the lithographers' union, which he also blamed for losing his job.

'A useless crowd. Hopeless, hopeless, hopeless!'

And then there were the ways his attitude had changed towards his home islands. Instead of criticising them for the narrowness of their geography, the narrowness of the minds of those who inhabited them, he was, by all accounts, beginning to sound a little like my mother who – when she was in a cheerful mood – praised the islands from which she came. Like her, he would speak for hours about the honesty and decency of its people.

'You can leave your door open all day when you're there. You know that no one's going to touch or take any of your property. Decent, honest people, like most small islanders everywhere. They will see no one starve or go hungry. Instead, they will leave food out for anyone they know who's in that kind of desperate position. And no one will ever know who's responsible for that act of kindness. The giver wouldn't want any kind of glory for themselves.' He would pause, shake his head in wonder before moving onto matters that would never have occurred to my mother to mention. 'That's why places like St Kilda in the Suðereyar are quite remarkable. Far away from civilisation and all its crime and corruption. Full of fine, upright Aryan people. No other races mingling among them. All we could and should be.'

It was a part of him that had been there a long time. Even when he was in school, he was full of talk like that. He'd speak about Jules Verne and Ignatius Donnelly a great deal, mentioning that US congressman again and again in his conversations. And then there was Madame Blavatsky and all her talk of the Fifth Root Race and their descendants, the Aryans. She, too, asserted that Atlanteans were bigger, more intelligent and a considerable improvement on today's humans, and Karl would say, 'You know they invented aeroplanes and electricity. They also passed on their secrets to Druids, ancient Egyptians, the people who inhabited Mexico. It's because of them that high temples and pyramids were built. Even stone circles.'

The clown even began to talk about reincarnation, how those from Atlantis were reborn and took on the identities of the smartest and brightest among us, our scientists and artists, our intellectuals. Once or twice, when I met him, I tried to discourage his nonsense.

'They'd laugh at you if you said that in Havn!'

'Havn doesn't get it right in everything. In fact ...'

It was for all these reasons that I resisted my mother's attempts to make me go and see him.

'He's one of us,' she would say. 'We know that some of us, after we move from the islands to the city, have difficulty in settling. It takes time to build the basis of a new life here. I know I needed help from cousins and relatives when I first came here.'

'We're not his cousins and relatives,' I'd proclaim.

'No. He's not. He hasn't any cousins and relatives. But our families are neighbours. It's good for neighbours to help one another. We don't live alone.'

'That doesn't mean we should help him.'

'It doesn't mean we shouldn't either. People sometimes need help to survive. It's our duty to provide it.'

'Nonsense.'

'No. It's not.'

'Karl's become quite a pain over the last few years,' I'd say. 'He talks complete and utter drivel. Behaves in the strangest ways. Needs to learn to live by himself and not depend on our damn rations.'

Mother would look at me, saying nothing.

'So what if he comes from Havn? He's not really from there!' I'd yell. 'His father was the oddest man to ever settle in the place. That's the stock the idiot comes from.'

And she would try and counter all my arguments, night after night bringing up my duty to look for him.

'We owe it to any young man from Faroe to look after him, especially one with a father dead, without a job, receiving no money from home, rarely hearing from his family. I'd expect people in our situation to help anyone like that. Far less someone from my native place.' She would snort then, jerking her head towards the empty room upstairs where my sister, Gretchen, slept before she married a year or two before. 'We have enough space and money to look after him if we need to do so. Just a little while, to make sure he gets back on his feet again.'

Eventually, I gave in, putting aside the sheet of paper on which I had been sketching plans for a set of new houses which a building firm planned to build in the city. I was following my father's trade, working for the same firm in which he had been employed for years, and finding it hard to concentrate. This was especially true these evenings I worked from home, a place where my mother used to urge me to go and rescue Karl.

'All right, I'll do it,' I announced, grabbing my jacket and heading out into the cold of a November day.

It was as I walked in the direction of the part of Vesterbro, where I believed he stayed, that I heard the newsvendors begin to shout, waving newspapers in their hands.

The war was finally over.

Armistice had been declared.

Christianna

'AND IT REPENTED THE LORD that he had made man on the earth, and it grieved him at his heart. And the Lord said, "I will destroy man whom I have created from the face of the earth; both man, and beast, and the creeping thing, and the fowls of the air; for it repenteth me that I have made them." But Noah found grace in the eyes of the Lord ...'

And so the voice of Pastor Lukas echoed around the white-washed walls of the church in Sandvágar as he spoke on the Sunday after we discovered the war had finally come to an end; resounding, too, over the acres of flat land nearby, virtually the only acres of their kind in the whole of the Faroes. Despite the wildness of the weather, the whole congregation seemed to be crammed in there. Only I – and those like me – had been given a little extra room. I was expecting my second child, my hands crossed in front of me.

In his ability to tell a story, the pastor reminded me once again of my father. He would wave his hands in the same way, pounding the pulpit with his fists. It was also the case that, like my father with his strange notions about the drowning of Atlantis, Lukas suffered an obsession with moments when the physical world was transformed. He returned to these events time after time, perhaps relating them to the morning his own life had been overwhelmed by grief, when his own wife had been lost, her heart shuddering to a halt one day when she was preparing dinner. The Great Flood. The opening of the Red Sea. Jesus calming the waters. The destruction of Sodom and Gomorrah. Like my father, he saw meaning in events like these, moments in which the earth experienced physical transformation, giving substance and direction to his faith.

To some extent, I could understand that, even without experiencing the loss that he had suffered. We lived in a world where storms arose from a cloud on the horizon, where – like my father talking about his early life in Iceland – there was an awareness that fire could split and slice the surface of a land that had lain still for centuries, where each day we saw the tide's rise and fall encroaching upon the edge of our small world.

'We, too, have found grace,' the pastor continued. 'On the edge of a continent where the people have seen war and terror, our lives have been fairly calm and peaceful. It is true that we have known want and sometimes pangs of hunger, but it is largely the case that we have been immune to the worst of this. The fish that swim around our islands have provided for us. The birds that fly. The sheep that graze. Even the occasional whale that made its way into our bays has helped us survive these last few years. The Lord knows we have not had plenty, but compared to those who live in Denmark, we have had enough. Compared, too, to those who live on the other groups of islands – whether Suðereyar to our south, our neighbours in Hjaltland and Orkneyjar – we have escaped the worst of these years of conflict. We may have glimpsed what war has done to others, but its horrors have rarely filled our eyes.'

Heðin nodded, sitting beside me. Quiet as stone. He rarely said much, but occasionally he had made me aware of some of the ghastly scenes he and the other fishermen had witnessed over the last few years. The birds, seals and whales feasting on corpses. The steel hull of a sunken vessel among waves. The sound of explosions in the distance as another of their vessels was sunk by German planes or boats. The way in which some who had volunteered for the British Merchant Navy had been killed somewhere, perhaps, in the Caribbean or the North Atlantic. So, he had been lucky. He had escaped injury. There was this time his boat had been fishing near North Rona, our closest island to the south. They had seen a German U-boat anchored there; its crew hunting the sheep grazing on its empty shoreline. They were flapping their arms and yelling, unable to control them.

'Don't blame them for doing that,' he'd muttered. 'Some fresh meat at last.'

'In the next year or two, there will be many more ugly changes,' Lukas declared, 'There is little doubt about that. Already we have seen angry citizens tear down the kings who have sat on their thrones for generations. In Russia, we have even seen people seek to tear down God from His place. They may think that they have succeeded, but they are wrong in this. The Almighty still has His throne – both in heaven and in people's hearts. It will remain that way.'

I must admit I quivered sometimes as I listened to him. His words made me realise something about myself – how much I was drawn to men who could master language. They could either be – like the Prince of Suðereyar I had met in Havn – at the centre of their own stories, washed far from the shoreline of their home, or men like Lukas, bright and eloquent in their speech, their faith burnished and golden as they stood before us in the pulpit.

So different from the man I married with the scar that heat had marked upon his cheek.

So different from the silence I had so often encountered in his world.

Karl

WHEN THE WORLD WAS IN CHAOS, my life was filled with a new kind of harmony. I stayed in a house where the wind did not whistle through gaps in doors and windows, where the walls were not stained with patches of damp. Each day I could sit at a table and be fed, my stomach no longer rumbling and empty. There were no yells that echoed outside. No screams and shouts of drunks taking part in a fight. Or women calling out in distress.

Yet I was always conscious that this time of peace and stillness would not last forever. Everyday, Verner, Kasper's father, brought a newspaper to his home in Frederiksberg, its pages filled with new dark headlines. One morning I might read of the Bremen Soviet Republic, our near neighbours waving the red flag and proclaiming themselves socialists. After that, it might be the Hungarian People's Republic or the First Austrian Republic, with fighting on the streets of Vienna between Reds and Whites. Perhaps, too, the Finnish Civil War with all its bloodshed. Or the short-lived People's State of Bavaria, led by Kurt Eisner, a German-Jewish journalist who spoke of a 'government by kindness' that would create a 'realm of light, beauty and reason'.

'That didn't last long.' Verner shook his head the day that Eisner fell. 'Looks like the human race aren't ready for light, beauty and reason yet.'

I said nothing to him, aware, in my view, that the world had seen light, beauty and reason before, way back in the age before Atlantis had been destroyed. But I knew Verner would not have been convinced of that, regarding my father's fascination with that time as illusion and fantasy. Instead, his view of politics was pragmatic and careful. Unlike some of my friends, he rarely gave vent to his own opinions. His brow only wrinkled when he saw that Carl Theodore Zahle had decided to give Iceland a measure of self-rule.

'So many of them are peasants and fishermen. Are they ready for that? What would your father think?'

'Depends on the day,' I answered. 'One day he might complain about how little regard the government in Denmark had for the poor of Seyðisfjörður. The next, he'd sniff and say, "Do you think those living there are capable of self-government?"'

'And the answer would change day by day too?'

'Yes.'

I looked in the direction of Kasper as I answered. He treated me with a little disdain these days, looking down on me for failing to cope living on my own. This was even more remarkable as he had never attempted to leave his own home, travelling the short journey between his house and his father's office for work most days of the week. Unlike many of his workmates, he had never been laid off during the years of war, protected by his father's elevated position in the firm.

'Kasper doesn't know how lucky he is,' his mother whispered once to me. 'Protected by his place in the world. Not even a decent storm to stir him. Sometimes I despair of him. So long sheltered I worry if he'll ever be able to stand upright on his own.'

He did know, however, how Danish he was. He used to talk about it all the time – how soft the Zahle government had been in its dealings with Germany throughout the war, how Flensburg along with Southern Schleswig should be returned to Denmark now that the conflict was over.

'These bastard Germans,' he would declare. 'We have to watch them all the time.'

Saying nothing, I would nod my head while his father grinned at his words.

'Whether you like it or not, Kasper, they are our larger neighbours. If we make too great an enemy of them now, we'll have to deal with them later. Whether King Christian and his kind like it or not.'

'It doesn't help when we're soft with them,' Kasper muttered. 'We'll pay a price for that too.'

'Perhaps.'

I was careful not to say anything to Kasper. I was conscious of the fact that not only did he resent my presence in his home, he also regarded Germans in an identical way to how many Faroese and Icelanders saw Danes. The colonial masters. Those that puffed out their chests and strutted as they strode around the boundaries of the islands they owned and occupied, claiming each inch as their own. There were still old men and women in Havn who recalled how everything on the island had to be bought from the Royal Danish Trade Monopoly, the ones who had owned my father's store before him, limiting the people's ability to make a profit from both the sea and the wool upon the backs of their sheep. There was a time when a Faroese man would be punished severely if he rowed out to a Dutch ship to exchange a pair of woollen socks for a few handfuls of flour. When I imitated an aristocrat, it was the swagger and pomp of these people that I had in mind, their ways and manners I copied, even the way some juggled a walking stick in their fingers. It seemed to me that Kasper had the makings of becoming one of them. That kind of arrogance was part of his inheritance, for all that his parents had never intended it to be so. He made his sense of his own rights clear at all times, even making it apparent he did not want me to be part of his home.

It wasn't long before he had his way. Verner sidled up to me one evening, his face stern and serious.

'You can have your old work back,' he declared.

'Really?'

'I've spoken to Brandes in Kronprinsessegade. They're happy to give you your old job back there. Things are picking up. Slowly, but it's happening. They also rate your talents highly. Brandes was saying that he thinks you're one of the most talented young men who's worked there in recent years – both in terms of language and artistic ability. It upset him a great deal when he was forced to pay you off.' Verner smiled in my direction. 'What do you think of that?'

'I'm delighted,' I said. 'Really glad to be back there!'

Sometimes the poor have no choice but to pretend.

Often there is no other option.

Copenhagen
1919–1925

Karl

IT DIDN'T TAKE LONG for Brandes to let me know how and why I was back there.

'You can thank old Verner for this one,' he told me within a few days of starting. 'He asked for you to be taken on again. I agreed reluctantly. I couldn't forget how guilty you made me feel the day I had to pay you off. It was bad enough to have to do that without having your sulky face looking at me and making demands that I couldn't accept.'

'Sorry about that,' I muttered.

'You will be even more if you cause me the slightest inconvenience or make a single silly mistake. You'll be out of the door faster than your two feet can carry you. And if I ever hear of you mimicking me behind my back again, it'll be worse than that. I'll make sure you never get a job again in this city. Or even the bloody country. You remember that!'

His arms were flailing as he said this. It looked as though he was performing some impersonation of the printers' drums, spitting out his words as he spoke. I trembled, not having been aware that he knew I was doing this before. One of my 'friends' had probably betrayed me, bringing this tale to the boss.

'I'll remember that,' I promised.

'Good. Good. Good. I don't want to give into the temptation of sending you out the door.'

'I'll behave this time,' I said.

And I did so, making sure I did not trouble him at any time I was working there.

Even when my workmates asked me to forge documents, I'd shake my head. 'It's not worth the risk,' I'd say, turning away from them. 'I don't want to lose my job.'

Despite this, I hated living in Copenhagen now. I was back once again in a cramped apartment in Vesterbro, this time not far from the railway station in a street called Helgolandsgade. Outside its entrance, drunks often gathered, sidling up to one another for the occasional fight, joining together in the chorus of a song. The poor here had a different smell from the ones to be found at home in Havn. There it was the reek of smoke and salt fish in their clothes. In Vesterbro, it was a stranger concoction. The stink of dried sweat half-hidden by perfume and layers of dried body powder among the women. Breath that reeked of beer and rotten meat among the men. Walking among them, these smells were as regular and persistent as waves that washed against the coastline of my home island, broken only by their mockery and attempts to beg money from strangers.

'Any change?' they would ask.

I used to wonder how many of them came from small communities like mine – Fanø, Bornholm, Lolland, Møn, Fyn, even the sweep and scale of Greenland – and had arrived in the city in the hope that their lives would be transformed. Like me, they were the lost kings and queens, princes and princesses of this country, coming from tiny places in which they had been adored and loved during their childhood, recognised and valued wherever they wandered within the boundaries of these places. Now their heads were heaped with sadness, their shoulders hunched because of the burden placed upon them.

Alongside them were the whores. Some of them had similar upbringings, given attention and notice wherever they walked during their childhood. Now, often fat and wrinkled, they only jiggled their hips energetically, hoping in vain that they might capture a glance from those men who were walking by, staying, perhaps, for a few nights in one of the hotels that lined the street.

'Fancy a good time?'

It felt worse because I had been orphaned once again. I had enjoyed my time with Kasper's parents, their presence strengthening me after I had gone through a dark and desperate period in my life. This was especially true of his mother, Nita. For all that she was far better groomed than her counterparts in Havn – her grey hair less often dampened and flurried by the wind, her clothes more tailored – there was still something that reminded me of the women I had known at home, the ones that often sheltered in our store and spoke to my own mother. There was the way her eyebrows arched when she told a story, the way her blue eyes sometimes sparkled like the small birds in the trees and shrubs that surrounded her home. There was the way too – for all that she relished the luxuries of her life in Frederiksberg – she longed for some of the realities of her existence back in Faroe.

'I miss the wind,' she'd declare. 'And the chill. Reminds me I'm alive.'

'It would be great to be far away from all this … politics,' she'd announce, shuddering when names like Zahle, Neergaard or Stauning were mentioned. 'Life would be so simple without them.'

And then there was the story she told, one I had first heard from my father's lips many years before, about how giants who lived in Iceland had been envious of the Faroes and wanted to take them home to their shores. They had sent one of their number – Risin – and a witch named Kellingen to tug the islands away from their location in the North Atlantic, arriving on the northern coast of Eysturoy to perform this task. They hitched a rope around Eiðiskollur, the most north-westerly mountain. Kellingen fastened all the Faroese islands into one tight package, stacking them onto her partner's back. It was at this point that some of the load crumbled and broke away. And the rest remained fixed where it was, defying all their efforts to shift it during the night.

They were still there in the morning, transformed into stone stacks by the first shaft of sunlight, looking back in the distance at the land from which they had come.

'I understand what they were up to,' Nita said, smiling. 'There have been times when I've wanted to hire some kind of ocean liner and try to pull those islands a litle closer to me. It would be wonderful to have them nearby. Only a short journey away.'

She would laugh then.

'Not that there's any chance of that ever happening.'

I knew exactly what she meant. I missed Havn too – the space between people, the possibilities of silence, the way in which you could take a short walk, scaling, perhaps, a vertiginous slope and discovering there was no one else in sight or earshot. To some extent, when I was in Kasper's home, I possessed the means to feel that way, strolling into their garden, helping them with their lawn or digging up the soil. There was no opportunity to do this in Helgolandsgade. Not only were there shouts from the street outside but occasionally there would be rumbling noises reverberating across the ceiling of my apartment, a cry, a scream echoing through the building. Police officers walking up and down the street, perhaps making their way up stairs that were filled with the stench of beer and urine; reminding me, too, that for all that many of the residents were good, kind and hard-working, there were others who were dangerous and violent. There had been a murder at the local cigar store, a window looked out from an apartment where a little girl had been killed by her father.

All unimaginable in my old life in Havn.

I tried to wish away the realities of my new existence through a variety of means. I stepped around the banks of just about every lake in Copenhagen, drawing the birds that clustered on the waters. There were geese, ducks and swans. I sketched them all, having the odd notion that I could transform the drawings into a notebook that told the story of Hans Christian Andersen's *The Ugly Duckling* for my young niece back in the Faroe Islands, underlining certain words which I thought might bring a grin to her mother's face, cold and cheerless in Sørvágar, the distant place she now called home:

To be born in a duck's nest, in a farmyard, is of no consequence to a bird, if it is hatched from a swan's egg.

Each day I would watch the cygnets, grey and darkened by the shadows of their mother and father as they swam, coming to know the edges of a lake. I would gather their feathers too, using them occasionally to sketch the birds, the darker colour of these tiny birds, the bright shade of their adult plumage, gluing these quills too on certain pages, providing texture to the tale. And then the transformation – the days when they shed their smallness and their size to become that bird that Christianna had rarely glimpsed but loved each time she saw. I could recall her grasping my hand and dragging me outdoors to see two of them passing overhead when we stayed in Havn, tearing the air apart with the power of their wings, as if the sky had been transformed into the depth and surge of water.

'It's beautiful,' she had said. 'Like a strange star settling over us in daylight.'

Or I might walk down to the harbour and hear the medley of languages that echoed there. The Swedish and Norwegian fishermen that were often found among its quays and warehouses. Their counterparts too from the Baltic states of Lithuania, Latvia and Estonia. The visitors from England and France that might sometimes be found there. There was one time, too, a merchant's ship was tied up there, filled with sailors from Orkneyjar, Hjaltland and the Hebrides, exiled from their native islands. There was someone from the first group with whom I shared the tale of Hether Blether, an island in Orkneyjar which I had heard about from my father, one that rose from emptiness every year or two, appearing and fading on the horizon.

'Never heard of it,' the Orkneyjar seaman declared.

There was another time I tested out my father's Gaelic with a crewman whom I encountered on the quay.

'*Tarbh, tarbh, tarbh!*' I said, imitating a bull.

The poor man looked at me as if I was crazy, walking away as briskly as he could.

It was after that I made a couple more drawings for my sister Christianna. Each one seemed to emerge from my memories of Havn. Some days they originated in the grey mist and heavy rainfall that so often clouded that port. A blurred line would appear in my imagination which I would imitate with my pencil before colouring it in, adding more detail until it was transformed into the curl of a fish or the sweep of a whale. At other times I might encounter a particular vision in the spume and foam of a wave I remembered crashing against rocks on the shoreline, concealing all within a whirl of white. Or it might be the depths of the ocean in the distance, its mysteries hidden for a moment before shape and shade emerged. Pale, perhaps, like the shell of the egg from which the Ugly Duckling had emerged.

And then there might be the Count of St Kilda in all his pomp, striding along a shoreline, his feet larger than any other individual I had ever met, made huge by the climbing of cliffs on the edges of those islands, tilting the world's axis as he stepped along. Nearby there was a yellow waterfall, turned that shade – I imagined – by the piss of trolls. A clutch of gannets, too, swathed through the sky, their sharp beaks and wings cutting cloud and wave like they did, perhaps, on Mykines, an island on the western edge of Faroe to which I had never ventured, whose inhabitants were said to feast on those birds.

I also drew two more sketches. One was of Emperor Cormorant of Atlantis, his nose like a dark beak, a raucous laugh echoing from his beak, his gown possessing the oily sheen of that bird's feathers. His arms were thrown wide and resplendent like the bird's wings when it stood on a rock to dry as the wind swirled all around in a chilling, ghostly dance, disturbing a sea-dragon from its place among the depths, its head appearing above the water's surface. Another was of the Prince of Suðereyar, that figure whom my sister had loved for many years. A sheepskin cloak hung around his broad shoulders, a tartan-coloured smock on his chest, a claymore clenched tightly in his hand, a face with a wide smile as he stood before a stack of stones, some glistening green and blue after being shaded that colour by the ocean.

Brooding on all I had lost since I left my home in Havn – even the mother who I rarely heard from these days, her letters becoming less and less frequent with age – I was walking back to my apartment from the post office after sending my drawings to Christianna when someone from that existence came into view.

It was Ásla, that strange girl from my schooldays in Havn. I met her walking down the street that winter's evening. Instead of the fishing line I had seen around her shoulders in Havn, she was now wrapped up in a heavy woollen shawl and a thick coat, an uncomfortable and ungainly pair of leather boots on her feet. Her face, however, was recognisable instantly. Green eyes. Fair hair. The slope of her cheeks. Features that hid all the hurt and inhumanity she had suffered since she was born under a mask of quiet beauty. It was not only an absent father that had done this to her, but also a mother who was unable to conceal all the resentment and rage she had experienced since her illegitimate child's arrival. I recalled the boys in the class talking about the story of Rannvá, a young girl who had been exiled from Havn after having a child out of wedlock in the sixteenth century.

'She was lucky,' one of my classmates had hissed. 'Back then they sentenced women to death for that.'

Yet for all that, she was not unfriendly to me, being the one who spoke first.

'Karl?'

'Ásla?'

And then we had stammered and spoke. Going to a café, we engulfed one another with news. I informed her about my life, all that had happened in the years since I had left Havn. She told me she was staying in a home for unmarried women in Helgolands-gade which I had passed on many occasions, having moved there a month or two before. She was working in a nearby restaurant, helping to prepare the food.

'It's all very different from working down at the harbour,' she said.

'You don't miss it?'

She took off her gloves, showing me hands that still bore the marks of old cuts and blisters, her mouth twisting into that look of sullen resentment I recalled from my youth. 'What do you think?'

I grinned and nodded.

'It isn't the only thing I don't miss. I can make a new beginning for myself here. Back in Havn, I was always going to be the lovechild. Even if I lived till my seventies and had a brood of children of my own. They weren't ever going to forget that.'

'Who did that to you?'

'Some of the old men and women. They'd either say something harsh and unpleasant or else look through you as if you weren't there. People like your sister Bedda's husband, Jacobsen. If you bought anything in their shop, they'd stare at each øre that was handed over as if it was tainted in some way. '

'"You're taking an age about this,"' I said, impersonating my brother-in-law. '"You'd think every coin was being sent by post from Spitsbergen instead of being taken out from your purse."'

Ásla laughed at this, loudly and cheerfully, a sound I don't think I had ever heard when we both lived back in Havn. In order to hear it again, I began to mimic some of the sayings I had heard from the lips of some of the old men and women back home.

'"Old ravens are not that easy to fool."'

'"Small fish are better than empty dishes."'

'"Wool is the gold of the Faroes."'

'"A chicken likes her own eggs best."'

'"There often lies falsehood beneath a pretty skin."'

Ásla roared at all of these, tears flecking her cheeks as she listened to these remarks, noting too the names of those who were their source. 'Greta … Rasmus … Sigurd … Agathe.' Once or twice, she even applauded me for the exactness of my impersonation. Finally, sore with laughter, she waved her hand back and forth.

'Stop it! Stop it! You're making me think I'm back there again – and it's painful!' she declared.

I halted. 'How do you think my mother and sisters are getting on? It's been really hard to see them for years. I'm better at keeping in touch with Christianna, but even then ...' I shrugged my shoulders.

'Bedda? She's fine,' Ásla said, answering her own question. 'She's probably met her ideal match. They've the same priorities. Kroner, kroner, kroner.'

'She's not very keen on letting a single one slip from her fingers.' I said, recalling the letter she had sent soon after father's death. I still resented every word of that, all the changes it had imposed on my life.

'That much is obvious.'

I shook Bedda from my head. 'Mother? I don't often hear from her. She relied on my father to do all her writing. She isn't very good at it.'

'Oh, she's fine too. Slowing down with age. Helping out in the shop sometimes.'

'Like she's always done.'

'Just that.'

'What about Christianna?'

Ásla was silent for quite some time before she answered. 'I'm not sure she's that happy. Not from what I've heard.'

'What do you mean?'

'Some of the fishermen who've gone to Sørvágar have seen her there. Ask her how she is, and she just shrugs and looks miserable. Push her for a while and she'll say she's fine, but she's not entirely convincing.'

'Oh.'

'That's what I've heard people saying. It might not be true.'

'It probably is.'

'Well,' – again she paused – 'she never struck me as someone who'd be that happy in Sørvágar. Even Havn was too small for her. Anywhere in those parts. More a Copenhagen girl. Or a Paris girl. Or a London lady.'

I nodded. 'Yes. I can see that. A little like me.'

'Perhaps not the lady part,' she said, giggling. 'But no doubt that's true. A little like you. You never really belonged in Havn either.'

'No. I don't suppose I did. Just someone who'd washed up on its shores.'

She frowned. 'Mind you, I don't think your father ever brought you often into the harbour. Just left you bouncing around on the waves nearby.'

I looked at her, wondering what she meant by these remarks, but I determined not to ask her.

'Let's go for a walk,' I said. 'There's lots around Copenhagen I can show you. Perhaps the day will come when you might feel you belong here.'

Christianna

I WEPT WHEN I LOOKED at the pictures that Karl had sent me. Not just the Ugly Duckling ones, which my daughter Dagrún wanted me to show to her all the time, but the Emperor Cormorant drawing with the words etched below that, he claimed, came from Atlantis, an ancient sea-dragon staring in his direction as if wondering what a strange and unearthly phenomenon this man was. The Count of St Kilda, his steps shifting the world until its northern half was pitched and sheltering under the dark rafters of our sky in winter, the walls of cliffs trembling and moving below the impact of his feet. The Prince of Suðereyar, with his garment made of wool, standing beside a cairn of stone. In the distance I could glimpse the houses of St Kilda which I had once seen in a photograph, shawled women with creels upon their backs moving among them, their men nearby mending fishing lines, shifting stones.

Each image took me back to a life I had left behind. Back to Havn. Back to days filled with my father's tales and stories, when laughter gusted around the house as frequently as the wind that howls around my new home in Sørvágar. Back to a time when I could dream and not wake each morning to a dull and cold reality, the various cries and noises of the fowl I fed each morning, the eggs that I went to gather and fetch. Back to an age I did not share much of my life with a sullen, silent fisherman. Or the two daughters with whom we occupied our home. Everyday seemed to be a war with shadows that were as large and dominating as the hills that surrounded our house.

I tried to shake these thoughts from my head. There was work to do while my youngest child, Malvina, slept. Her name was in itself a symptom of my restlessness, one that might have been reflected in the way she found herself unable to sit still, constantly moving in the direction of whatever had caught her attention. I had my daughter christened with that name because of a character in the book *The Prince of Suðereyar*, which I had read so many years ago. As I looked down at the baby curled in my arms, I had seen her as she might look when she was an adult. There was a glorious mane of dark hair, a blue-eyed piercing gaze, the same tartan shawl the character had worn, long leather boots which she had worn to stride across the length of her kingdom, from Inverness to Loch Lomond, Edinburgh to Perth, accompanying her prince in a way I had never dared to do.

It was a decision that Heðin had disagreed with.

'Malvina?' He had looked at me. 'What on earth kind of name

is that? It's got no connection with your family or mine.'

'It doesn't have to have,' I said. 'There's no law that declares all children should be named after our ancestors.'

'No. But it's the way both your and my family have done things for generations. It gives a sense of being rooted to a place if you give them a name like that.'

'And what's the advantage of that?' I hissed.

He gave into me, accepting my choice of name. 'Oh, all right. Have it your own way. I'll choose the name of the next one that comes.'

'That's fine.'

Yet even as I said this, I knew that the reason I planned to christen the child Malvina was a tiny act of adultery towards my husband. The character that had been pictured alongside the Prince of Suðereyar was a reminder of the day that MacCusbic arrived in Havn, when there seemed to be the possibility of a new turn and direction in my life, when – for a short while – I saw my existence as one that would no longer be confined by the shorelines of these islands. And then storm clouds had closed once again around the harbour, walling me in, trapping me on the narrow strips of land I came from.

So, I shook my head again, doing my utmost to banish all thought of this. Picking up a bucket filled with crumbs and seed, I went out to feed the hens and ducks.

It was when I was out there scattering grain that I saw the other man that had awakened such thoughts. Pastor Lukas was making his way down the slope of the hill a short distance away. His fair hair was flapping in the strength of the wind. He was trying to dodge pools and puddles while still heading in our direction, like a small boat sailing towards harbour while seeking to avoid the worst of the wind and waves. He waved to me when he saw me among the ducks and hens behind my home.

'Christianna!'

'Pastor.'

I waited for him there, knowing he could only be heading in the direction of our home.

'I have a favour to ask,' he said. 'Only you have the skills to do it,' he added a few moments later.

And then he slipped on a damp patch. I stretched out my arm to stop him falling, saving him from landing in a shit-spattered stretch of land by clasping his hand. It wasn't the first time I had done this. We held onto one another's fingers a long time sometimes when we met at the doorway of the church, unable – it seemed – to allow the other to go.

'I'm all right,' he said, blushing.

'You sure?'

'Yes. I've got my balance now.' He coughed before he spoke again. 'Let's go into the house. I've got something I have to show you.'

'Sure.'

The moment passed – as it always did. On rare calm days we could hear the knocking of each other's hearts. He was aware, too, of my warmth towards him in the ice-cold cluster of houses where we sometimes met, the church in which he would speak so eloquently every Sunday.

Yet neither of us would ever do anything about it.

Sometimes, small places can be like that. People are forced to conceal their own needs and longings, muffling the words and thoughts they yearn to bring to their lips.

Karl

ÁSLA HELD MY HAND when we watched some of the films shown in the Empire and Grand theatres during those years, squeezing my fingers as we followed the performance of John Barrymore in *Dr Jekyll and Mr Hyde*. And again when we were being taken to various locations that were almost familiar to us. My father's old life in Iceland being conjured up in *Eyvind of the Hills* or *The Outlaw and his Wife*, with its words and sights – in so many ways – recalling our past existence in Faroe. A farmhand's words on screen declaring, 'The sheep have been restless today,' or the character Arnes recalling the men and women who stride across the moor or the shoreline, collecting some of the small plants or sprigs of seaweed to be found there: 'Have you ever seen such fine lichen? I have a whole bagful. It tastes delicious boiled in milk.'

And then there would be an occasional film that would remind me of darker moments in my existence. Such as a room in which a rich man's suicide occurred, the streets of a town just across the Baltic Sea, complete with a graveyard I half-recognised one New Year's Eve in *The Phantom Carriage*, directed by Sjöström, who had acted in the previous film. Or *The Cabinet of Dr Calgari* with all its dark distortions, the mad hypnotist who hoodwinks and compels a sleepwalker to perform his murders. The words of Count Orlok in *Nosferatu*, declaring, 'Your wife has a beautiful neck' – a moment when I would deliberately look down on Ásla's naked throat, licking my lips and giving my most chilling smile.

'Oh, stop it!' she would half-shriek, half-laugh.

And then there were the moments of comedy. Films like *His New Job* and *The Kid*, with Jackie Coogan and Charlie Chaplin. The last-named was someone I felt I had started mimicking long before I had seen him, twirling either a walking stick or my father's ancient rifle between my fingers as I strolled down the road in Havn, pretending I was part of the aristocracy. All that was missing were his deep, mournful eyes filled with shadows, his dark moustache and the penguin-like way in which he walked down the road. For Ásla's amusement, I did my best to imitate all this, smearing my upper lip with coal, wearing over-sized boots.

'That's great,' she would giggle. 'You can play any part you like.'

I was beginning to think she might be right. There were days when I would put on my best clothes and head out to the centre of the city, sometimes accompanied by Ásla. I might stroll around places like Thorvaldsen's Museum, near the canal. Standing in front of sculptures like 'Adonis' and the 'Three Graces with Cupid', I would talk loudly about Thorvaldsen's skills and accomplishments, drawing on knowledge I had gained way back in school. I would speak, too, about the paintings of the Norwegian artist, J.C. Dahl. Much of his work recalled my own years in Havn. The steep eastern slopes of Jordalsnuten in Norway. Telemark. The coast at Laurvig. The heights of Mount Vesuvius. Even the Bay of Naples in the moonlight. On the flat, green land that surrounded me in Copenhagen, there was something about his art that sparked tears in my eyes.

'His father was a fisherman in Bergen,' I would tell Ásla. 'Just like some of those that we saw on our shoreline growing up. Apparently, there were times when he felt really bitter about that. Claimed it held him back. That he would have done far more with a better start.'

Sometimes, visitors would stop to listen to my explanations. Englishmen, Austrians, Swedes and the occasional Frenchman – they would all sidle up to me and ask questions.

'How come you know so much about the artwork here?' they would say.

Ásla would do her best to conceal her smile as I came out with my answer. I would tell them that I had aristocratic connections here in Denmark, going back for many generations, but that my people first came from Scotland, being linked to the Stuart dynasty which had come to an end in 1746 with the Battle of Culloden in the Scottish Highlands.

'My family name is Dunganon,' I might announce. 'Named after Dun Geanainn, or "Geanann's fort", a man who was my distant ancestor many hundreds of years ago.' I would say this dryly, knowing all too well it was a lie. 'But I'm also the Duke or Count of St Kilda as my people possessed a family estate both there and in the rest of the Hebrides. Skye. Harris. Uist. Lewis. At one time, we were known as part of the royal household of Suðereyar, the aristocracy of the north.'

'Oh? That's remarkable,' they would say to all this. 'We're really glad to have met you.'

And they might slip a few kroner into my fingers.

'Thank you very much,' I would say, smiling. 'I'm very grateful for your company.'

Or treat both Ásla and I to a meal, a glass of wine or two.

'You're really good at this,' Ásla might say.

'I'm getting better,' I would grin. 'But I've still a little work to do. Neither Danes nor Norwegians are fooled by me yet.'

'Why do you think that is?'

'I don't know. I can only guess that they can hear something in my accent. A sound that's not quite right.'

'A little touch of Havn?'

'Probably.' I grinned. 'The Germans and Swedes are easily fooled. They might even imagine they can hear slight echoes of the days when the Faroes were "the islands of sheep and the paradise of birds", before the Vikings came to either kill or chase the Irish monks that lived there in the ninth century. But the Danes and Norwegians? They know exactly where I'm from. The Faroese accent they can spot no matter how hard I try to disguise it.'

There were one or two times, however, when this was to my advantage. Sometimes, even city-folk trusted me automatically when they heard my voice, especially when I laid it on thickly, slowing and emphasising each vowel and consonant till they recognised where I was from, shedding my usual disguise.

'You're from Faroe, aren't you?'

'They're fine people there. Men and women of faith and decency.'

'I'm jealous of you. To come from such a good, honest and decent place.'

And then there was the moment a restaurant owner called Rasmussen approached our table when Ásla and I were eating one night in Restaurant 1756 in Strøget, the longest street in Copenhagen's centre. He had served us his best produce – ox tongue, wine, the tastiest butter and bread he could obtain – and he was spending time talking to us, having worked out where we were from. He was an unusual-looking man who had thick, dark hair, a pince-nez that rested on his nose because of a dark gash in one of his ears, and a tight neat beard. He spoke in a scratchy, high-pitched voice, asking us various questions about the seabirds and other creatures we had eaten.

'Whale?'

'Yes. Many times.'

'Seal?'

'Often. I even used to go out and shoot them sometime, using my father's rifle.'

'Dolphin?'

'Occasionally. Once or twice.'

'And what about seabirds?'

'Lots of them, too. Guillemots. Shags.'

'Puffin?'

I nodded, recalling how Pastor Anders blessed the men who went on the hunt by quoting a few verses from Psalm 91. 'Surely He shall deliver thee from the snare of the fowler, and from the noisome pestilence. He shall cover thee with His feathers, and, under his wings, shalt thou trust.'

'What about gannet?'

Ásla looked in my direction. 'I've tried them a few times. My mother's father originally came from Mykines. They eat loads of them there. He used to get some every year.'

'Not only there,' Rasmussen said. 'In other places too. I've heard they eat loads of them in the Suðereyar. Especially their chicks. Islands like St Kilda. The tip of the island of Lewis.'

'I've heard that too,' I nodded. Hearing my favourite place being mentioned, my chest swelled. I sat up straight, my shoulders pinned back in my chair. 'They call them "guga" in that part of the world. It's just about their favourite food there.'

'Yes, yes,' Rasmussen declared. 'You know, I've had a few customers asking for them. Especially from the British Embassy. The ambassador there apparently has connections with Suðereyar in the north of Scotland and wants to see what they taste like. He thinks here in Denmark is his best chance of doing that.'

'He's probably right in that.'

Rasmussen looked at me intensely, his eyes glinting behind the glass of his pince-nez. 'He'd pay a lot of money for the privilege of eating it.'

'Would he now?'

'Ambassador Morrison? He certainly would.'

Rasmussen rubbed the tips of his fingers together to underline his words, licking his lips as though he could taste the flavour of guga in his mouth. I responded by imagining how my wallet might swell and grow fat if I managed to obtain this seafowl for the ambassador's dinner plate.

'It could be done,' I said.

'How?'

'I'd need to write a letter home first. To one of the fishermen there.'

'You think that?' His eyes gleamed again.

'Yes. Mykines is quite a small place, but they'll all know someone there. They'll be able to get the birds for you. Who knows? They might even have some of them on board.'

'Really?'

'Really.'

Rasmussen leaped to his feet, grasping a handful of kroner from the restaurant till. He squeezed them into my fingers.

'There's more of them waiting for you on your return. Just bring me the gannets. I'll reward you when you do.'

*

It was Ásla who pointed out the problems with all I had promised.

'Who are you going to write to? You know what they're like. They won't bother answering. Besides, there's not many young people in Mykines anymore. Only around two hundred folk in total. Many of them old. They won't have too many gannet chicks to give.'

'I know, I know. I should have thought it through.'

'It's also a bit far away. Farther west than I've ever been. Do you honestly think they're going to bring a few pails of gannet over to Denmark for you? Surely they have better things to do with their time. And then there will be other consequences.'

'Like what?'

'You won't be able to go to Restaurant 1756 anymore. Or even to Strøget. Rasmussen knows everybody there, and they'll give you quite a hammering if you let them down.'

I shook my head, thinking of the prospect of living in a city where I would not have the opportunity to visit the main streets, where I would be condemned to wander the likes of Vesterbro day after day. I was aware that I would feel just as imprisoned as I ever had in Havn. At least there the sea changed shades with the seasons. Sometimes, it would be streaked with silver or touched by the gleam of the lighthouse at Skansin, the flicker persistent in the darkness. At other times, the sea would be calm and coloured blue or green, the crests and peaks of the islands also reflecting the prevailing light, touched occasionally by sunlight. Unlike the grey bleak apartments that surrounded people like us in Vesterbro. Our walls changed little day by day, month by month.

'I'll write the letter anyway. To someone like Arno. Let's see if we'll hear from him. I'll also have to think of another plan if that goes wrong.'

'What do you mean? Some kind of swindle? Some kind of trick?'

'I think so.'

She laughed. 'Well, you've been training for that for much of your life. Let's see if it all works out.'

It took me a while to think it over, to settle on a strategy that I could rely on if no gannet arrived from my native islands. I planned it thoroughly, borrowing a rifle from one of my colleagues, going to a local gun-range to rediscover long-forgotten skills. Eventually, after hearing no news from Faroe, I decided to travel across to Ribe, on the other side of Jylland. I knew there were barnacle geese there, flocks of them settling on waters near the shore and inland. I remembered seeing their white faces and black heads, their silver-grey wings which made them look as if sunlight gleamed and sparkled on them even on the most dull and gloomy days when they took to flight. The sight of them had marked my arrival back on that first morning in Esbjerg, as if I had left the fulmar and guillemot, puffin and skua that had dominated my earlier days behind. They were less common than some of the other wild geese found in Denmark, the greater white fronted, the greylag, the pink-footed goose.

When I reached the shoreline, I took the rifle out, waiting for geese to appear. It didn't take long for them to do so, their wings scissoring a thin layer of mist as they touched down on the flat land just below the fields of a nearby farm in which cattle grazed, their squawk cutting through both cloud and silence with the sharpness of a blade. The contrast between all this and the last time I had hunted seabirds came to my head as I lay stretched out on the ground there. In the Faroes, people ate fowl of that kind because they had very little option otherwise. There were few acres that could be ploughed, only small patches of ground that could be cultivated, a handful of fruits or vegetables that would not be susceptible to the cuff and clout of wind, the smack of salt. Apart from the hardiest of sheep, most animals, too, would shiver and cower in its crests and valleys. So unlike this place. So different from much of the country which laid claim to its shores. All around me now was flat, cultivated, arable land with a density of rich soil. Yet I had met too many of its citizens that shrivelled their noses at the diet which those in the islands had little choice but to eat. Dolphins, whales, seabirds.

'How can you possibly put that in your mouth?' they would ask, the very question a sign of the choices they had before them, evidence that they rarely felt any great need for food.

It was a question I found hardest to answer when someone asked about puffins. Orange-beaked. White-breasted. Hopping up and down. Scurrying into burrows. About the size of one of my father's books. Even the curious way they looked as if they were sizing you up and capable of thinking for themselves. It was easier to answer the questions of strangers when it came to barnacle geese, cormorants, shags. Each of these birds looked more soulless and alien than the puffin, their beaks as sharp as the swords of the Three Musketeers.

'How can you possibly put that in your mouth?'

'For our survival in these parts. You have no choice.'

The words were in my mind as I pulled the trigger for the first time, aiming it at a nearby bird.

*

It was Ásla who plucked the dead birds when I arrived home, all too aware that I had shed many of the skills I associated with my past life in Havn.

'I'll just make a mess of it,' I said. 'I was never any good at it and I've forgotten everything I ever knew about it all.'

'Really?'

'Really. I wish it were otherwise.'

In contrast, she sang as she performed the task – the words of a song I had never heard before, one about how night had severed the last strands of light that bound the day to land; how its last beams clung to ledges in cliffs, filling chasms and clefts found around the island's shores until over time their grip loosened, giving way to the dark; how soon the only source of brightness that might be found would be that of a lantern, winking its way round the shadows of a house or barn; how, too, we should draw comfort from its existence. In itself, it was a reminder that day would soon return.

It wasn't only the unfamiliar song that reminded me of Faroe. There was, too, the way she sat, a cloud of feathers forming around her as she plucked the birds, just like I had seen happen back in the harbour in Havn. Both old men and women used to do this, the mist of down clouding and veiling their bodies and faces as if they were caught within a giant spider's web, their voices – either shouting or singing – occasionally breaking through the swirl of white or grey. She completed this exercise by filling a small tin with methylated spirits, burning the last remnants of the birds' plumage away.

And later, too, there was the smattering of salt Ásla lifted in her fingers, sprinkling this on the bare skin and dark flesh of the birds like a crusting of snow at the same time as she tugged out any remnants of bullets that could be found within the corpses. The memories that all this stirred within me made me choke back tears. I thought of the men and women coming into my father's store and how the plumage of dead birds still remained stuck in parts of their clothing – the collar of a jacket, the pockets of trousers, the inside of a boot. My father, too, grinning when he saw one with a quill or pinion wedged in their hair, looking as if they were about to take flight in the fury of the winds that roared outside.

'Sometimes I think I've got Icarus and Daedalus among my nearest neighbours here. Either that or mermaids,' he declared once when he saw a young woman coming up to the counter, her fingers and legs sparkling with fish-scales.

And then, too, there was that other aspect of life in the Faroe Islands that I had almost forgotten. The smell that arose from the salty seabirds as they lay in buckets in a corner of the kitchen. Their tang followed me everywhere. I could trace it in my clothes when

I went to work in the morning, its scent almost overpowering me. Its reach competed with all the other smells that surrounded me in the vicinity of Helgolandsgade. The stink of the sweat of others. The reek of alcohol. The smoke from the chimneys of nearby factories. A dark and ugly kaleidoscope of smells.

'At least we're going to make money from this one,' I said when Ásla complained about it. 'There's some comfort in that.'

She cast a doubtful look in my direction. 'You sure about that?'

*

She was right.

We didn't.

I was forced to act one day I passed Restaurant 1756 in Strøget. Rasmussen was standing in the doorway, his old-fashioned spectacles still clamped on his nose, his high-pitched voice calling in my direction.

'Hey, Faroe man! Come here, please.'

I tried to avoid hearing him, but his call was much too loud and persistent. It would have alerted everyone in the street to my presence if I had pretended to ignore him.

'You heard anything yet about the gannets from your fellow islanders?'

'The guga? Yes. Just yesterday. They're delivering them to Esbjerg in a day or two. I'll go and collect them then and bring them to you.'

'Oh, wonderful!' He clapped his hands together. 'I was beginning to doubt your word, but I should have been more trusting and had more faith in a man from Faroe.'

'We won't let you down.'

'No. You certainly won't. You'll be true to your word. Just wait there a moment.' He went back into his restaurant to grab a few more kroner from the till. Once again, he crammed them into my fingers. 'Here. Have that. I'm looking forward to seeing you soon.'

'Thanks. That's really appreciated.'

'Not as much as your gannet is going to be.'

As I walked away, the notes scorched my fingers. I could still feel that wound searing me when I returned to the restaurant a few days later. It was almost as if the handles of the two pails were scoring the injuries deep within me, not allowing me to escape its effects. I was aware, too, of the fact that Rasmussen was part of the hurt. He was a decent, kind individual, one who was pleasant and charming to meet. I felt my stomach churn as I approached the door – and not only because of the stink of salt and wildfowl I was carrying. My face turned pale as I entered, my usual ability to act and pretend deserting me when I saw Rasmussen standing in front of me.

'Oh, it's the Faroe man,' he said, grinning and tilting his head towards the pails I was carrying. 'And these are the gannets?'

'Yes.' I gulped.

'Good, good, good.' He reached for them, taking both pails from my hands. 'I'll bring them to the chef.'

'Fine. Fine.'

He almost danced as he made his way to the restaurant kitchen, pushing open the door.

'I'll be back in a moment,' he said.

My fingers clawed towards an empty seat as I stood there. Leaning on it, I was all too aware I was sweating, that my legs, too, were in danger of giving way. I was conscious that the eyes of the restaurant's customers were on me, following every shift and movement of this man from the Faroes who had just arrived in their domain with two stinking buckets in his grip. It was almost as if I retained the smell around my body. One woman gazed at me while pouring out a pot of tea. In a corner of the room, a fork faltered, held between the fingers of an elderly man who was gazing in my direction, wondering, perhaps, what on earth a man from the seabird-swallowers from the far west was doing mixing and mingling with his colonial masters. It was at that moment I realised what was wrong with this plan I had thought up. I was not pretending to be someone other than myself. I was not wearing a guise or mask. I was simply being myself.

I decided to turn and run out of the door.

My race continued the length of Strøget, passing all the shops and customers there, jostling my way between them, feeling my stomach reeling as I did so. And all the time I was praying, reciting words I had heard as a child, changing them to suit my purpose and the panic I was feeling.

'Deliver me from the snare of the fowler, and from the noisome pestilence. Cover me with His feathers. Only under His wings, shall I trust …'

I stayed mainly in Vesterbro for months after that, spending much of my spare time in Ásla's company, enjoying her laughter, the way she reached for my hand as she often did when we walked the streets together. We provided protection for one another. In my case, the eyes of men rarely fell upon me when she was in my company, diverting the gaze of, say, any policemen who might have been looking for some charlatan who had attempted to swindle the owner of a restaurant in the city's centre. I provided a different type of guard. Drunks rarely whistled at her or made crude remarks when she was in my company, though occasionally there was a shout directed towards her.

'What the hell are you doing with an ugly-looking brute like that? Why don't you choose me instead?'

It was a question I often asked myself. I would look at the short fair hair she had adopted soon after arriving in Denmark, the cloche she wore, shaped like a bell or flowerpot, the coat with intricate patterns on its hem, the end of her sleeves, her fine stockings and buckled shoes and wonder why she spent any time with me, a man with a dull and nondescript face, average height, average breadth of shoulders, neither handsome nor ugly, the only thing distinctive about my features the wings of dark hair I had inherited from my father. I saw her beauty most clearly in the tiny apartment we decided to share, having each other's company a way of saving money on the rest. There were the occasional warm, still evenings when she would undress and allow me to draw her naked body – something which would have been impossible to do if we lived in Havn. I loved the paleness of her skin, the beauty of her legs and arms, even the birthmark on her left shoulder blade, the curve and swell of her breasts. It was something she had suggested she might do when we had stood before the statue of a naked Cupid in Thorvaldsen's Museum.

'Would it help your artwork if you drew me naked?' she asked.

'Well, I suppose so ... if that's all right ... it would be great,' I stammered.

'As long as you keep my face blurred. Or even use someone else's face.'

'That's fine. I'll do that.'

'Just in case someone from the Faroes ever steps into a gallery and sees it.'

'I don't think that'll ever happen,' I laughed.

'You never know, Karl. After all, a fisherman's son from Bergen clearly walked into one at some time.'

'The Havn ones are a different sort.'

'Don't you believe it – they're as bright as those from anywhere else.'

'All right,' I said, laughing again. 'I'll do as you want.'

And so I drew her with her features blurred, the birthmark on her shoulder blade cleared from view. Behind her I sketched landscapes that no one could possibly confuse with our home islands or even anywhere in Copenhagen. The naked, vulnerable form of Ásla crouching to lift a flower with the towers and columns of Atlantis crumbling in the background, each stone broken or misplaced, the smoke rising from lost battlements. Her unclothed figure standing with Hether Blether on the horizon, barely seen through mists, a few swans floating on the depths of the waters nearby. Naked, too, she lay outstretched on the long, sandy beaches of certain parts of Suðereyar, based on a few photographs I had seen of the coastline of Harris several years before. My fingers sometimes shook as I sketched her outline with a brush or pencil, taking note of each shade and glint of light upon her flesh.

'You're giving me a kind of immortality,' she giggled one time.

But there was one condition to all of this. I was not allowed to even attempt to make love to her. If I ever did, she would pack up her bags and be gone. She had told me this when she first decided to move into my apartment.

'I don't want to end up like my mother,' she said. 'She slept with a man before she was married. Her story was like that statue that used to be up on the edge of Copenhagen. The one of Leda and the swan.'

I nodded, aware that there had been a sculpture like that on top of a tall tower near the city's Arsenal harbour until the end of the nineteenth century, the one that illustrated the story of a woman being raped by a swan. I had heard people talking about its disappearance a few times, wondering where it had gone.

'She trusted this fisherman from Bergen she met one day in Havn. Went walking with him round the harbour, believing all his stories of how he was unmarried. Had no woman waiting for him at home. He filled her head with dreams.' She used a finger to wipe away the tears spilling from her eyes. 'And look what happened to her – her dreams brought her a life full of regret and misery. That's why I'm terrified of my own, every time they come into my head.'

'But we all need to dream. Life clouds over if we don't.'

'That's not my experience; it's exactly the opposite. Besides, it's not the only reason. I don't want to ruin you either.'

'What do you mean?'

'If you sleep with me, you might feel obliged to stay with me. You were designed for a better life than this. I don't want to hold you back.'

'But it might be worth it.'

'Don't delude yourself,' she said, grinning. 'You'd feel trapped eventually. From what I've seen, a lot of people do.'

I nodded, knowing exactly what she meant. I had seen a lot of people ensnared by marriage during my time in Havn, as trapped as fish caught upon a hook or a whale being bludgeoned in a bay.

Despite this, we still held each other in the darkness – with me struggling to control myself as I wrapped myself around her in the chill of winter, feeling the weight of her breasts on my forearm. Or else when she curled around me during these hours when we could hear noises through walls and ceilings, the thin glass of windows. There might be curses or crying, the boom of fists. Sometimes, there might be the monotonous rhythm of a couple making love in a nearby room, the creak of bedsprings, the thud of a headboard, a sound and echo that was carried across from one apartment to the next, waking up children, making parents stamp around the room to try and get them to sleep once more.

Ásla turned and looked at me. 'It's enough to put you off it for life.'

There were others who clearly thought differently from this. One of our neighbours, old Mathilde, spoke one time she met me on the stairs.

'How come there's never any sounds of sex from your apartment? I'll tell you what – the silence is really disturbing.'

Christianna

PASTOR LUKAS TOOK an envelope from his pocket when he arrived in my home, flattening it on the table before he handed it over.

'This came the other day. Someone told me you were very good at reading and understanding English.'

Then I could barely speak for a moment. My legs seemed to have filled with flame. There was the glow of warmth in my stomach. Standing near him was like being in a rush of wind, those that often arose suddenly and unexpectedly in places like Sørvágar, sending people reeling for a moment or two before they could catch their balance again. It was strange that Heðin had never had this effect on me. Instead, there had only been a mild curiosity to discover what it might be like to kiss his lips, feel his arms around my waist or shoulders – none of the tumult Lukas sometimes inspired.

'I think they're probably exaggerating a little.'

'Oh, I doubt that. Your family has a reputation for being really good with languages.'

'That's my father,' I said, blushing. 'It isn't always like father, like daughter.'

'I'm sure it more often is than it's not,' he said, taking out the sheet and giving it to me. For a moment or two, the words blurred and became indistinct before me. I was unable to make out a sentence on the page. After that, things cleared. I could make out a mention of St Brendan coming north on his boat to these parts, encountering mythical creatures on his voyage and then there was a reference to an Irish monk called Dicuil, telling of how in this part of the world:

There is another set of small islands, nearly all separated by narrow stretches of water; in these, for nearly a hundred years, hermits sailing from our country, Ireland, have lived. But just as they were always deserted from the beginning of the world, so now because of the Northman pirates they are emptied of anchorites and filled with countless sheep and very many diverse kinds of seabirds. I have never found these islands mentioned by the authorities.

'He wants to come here,' I said.

'Oh? For what reason?'

Then I skimmed the page again. 'He's a scholar from Cambridge University. In search of the lost land of Thule. He wants to find out if there's any evidence that it was Faroe. Or if it was Hjaltland or Iceland, where people whose communities were washed away lived in and settled. He wants to find out, too, if there's any evidence in these parts of monks settling here. Wants our help to find out.'

'He'll be very lucky to find anything.'

'No doubt. My father used to say that there was some evidence that monks had lived in Iceland, a place where darkness reigned in winter but where the summers were bright enough to pick lice from your clothes.'

'That's a strange thing to notice. You wouldn't think it was the first thing to catch your attention.'

I blushed, aware that could be said about me too. I was attempting to focus on the frayed end of the sleeve of his jacket, conscious that I might shake if I looked for an instant on the rest of him. Despite this, my gaze kept shifting, taking in every swirl of his hand, turn of his chin. Each look brought me a pang of pleasure. I was both troubled and delighted to be in his company.

'Well, will you write to him?' Lukas asked.

'What will I say?'

'Oh,' – his brow furrowed as it did sometimes when he was in the midst of a sermon – 'just tell him he's welcome to come here at any time.'

'Yes. I'll do that.'

'But I suppose we should also warn him that he's unlikely to find anything here. As far as we're aware, there's no trace of any Irish monks ever being here.'

'All right. I'll do that too.'

He nodded. 'Thanks very much, Christianna. That's very helpful indeed.'

And then he was off, back to a house where he lived alone, accompanied within its walls by the desolation of the loss of his wife, the grief he had suffered back then; leaving me with the company of my daughters, living in a home where my husband was most often absent, where, even when he was present, he was often trapped in the brooding silence which usually accompanied him, without hope of relief or escape. There were so many times when I wished I could follow Lukas to his house, to be swept up in his arms. There were occasions, too, when I was aware he longed to do much the same to me, making my life part of his own.

But with his faith, and all the constraints of small places, we both knew that was impossible.

It could never happen now or in the future.

Karl

'YOU WERE DESIGNED for a better life than this. I don't want to hold you back.'

Ásla's words kept returning to me most nights, coming back into my head time and time again. I could see there was truth in them, even when I was in my workplace in Kronprinsessegade day after day. I still often watched people gathering in the Rosenborg Castle Gardens opposite, taking shelter from the rain beside the Hercules Pavilion, alongside the statues there, picking up the accents and attitudes of those who sometimes sat during sunlit days in nearby cafés and inns. There would be a strange concoction of individuals there – members of the Swedish aristocracy in Copenhagen for a short holiday, the Russian nobility and landowners in exile after the revolution, those nobles who had fallen out with Piłsudski in Poland. I played their conversations over and over in my head, recording and noting their every affectation and word.

More and more I was able to blend in with them, speaking to them about the weather, fashion and the latest film and theatre performances. The latter was largely an act of deception. I did not have the money to attend too many theatre productions; unlike them, I never stepped once into the Royal Danish Theatre on Kongens Nytorv. Instead, I scoured newspaper columns, not only in Denmark but in other countries where the plays had appeared, noting the opinions of critics, reciting their views as if they were my own.

'Oh, I thought it was a tremendous play right until the third act. But then the climax let it down. A bit of a non-event.'

'I didn't find the stage-set too convincing. Clearly they were trying to save money.'

'The opening was incredibly slow.'

And then, too, there was my artwork for the company in Kronprinsessegade. My colleagues praised it constantly, their words rattling away like the drum downstairs. Even Brandes would do so. Despite both his race and general mood, he would squeeze out a compliment from his lips on one or two occasions.

'Rarely does a day go by when I am not astonished by the standard of your work.'

And then there was Ásla's constant prompting. She would remind me of the work we had seen in Thorvaldsen's Museum, the paintings of the Norwegian artist, J.C. Dahl on its walls.

'How far would he have got if he had stayed in Bergen? They would just have sniffed the air and pretended he had no talent. What else would you expect from a fisherman's son?' She raised her eyebrows to express her horror. 'And it'll be the same for you. As long as you stay here, you'll be the boy from Havn and they'll never forget that for a moment. "Can anything good ever come out of Nazareth?" they'll say every time they see your work. There's only one answer they'll reach.'

'Is that from the Bible?' I asked.

'Aye. John 1:46. My mother used to say that each time she mentioned my father, cursing the port he came from and telling me it taught him how to behave. All the place's fault. Most of the time she claimed he came from Bergen. Sometimes, though, it was Trondheim, Florø, Rørvik, Stavanger. She would change the location to match her mood.'

'You never knew for sure?'

'No. She never wanted me to know. She wanted to keep a whole range of possibilities. There were times when I wondered if she really knew herself.' She paused before speaking again. 'The trouble with that is you become never quite sure of yourself, where certain things you say, or feel, come from. It's as if all your life, you're playing a part.'

'I know how that feels,' I said, smiling.

'Oh, no. You don't. It's because you know exactly who you are that you're able to put on a mask. You're the son of Magnus Einarsson, storekeeper in Havn, native of the east coast of Iceland. No. It's because you're so firmly rooted in that world that you pretend to be someone else if you need to do so. Something a person like me will never be able to manage.'

I shook my head sadly. I had grown very fond of Ásla over the last year or two. This was even though there were times her company undermined some of my actions and pretences. I would glance at her while I was passing myself off, say, as a Swedish aristocrat, and see her suppress a giggle, laughter flashing across her eyes. At other times, there would be a frown, a pouting of her mouth when she thought what I was doing was wrong or immoral. There would be occasions, too, when she might lecture me after I had tried to hoodwink an individual whom she thought was too young or poor for me to take advantage of.

'You're wasting your time there,' she would declare. 'There's no rattle in that one's purse.'

For all that she was occasionally wrong about these matters, mostly she was right. She could see more clearly than I did the effect of my words on others, an observant eye on all our discussions. At the same time, though, she was a distraction. When I was seeking to fool others, I was always forced to cast an occasional glance in her direction, to see if her presence was undermining my act of deception. A quiet grin at the wrong moment could do that. So could a slight knotting of the brow.

It was during my final months in Vesterbro that I began to plan for leaving. It was something that several people whom I worked alongside had been urging me to do for years.

'Your talents would be more recognised if you lived elsewhere,' one declared, 'Paris, Berlin or London – anywhere where people with a variety of tongues mix and mingle. Anywhere that's a bit more central.'

'Berlin is interesting these days. Lots of films going on there. They need people with your skills there.'

'What about Paris? The centre of an empire.'

'There's other ways you can make money,' another of my workmates declared, his thumb circling the tips of his fingers. 'Time to travel and do exactly that.'

'While you're here, you will always be that strange man from the Faroes, judged by your address rather than your abilities. Leave here and you can become whoever you want to be.'

I twirled all these words in my mind as I had once done with my Charlie Chaplin stick, thinking them over again and again as I lay restless in my bed. There was still a part of me that was like my father, reading about the world in books but reluctant to confront it in reality. There was a part, too, which was like the swans I encountered in the city, staying on still, safe waters and reluctant to rise up in case it meant another clumsy, uncomfortable landing elsewhere. I dithered continually until one day I was approached by a man called Larsen. He was someone I barely knew but instantly recognised. With his snow-white hair, massive head and thrusting jawline, he was well-known in Copenhagen for his smuggling activities.

'Move to Berlin,' he said, 'and I'll give you work on the side. There's a group of us who are looking for someone with your skills. You can help us get wine from Bordeaux, coffee from the Netherlands, anything else we might need. Your language skills would come in very handy indeed.'

I thought about it for a moment. 'Can I speak to you about it tomorrow?'

'Of course. But no longer than that.'

I nodded.

That night I talked it over with Ásla.

'What do you think?'

'I think this is exactly the opportunity you need,' she declared. 'This country is too small and narrow for the likes of you.'

'You mean, I'm a Parisian?'

'Or a Berliner?' She laughed. 'It's up to you to make the decision.'

'Just not a chap from Copenhagen,' I said in my best English accent.

'Certainly not that!'

I went back the following day and told him of my decision.

Larsen nodded, shifting that white head of his, looking for all the world like a flurry of sleet or a blizzard. 'Good,' he said. 'We'll be very useful to each other.'

I smiled in response, aware exactly what had made me come to the decision. The opportunity would give me the chance to travel across the continent, visiting cities where my voice would not be recognised, the undertones and expressions of Havn unnoticed and unheard – even if they were still present in my speech in cities like Paris or Rome. I would no longer even be recognised as a Dane, but instead the descendants of Highland Scots who had fled their home country for Scandinavia during the eighteenth century.

I even designed my own passport for the occasion – the names 'Dunganon' and 'The Count of St Kilda' printed upon it together with a self-portrait. Along with this, there was a medallion and chain that I created for myself, conscious it might help me in any act of duplicity I had planned. On it, a jeweller had etched out the words that were the motto for the Clan MacGregor – *'S Rioghal*

Mo Dhream, or 'Royal is my race' – around the plunging outline of a gannet. On the other side, there was the outline of an island, complete with the tiny village most knew as 'Main Street' but I termed 'Port Nirvana', circled by a ring of foam and seaweed. The chain for my neck resembled a rope, one that those on that island might employ to hoist them downwards to capture the seabirds nesting on its cliffs.

And then there was the notebook in which I scrawled observations about *How to be a Mountebank and Charlatan*, duping and tricking the wealthy people I met, dealing, perhaps, with those like Larsen who operated on the shadowy side of the world's existence. Each one was a small reminder of my observations when I had either succeeded or failed in my ruses and gambits. I jotted them down, reminders to myself about how I should behave when undertaking these various ploys. I would need them even more when I dealt with people elsewhere on the continent, far from the sheltered existence of my early life in Havn or later days in Copenhagen.

- Practise your gaze every morning by staring into a mirror. Repeat this exercise several times a day.
- Never scold others – no matter what they do. Always praise and compliment.
- Always be at your most guarded when you experience joy or sorrow. They will set you off balance.
- If you see someone crying, move to offer comfort and sympathy. People are always at their most vulnerable when they are suffering grief.
- Do not employ disguises. They invariably fail.
- Keep your language simple, if at all possible.
- Pity softens and debases. Do not succumb to it.

- Be guarded with your opinions. Others may be listening.
- Imagine aristocrats, nobility and millionaires completely naked. It will help you see through both their clothes and airs.
- Make sure the role you play is at a little distance from yourself. It will prevent you becoming confused – The Guga Lesson!
- No one is so stupid that you can't convince them they are a genius.
- Keep things simple.
- Trust nobody else.
- Do not have a family. It will make deception impossible to sustain.
- Do not live with anyone. The day will come when their presence might undermine your pretence.

It was all this that made me look more and more at Ásla with a mixture of suspicion and regret. I could see that, almost without being conscious of it, I was becoming ensnared by her fair hair, her beauty, the mildness of her manner. Even the way she tended to me played a big part in my enchantment by her. She would wash my clothes and prepare my food on most days. Everything apart from – of course – running the risk of becoming pregnant by me, the coldness of her childhood preventing her from ever being scorched by the warmth of naked flesh.

Despite her consent, I would find it difficult to leave her. There was no doubt about that. Something about her drew me like no other person I had ever met.

But I had spent long enough in Copenhagen.

That night, I sat down and wrote two letters – one to my mother and the other to my sister – and told them where I planned to go.

The Weimar Years

1925–1933

Karl

'THEY'RE NOT GOING TO PUT UP with this forever,' my friend Egon said as he glanced at all the people who were in the Romanisches Café. They were all there – some with names that were familiar to me even from my days in Copenhagen. Bertolt Brecht, Otto Dix, Alfred Döblin, Hanns Eisler, George Grosz, Erich Kästner, Irmgard Keun, Else Lasker-Schüler, Erich Maria Remarque, others with names that even then I was aware were going to become known to me during the years ahead. My gaze would follow them all as they moved in and out of the building, especially occasional visitors like the writer Joseph Roth, weary from his travels around Europe, the small fat Berliner Kurt Tucholsky, whom Nazis hated with an indescribable venom, Sylvia von Harden with her monocle and short, bobbed black hair, a cigarette poised within her fingers.

'Who?' I asked.

'The people around here. Those hurt and damaged by the war. Those who've been wounded in their bodies. Those who've been damaged in their minds. It's full of the type of men and women they most detest. "Café Megalomania", they call the place behind their backs.'

'Do they? I wonder, would they include me among that number?'

Egon laughed, his overlong fair hair flopping as his shoulders shook. 'They certainly would. I think you would be first in that particular group. A mad toff and a Jock in these parts. You'd be first in line for the scaffold.'

'Or the guillotine.' I grinned.

'Oh, that would be too kind for you. They'd want to stretch out the experience, leave you flinging about on a length of rope for ages on end. Only suitable punishment for a man who looks like you.'

I laughed again, aware it was my clothes which gave that impression, those I wore in places like the Romanisches Café, allowing me to pass myself off as the Count or Duke of St Kilda in the Kürfurstendamm and other places when I strolled through Berlin. It consisted of a fresh, green velvet cloak, Arabic leather on its edge, and a pair of tartan trousers. The odd member of the aristocracy – including Sophia of Prussia and Alfonso of Spain – whom I encountered during these walks was convinced by my appearance.

'It is wonderful to meet someone with connections to such a distant island,' the former told me, frail and weak by that time in her life, her connections to those in power tattered and frayed.

At moments like that, I recalled the old Irish legend of the Children of Lir – the offspring of an old Celtic king transformed by their father's new wife into swans and condemned into exile for hundreds of years. I would think of them when I walked to places like the canal in Kreuzberg, feeding the swans breadcrumbs, watching as the birds dipped their necks towards the water or swam up and down the dark currents found there. Some of the time I identified with the swans in the Irish story, knowing that I, too, was exiled from my own past homelands in Faroe and Iceland, unlikely ever to return. Most of the time, however, I saw that tale reflected in the lives of others, the victims of loss and exile shuffling and wandering throughout Berlin.

Some had travelled from Italy, Russia, Austria or France, unsettled in streets that looked darker and more unpredictable than most of the cities and towns from which they came. So many hungry, crippled, wounded soldiers, pale-faced and bald, eyes deep within their sockets. There were legions, too, of Poles and Russian Jews sent into exile by the events of the last decades, stretching out hands to all who strolled by. A number sat in wagons, their legs blown off during the war.

'A pfennig?' they pleaded. 'Can you spare a pfennig?'

And then there were the other kinds of men and women – those males dressed in female clothing, wearing high heels and thick coats, the hordes of prostitutes blocking the pavement as I walked along, the fishnet stockings on their legs stretched out to catch any likely customer passing by. At night, they would be found in other locations, lying on the grassy acres of the Tiergarten, with their clients half naked and heaving on top of them. In my head, I could sometimes hear Pastor Anders back in Havn talking of such locations, using words like 'Babylon' and 'Gomorrah' to describe them.

'Places of depravity. They lie beyond our understanding or the reach of our imagination. Let them remain there. Let them stay at a distance from these islands.'

There were other things about these streets and boulevards those aristocrats with whom I came into contact must have noticed. The fact that, being a Protestant place, there was no sound of the Angelus ringing the length and breadth of the city at certain times of the day. 'Berlin,' as one of them said to me, looking in the direction of some drug-addled men standing on a street corner, 'looks like a place which Christ has left. You look as if all these changes have passed you by.'

I would nod my head and smile when they made remarks like these. 'I do my best to remain above it,' I'd say.

The odd Russian one I met was also charmed and enamoured with my company, mistaking my Faroese accent for that of the Scottish Highlands when I mentioned that part of my family estate included not only much of the Suðereyar but also Braemar.

'Oh, doesn't the king live near there?'

I would provide them with a short, baffling geography lesson before finally informing them, 'He's one of our neighbours.'

'Really?'

'He sometimes calls at the family estate for tea or a glass of whisky.'

For a time after that, they would babble on about how many Scots, the descendants of former Jacobites, they had known around St Petersburg and Moscow, mentioning names of which I had never heard – governesses like Jane Lyons and Catherine MacKinnon, soldiers like General Patrick Gordon, the Cock of the East. I would nod my head as if I had heard of them all.

'I know his distant cousins,' I might declare. 'They're friendly with us.'

They would grin when I said this, offering me an invitation to a party in their homes. It didn't take much to convince them that some connection between the Highlands of Scotland and Russia still existed, enshrined in this strange-looking man garbed in tartan whom they had met in a boulevard in Berlin. I would even describe the mountains of Scotland as if they were a mixture of the peaks and slopes of my native Faroe and the Alps or Pyrenees I sometimes had occasion to cross for my 'work'.

'They're quite magnificent,' I would say, 'crested with trees and heather. Snow on their tops in winter. As mystical and marvellous as the tales of Atlantis in their own way.'

Sometimes I would go further than that when I talked with the rare members of the English aristocracy I encountered, informing them in their native language that my ancestors had taken part in the Battle of Glen Shiel in 1719, leaving those shores in haste after the Jacobite forces had been defeated.

'They fled to Denmark after that, serving in the Great Northern War with the Danish Army against the Swedes. It's the reason I can speak in both the German and Danish tongues. We stayed near Lübeck for generations before returning to the Highlands, our old home.'

They would nod their heads as I said this, accepting this fantasy biography of my people as if it were the truth.

'Well, well, well. I never expected to meet the likes of you here,' they would say, again proffering me an invite to their apartments or their hotel rooms in the city, convinced that I was one of their kind; unaware that I lived in an attic room in Bahnhofstrasse, paying an extra twenty-five pfennigs for heating when I was there. Otherwise, the winters within its walls would have been chillier than those I had left behind in Havn. 'Really delighted to meet you.'

In the café, Egon and I would have different kinds of conversations, pointing out to one another the different groups that gathered there. In one corner, there might be earnest Talmudic scholars, writing out their plans to publish thick Hebrew publications on the black marble tabletops. In another, there were Yiddish speakers, talking of their days staying in Moscow and St Petersburg, the *shtetls* of the Ukraine and how they were now in exile from the lives they had known.

There were others in the room who could not have been more different – left-wing intellectuals who despised the worlds these men had left behind and wanted to create a new one of their own. There were also homosexuals, the group to whom I always suspected Egon belonged, for all his childhood as a pastor's son in a small town near Plön in Schleswig-Holstein had restrained him and curtailed that form of behaviour. His thick, round glasses would linger on them, both within café walls and in places like Kürfurstendamm, where young men caked with make-up and possessing tight artificial waistlines would parade the length of the avenue. For all that his upbringing restrained and confined him, it was often clear that this was the group to which he wanted to belong.

'He's very striking,' he might say. 'Looks a fascinating fellow.' He would grin, too, if he saw another young man wearing a tight dress or a woman wearing a three-piece suit. 'I'd like to work out the puzzle of who or what they exactly are. It would be a wonderful challenge for me.'

I shook my head when he spoke like that, steeling myself against any thoughts of involving myself with others. It was all part of allowing myself to be guided by the rules I had established for my behaviour when I stayed in Copenhagen – to stand remote and isolated in my life, trusting no one and expecting no one to trust in me. Besides, something remained within me of my early days in Havn. I saw people in simple, straightforward ways. The fisherman. The housewife. The storekeeper. These Berliners – and others from elsewhere – seemed awash with complexities, vivid and colourful but with no clear perception of who they were. They made men like my father seem dull and muted, for all his obvious eccentricities.

'I think it's a challenge I'll avoid,' I responded.

'You'll say that until it's forced on you.'

'Probably.'

Egon grinned and mocked me whenever I behaved like that, interpreting my existence as a disdain for others.

'We all know that you're an aristocrat, but do you have to look down your nose at people like that? It's really ill-becoming.'

'It's a long nose,' I'd say, smiling. 'I have very little choice.'

But my attention was truly drawn to those who displayed themselves in other ways – writers, actors, artists, film directors. We sat there trying to catch the attention of those who had already been successful in these fields, sipping coffee until it turned cold and bitter in our mouths. When someone we recognised passed our table, we tried to pretend what was still in our cups was warm and full of cheer. We would smile and raise a hand in greeting, muttering the first name of whoever was in the vicinity – Fritz Lang or his wife, Thea von Harbou, Stefan Zweig, Ernst Toller – hoping that the day would come when we might enjoy a long conversation with them, one that began with words like:

'Hello, Karl. Hello, Egon. It's great to see you.'

But it never happened. Occasionally, one of these famous individuals might make a brief nod in our direction, aware they were being recognised and unsure how to respond to this. Sometimes, we might overhear the odd discussion. Something about the ideas of Sigmund Freud. A few words about the politics of the time or the novels, say, of Thomas Mann. Mostly, however, I sat at the table with Egon at my side, sketching some of the faces of those I was aware were famous, occasionally earning a few pfennigs or even a mark or two for the likenesses I drew of Marlene Dietrich or Peter Lorre, whose faces were beginning to be recognised. Sometimes, I would even draw them the likes of Húsareyn and Kirkjubøreyn or Sørvágsfjørður, with their five stone summits in the background, yearning occasionally for the simplicities of my sisters' lives in the islands – a store somewhere in Havn, perhaps, or a tight, crammed cottage near the shores of Sørvágar. When anyone asked me where these places were, I would come out with a variety of answers, depending on whoever I was speaking to.

'It's somewhere on the edge of Zugspitze,' I might say, mentioning locations in Bavaria that I knew many Berliners wished to go and see. 'It's a peak near Sonntagshorn.'

'It's St Kilda, which my people own. Part of the Dunganon family estate.'

'An island I know.'

They would clap their hands together when I came out with answers like that. Some, of course, knew about St Kilda. The island was mentioned in a few Berlin newspapers sometime in 1930, when its last inhabitants left; photographs showed them crammed together on a boat.

'Oh, what a sad place to be connected with. It must have been heart-breaking to leave.'

Most, however, had never heard of it. Instead, they shared a strange nostalgia for peaks, crests, valleys and islands they had never visited. They had only seen them in films like *The Holy Mountain*, which were popular in the cinemas of that time, their vast expanses filled with snow, billowing clouds and trails of mist, a bird whirling around a barren, empty summit – like the gannets and gulls I had witnessed in my childhood, for all that their feathers were darker, their wings less smooth. It brought back memories of Copenhagen, those days when Ásla gripped my fingers as we watched *Eyvind and the Hills* and *The Outlaw and his Wife* together.

'They're not making you homesick, these films?' she'd ask.

'Not as much as these Copenhageners,' I'd answer. 'They're in tears wanting to go to places where they've never lived. Islands and mountains. At least I've lived among them. I know their dark side. The distance is hiding that from them.'

The longing for such locations among Berliners could be found in the way they often scanned adverts in the likes of the *Tägliche Rundschau* which promised 'Snow on the Slopes!', enticing them to spend Christmas and New Year skiing in the Sudeten mountains.

'We should go there!' they'd declare.

They would plot their escape, regardless of how much or little money they possessed, desperate to visit localities where only the occasional person could be seen, cramming into a car making its way for the length of an entire day down the autobahn or round a narrow, twisting road. In my conversations in the Romanisches Café, I summoned up such surroundings, all my words and actions taking place in the kind of vacancy I had left behind in my travels, the acres that surrounded my old home in Havn.

'High cliffs and summits. That's what St Kilda is like. The birds sweeping round them. Just like they do in some of those films.'

Fortunately, it wasn't in the café that I earned most of my living. I made as little there as I made from artwork during these years. I still worked occasionally with publishing firms, my gift for languages and art coming together in creating posters for the likes of the Deutsches Theater and the Kammerspiele, the State Opera and the hordes of cinemas around the city. This was some-times extremely lucrative for me, my various employers aware that people found my images arresting on the walls of various streets around the capital and beyond.

There were, too, my travels to different countries, something I only did from time to time. I would journey to places like Guipuzkoa and Navarra, Basque-speaking settlements near the Spanish border, when a contact heard that a large shipment of tobacco had been smuggled into Spain, something that happened from time to time when the nation was falling into the chaos that marked and defined these troubled years. Larsen or one of his compatriots would send me there.

'See what you can get,' he'd declare. 'But don't go over a certain price for the stuff. I don't want to pay too much.'

'Fine. I'll do that,' I would nod, aware what might happen if I ever failed in my negotiations with the Spaniards who were behind him. His snow-white hair was a mark of both his chill and ruthlessness. He'd sweep down on anyone who ever betrayed or disappointed him, something I was careful never to do.

'Good.' He'd raise his hand, dismissing me. 'You'll get paid for the journey there.'

To my credit, I did it well, my childhood performances preparing me for my role as middleman or negotiator in these matters. I would take note of the reputation of others before speaking directly to them, finding out if they were, say, Spanish aristocrats or those from the lower classes before I encountered them. I would mirror all this in my behaviour towards them. Sometimes I was the Count of St Kilda. On other occasions, a poor man from Copenhagen.

'You'll send it north to Bordeaux,' I might say. 'We'll take responsibility for it from there.'

'Yes. Yes,' they'd agree, aware of all the safe routes and trails meandering across the Pyrenees. 'We'll manage that fine.'

'Good.'

I would also travel to other countries, being paid in US dollars which I stored within a pair of socks at the bottom of a dresser in my bedroom, obtaining illegal wine from Bordeaux, buying goods like coffee to smuggle to the cafés and restaurants in Berlin – those like the Kit Kat Club, House Babylon, Moka Efti, trying to avoid the high taxes the Weimar Republic charged on these goods. Often this was done by visiting the Netherlands. The coffee there arrived in a factory in Utrecht from all over the East Indies, places like Batavia, Java and Sumatra, all bought there much more cheaply than their equivalents in Berlin. It was easy to hide away the odd container from those who supervised their movement. Sometimes, they even assisted us, those in charge making profits that the taxman would be unable to identify or spot.

'Our little secret,' they'd whisper, tapping their noses.

There were times, too, that I would be involved in groups organised to smuggle items – like alcohol, tobacco and certain drugs – between the north-western edge of Switzerland and the southern edge of Baden. There was a piece of woodland there they called *Eiserne Hand*, or 'the Iron Hand', that poked out of Switzerland into Germany like a prodding finger. Young men wound their way through the trees at night, concealing contraband around their person, trying their best to dodge the gaze of guards and dogs, bringing their smuggled goods to another state.

But I never took part in any of that. Not the carrying of goods. Not the smuggling of items aboard trains or aircraft. Not throwing them out of carriages or plane doors when a convenient moment came, allowing them to be collected by those who lived nearby, dodging tight controls and blockades, the sight of custom staff and soldiers. Not the carting of bottles of wine or vodka up and down hidden tracks.

My hands were clean and unsoiled by such tasks. There was only the occasional sniff of cocaine to check out its worth and value, a cursory examination of the strength of the heroin and the other drugs I helped to smuggle onto the streets of Berlin. Unlike a few years before, when I had been rescued by Kasper's family, I never indulged in any of this. Instead, I used my skills with the languages of the world, speaking Russian, Spanish,

English, Italian and other tongues to enable such exchanges to be made. They trusted me, too, because they thought I was a man of breeding, only indulging in such tasks because they assumed I was – like so many others at that time – down on my luck, out of pocket for a short time in my existence. Soon I would walk away from all of this, my decency and goodness restored, as distant and remote from all this crime as the islands in the Hebrides from which I obtained my title.

'It is good to see you, Count of St Kilda,' they would say, as if my character possessed the claim to sainthood that my aristocratic title seemed to assert. 'We know from even looking at you that you are a man of honour and dignity.'

Sometimes I'd blush at this, aware that I had never even been in Scotland, visiting, perhaps, one of the distilleries there, seeking to smuggle whisky to Berlin or Paris. It was an opportunity that someday I wanted to obtain.

'Thank you,' I said, 'I've always been blessed by my connections with far-off islands.'

'Yes, indeed,' they might say.

It wasn't always so. I remember sitting with Egon in the Romanisches Café one day, looking outside at the Kürfurstendamm where there were men gathering. Most wore brown shirts, brown ties, brown trousers that were so wide and flapping above the knees that they looked as if their wearers had sprouted wings there. Some had jackboots clamped tight upon their feet. They bustled and shoved against others on the street, especially the customers who were gathering round shops owned by Jews in the city. They created walls as substantial and forbidding as the Gedächtniskirche opposite us, its squat stone barriers like those of a dungeon.

'The Sturmabteilung. The SA,' Egon muttered.

'Who?'

'The gang led by someone called Adolf Hitler.'

'Oh, I think I've seen him. He looked a bit like this.'

I stood up. Daubing a little coffee stain on my upper lip, I flattened my forelock with water to make my hair look as if belonged to one of the local pimps, allowed myself to froth a little at my mouth. I twirled a fork, too, between my fingers, stepping round the table in the penguin-like way Charlie Chaplin walked. Someone in the café laughed. Egon slapped the table surface and chuckled, eyes sparkling through his glasses.

'That's him!' he said. 'That's the mad Austrian.'

A moment later a brick smashed through the nearest window. I ducked under the table to avoid the shower of broken glass. A riot had started. The men in brown charging down the street in the direction of the café, clubs and stones in their hands. The day of reckoning that Egon had prophesied had come. All of us who were in some way different – whether Jews, homosexuals, communists, fake aristocrats or foreigners like me – were clearly under threat.

Christianna

IT DIDN'T TAKE ME LONG to get sick of how Barratt, the archaeologist, was obsessed with islands.

He had visited so many in his working life and would list them sometimes in his conversation – 'Mull, Iona, the Farne islands, Skelligs, Orkneyjar, Hjaltland, even Heligoland off the coast of Denmark' – and talk about them all in countless ways. Some nights both I and his other chosen companions would suffer endless monologues about St Brendan's voyage, the sights that an Irish saint many centuries before had seen on his way around the North Atlantic, how he had celebrated mass with his fellow monks on the back of a sea monster they encountered during their voyage.

'They thought it was an island they had stepped upon. Imagine their surprise when they discovered it was a beast.'

And then there was the marvellous geography they had encountered on their voyage. Barratt's face coloured as he tried to recall the names by which they were known, counting them off on his fingers.

'There was the Steep Island, the Paradise of Birds, the Crystal Columns, the Island of Smiths, Islet of Paul the Hermit, the Island of Small Dark Fiends, the Isle of Sheep ...'

He broke off after mentioning the last named.

'People think that was the Faroes, that there were flocks of large sheep grazing on the shores here centuries ago. The monks caught one of them to make a meal for Easter. Soon afterwards an islander arrived, offering them a basket of white bread to accompany this. He was the one who told St Brendan that the reason the sheep were so large was that they were never milked but left alone in their pastures, grazing day and night.'

One or two who had heard the tale before nodded. Pastor Lukas even dared to interrupt him for a moment.

'Some say that he landed in Kirkjubøur, at the southern end of Streymoy. Its other name is Brandarsvik, linking it to St Brendan. Others say the man who brought him the food was an Irish priest who was already staying there.'

Barratt noted this with a brisk nod and continued his story.

'And then there were the other sights they encountered. The Hostile Whale. Jacontius, the Friendly Whale. The Sea Cat. The Arctic Hell. Till they reached the Land Promised to the Saints on the Borders of the Earthly Paradise. That was meant to be Newfoundland, on the shores of America. A great mist covered the islands there, shrouding them for days. It must have been a lot like sailing around here or near Hjaltland. A lot of fog to be found there. Much more than the islands further west in the Atlantic.'

'Like which ones?' someone asked him.

'Iona. Mull. The islands of the Suðereyar. There's a great deal of wind and rain there. Just like here. But not so much fog.'

I perked up on hearing this, sitting upright in my seat. 'Ever been to Harris or Scalpay?'

'No. Never had the good fortune. Someday the chance might arrive.' He gave me an odd look. 'Why did you ask that question?'

My face flushed before I stammered out an answer. 'Oh … some fishermen from there were washed up in Havn a few years ago.'

'They must have made a big impression on you.'

'They did.' I blushed again. 'Some of them drowned. Only two lived. Their boat was wrecked.'

'Oh … I'm sorry. I didn't mean to upset you.'

'That's all right,' I said, blinking back tears.

He moved on quickly, speaking about how different and distinctive all islands were, each one striking and unusual in its setting and history.

'They're wonderful places to stay. It's possible to live a good life in them. Much easier than it is in our cities, where evil and wickedness crowds in around you, blocking the path to righteousness. There are less temptations ahead of you, fewer prospects of sin. It's what makes places like these islands good and virtuous places in which to live.'

Then Pastor Lukas's forehead furrowed as it sometimes did when people spoke to him. He was troubled by the fervour of the

Englishman who sat at our table, waiting for me to translate his words. Barratt was an odd-looking man, eyes bloodshot and restless, face red and covered sometimes with grains of sweat. ('Like a shingle beach,' one of our neighbours said.) When he grew excited, as he often did, his fists would pound the air, warding off invisible assaults on his slim, slight body. Lukas watched all this, waiting for me to explain what he said.

'I disagree with what you're saying, Mr Barratt. There are no really good places outside of Heaven,' he declared. 'Places like this have their own dangers. You can grow complacent and smug here. Little to challenge your beliefs. We also see too clearly the faults and failings of our friends and neighbours. They grow large here, blocking our view of the goodness in them.'

Barratt laughed, smiting the air again with his fists. 'I disagree. The faults and failings of people here are much smaller than they are in London or Copenhagen. You can leave your door open and never even think of locking them. You know no one's going to steal from you. Try that in the city. Your belongings would be gone in a couple of minutes.'

'That's only because they think they can get away with it in cities. Lots of shadows and corners to hide in. Here ... ?'

'It's all open.'

'That's it. You're more easily caught. And yet small dishonesties exist. Boundaries are sometimes shifted. Someone's sheep can be stolen. People seek to get off with things if they can.'

'Small crimes.'

'And yet they happen. None of them are invisible to the eyes of God.' Lukas shook his head. 'The trouble with your argument is that it makes people think they can come to islands, shake off their past wrongdoings and make themselves anew. But that not true. You have to face up to your wrongdoings and repent for them, shake off your past and learn to begin a new life. Unfortunately, there's some who come to live on islands who think that it's the people already living on them that have to alter, rather than themselves. We've seen too many of them over the years.'

I nodded, agreeing with Lukas, something which, impressed by his fervour and eloquence, I did more and more often these days. I had seen a few over the years, men who had got into trouble in Stockholm, Copenhagen, Aarhus and Bergen, thinking they could set themselves right by coming to Faroe, fishing on a boat or working on someone else's land. It rarely worked out for them, toil and turmoil shadowed them even on these shores. Sometimes that may have been the fault of those living here – calling them the 'Swede', 'Dane' or 'Norwegian', never allowing them to dust off the debris of their past existence – but mostly it was their own. Their old lives and mistakes clung to them, holding them with the grim persistence of a chain.

'But you've seen some alter too,' Barratt said.

'No doubt. The ones who looked in the mirror and not just at their surroundings.'

'Oh ...'

Fed up with it all, I drifted off from the table, preparing some fish that Heðin had caught for our meal. When I did so, it wasn't the conversation of the men I was thinking about. Instead, it was the letters and postcards Karl sent me from the continent. My daughters Dagrún and Malvina really enjoyed the bird-feathers, drawings and artwork he sent, even the words in strange languages that accompanied them ('The tongue of Atlantis,' he declared). He drew his inspiration from the letters I had sent, sketching islands where ewes, lambs and rams were crammed together on a thin skerry of rock, another one which resembled Mykines, 'a paradise for birds' with fulmars and gannets spiralling through the clouds, or even the 'Island of Smiths' – Iceland, where we had come from many years before, with its mountains spitting flame.

And then there were the other stories I read aloud to Dagrún and Malvina from his letters, the ones that truly made their eyes grow wide with wonder.

Karl

THERE WAS A LESSON from that day in the Romanisches for me. It showed me how fragile the peace in Berlin was, how easily the people in its streets could turn on those who were different and unusual from themselves, no matter how valuable or precious some perceived their talents to be. I remember seeing Otto Dix shaking and trembling a short time after the riot, the uproar and turmoil clearly reminding him of the horrors of war he often portrayed in his artwork. Clearly the wounded and legless men found near the Hauptbahnhof, Berlin's central station, or places like the Wilhelmstrasse, had no idea how much he had tried to do for them, drawing attention to their suffering in his art, seeking to stir up compassion for those in that predicament. And then there was the writer Irmgard Keun with her thick dark curly hair, lips daubed with lipstick. She, too, looked upset that day, tears flooding her features. Both Egon and I tried not to react. I only paused a moment to wipe the coffee stain from my upper lip. He tugged his jacket collar upwards, trying to conceal his face.

'Best to get the hell out of here,' he muttered.

'The sooner the better,' I said.

He didn't get very far. At least, not the next time he encountered the Brownshirts. He was strolling round the Pariser Platz a few days later, not far from the Brandenburg Gate. Knowing him, he would probably have stopped in front of a flower bed, reaching out to stroke one of the flowers with his fingers, contemplating the beauty and symmetry of its petals. He was interrupted by a shout from one of the SA standing nearby.

'Hey! Haven't I seen you somewhere before?'

'I don't think so.'

'You were in the Romanisches the other day, weren't you?'

'No.'

'You sure of that?'

'Yes.'

And then the thundering began, the sound of heels and soles echoing on stone as they powered down the pavement after him. He stumbled. A moment or two later and they were onto him, these heels and soles powering down in harder, more brutal ways.

'*Warmer bruder … Tunte … Arschficker …*'

They shouted out their abuse without any sense of irony, as if they were unaware that their leader, Ernst Röhm, was himself a homosexual, denying themselves a knowledge that most of Berlin already possessed.

'*Tunte … Arschficker …*' their cries continued.

A whistle from the police probably saved Egon, sending the Brownshirts on their way. I saw him a few days later, his face broken and battered, shivering in the chill of tears.

'I'll have to go home,' he kept saying. 'To Plön. It's not safe for someone like me here. I'll have to go back to Schleswig-Holstein. Back to my father and mother.'

'But I thought you hated it there,' I said, 'that you never wanted to go back there again.'

'That was before all this.' He wept once again. 'That was before this happened.'

And then he turned to me.

'You should go away too,' he said. 'Back to the Faroe Islands. Or even Iceland.'

'There's no chance of that,' I snorted. 'I would only be miserable there.'

'Better to be safe and miserable than at risk. That's what made me decide to go back to Plön. At least there's a chance I might be safe there.'

'At what cost?'

'I know. But still, it might be a price worth paying. Even going back to Tórshavn till this storm is over. I'm sure your sister and mother would give you shelter there.'

'Nothing is worth that,' I said. 'There's a different kind of storm blowing there.'

I shivered as I thought of that, being trapped in my father's store with the likes of my brother-in-law lording it over me. Not to mention my sister and mother.

'Well, find somewhere else,' Egon said. 'Somewhere a little safer than Berlin.'

'Everywhere carries its own dangers. In some places they're just a little more visible than others.'

'Have it your own way, Karl. But don't say you weren't warned.'

'I won't.'

But for all my denials, those days altered me. I became more fearful of my fellow man, aware that on the lips of many, their language was changing and altering. They were starting to use words that I had never heard them speak before – expressions like *Volkengosse* or 'racial comrade', *Scholle* or 'soil', *Artfremd* or 'racially alien', *Untermensch* or 'subhuman', *fanatisch* or 'fanatical' – clustering on people's tongues in ordinary conversations. I stepped more warily among people. Conscious of their stupidity,

I leafed through the pages of the advice to myself I had written during my time in Copenhagen, reminding myself of its words.

- Trust nobody else.
- Do not have a family. It will make deception impossible to sustain.
- Do not live with anyone. The day will come when their presence might undermine your pretence.
- Keep your distance from everybody.

I also altered myself in other ways. I set aside in my wardrobe the clothes I wore when pretending to be the Count of St Kilda, conscious that it was not a good idea to stand out from others during these troubled times. One month it might be Jewish shopkeepers who were the targets. The next it could be Poles, the French, the English and their neighbours. Even someone wearing a tartan suit might not be immune to their attentions.

I kept my opinions to myself, too, and made sure that my face was as bland and impenetrable as possible when others spoke. In this, I probably had an advantage, having been brought up in a place like Havn. All those from small islands and communities have been practised in this tactic for years: suppressing grimaces when certain neighbours or relatives arrived, silencing the thoughts that flick through your head. It was only a few people – like my father – who defied these restrictions, seeing them as obstacles to be overcome.

'No one has the right to do that to you, neither pastor, politician nor priest,' he would declare. 'Always speak your mind.'

I would shake my head when this memory came to mind, wondering how he would react if the Sturmabteilung, these new brown Germans with their boots and baggy trousers, had surrounded him. Or if he had been in the company of men with murderous mayhem in their eyes, talking of 'Eastern vermin' and 'evil Americans' with a sneer. Once they had even turned on me when – against my usual judgement – I said a few words in defence of a Pole I knew.

'He's a fine man.'

'A fine man? He's a parasite, a leech, a maggot,' responded a broad-shouldered man with a bull neck and bulging eyes. 'Like all of his kind.'

'Where is it you come from?' another growled.

'The Faroes. Some islands off the coast of Norway.'

'A Nordic people, then.'

'Yes.'

'Like Iceland and Hjaltland. One of the places where some believe that ancient Thule was.'

I nodded, aware that there were some among the Nazis who believed in the truth of these stories, that the ancient Nordic race had lived in my native islands.

'You're such an innocent, Karl. You've not had to deal with being contaminated by the likes of Poles, Slavs, Jews. It's easy to stay pure out on the edge. The sea washes away all their filth.'

'I suppose so.'

The bull-necked man kicked a stone off the ground. 'A bloody islander. Bloody innocent. Easy to see a Pole being a fine man if you've not had to spend years dealing with them. Bloody vermin, the whole crowd of them.' He shook his head again, his gaze full of contempt. 'A bloody islander. A bloody child,' he declared.

I said nothing in response, all too conscious that I had broken my own rules in saying anything meaningful to these men. I should have remained silent instead of coming out with words that might resemble my own views.

'Don't worry,' the other man scoffed, 'he'll lose his virginity if he stays here in Berlin much longer. No doubt about that.'

I grinned, glad to have been the butt of a joke rather than a victim of their bad humour. I had seen the results of that in the crumpled and broken bodies I had passed walking through the streets of Berlin at night. The men in brown would crowd around them, beating their victims with boots and batons.

I even changed my ways of practising my art at that time. I wrote verse most often in languages like Italian, Spanish and Portuguese, conscious that if the Brownshirts ever tried to read it, they would be baffled by every word. There were times, too, when I wrote in my own Atlantean language, based largely on what the seventeenth-century Swedish scholar Olof Rudbeck believed. He claimed that Swedish was the language this tongue most resembled, that the mythical King Atle had once ruled Atlantis and that Atlefjell, a Swedish mountain, had been part of the real Atlas Mountains and had once formed the foundations of that lost continent. He even claimed the Øresund strait between Sweden and Denmark had been the true location for the Pillars of Hercules – something I disputed because I had always believed the heights of the cliffs on St Kilda possessed a greater claim to that title. They might, too, have formed the continent's edge. It was due to this that I wasn't entirely convinced by Rudbeck's argument. I would add little touches of Basque and Finnish to the Swedish I used in my writing, knowing that they were strange and different to the rest of the languages found at the edge of Europe.

I also altered my way of painting. I drew mountainous land-scapes, billowing seas, horses tugging ploughs behind them, tall muscular men with straight-lined jaws and hard-edged stares, fair-headed women with wide smiles and white blouses who resembled Norse goddesses, everything that the Nazis considered good and decent. It was only in my letters to my sister, mother and the occasional ones I sent to Ásla or Kasper's parents in Copenhagen that I revealed both my real self and the sweep of my dreams and visions.

Swans flew in them. Gannets, fulmars, guillemots – the birds I recalled from my youth.

Christianna

FOR YEARS I STORED AWAY my brother's letters. They were so different from the ones I received from my sister with her sharp, caustic stories about her customers, neighbours, the children she had parented; different from our mother's notes, too, with the list of ailments and illnesses that accompanied her ageing. 'I don't know why I'm lingering,' she kept saying. 'There is no point in carrying on when you're on your own.' Sometimes she used to compare herself to the dead cat that sat in the window of Father's store for years, clutching her heart in the same way it once held a fiddle. 'The pain in it. The pain.'

Karl's words cast a spell on me – as they did Dagrún and Malvina when I read the letters aloud to them. It wasn't only the drawings that appealed. The language was both striking and unusual, full of a noise and clamour that was alien to the stillness and quiet of the places where we lived. I rolled them on my tongue, tasting the flavour of the places where he'd been.

'The Deutches Theater, Kammerspiele, Volksbühne, State Theater, Tribüne …'

And then there was the sparkle of those other names, the ones who had their work performed in such locations.

'Shakespeare, Hauptmann, Werfel, Molière, Shaw, Galsworthy, Schiller, Unruth, Hofmannsthal ...'

The words, too, they had written:

- To be or not to be, that is the question.
- Beware of false knowledge; it is more dangerous than ignorance.
- Of all follies there is none greater than wanting to make the
world a better place.

He would write, too, about the music he had heard. The Philharmonic concerts led by Wilhelm Furtwängler. The Bruno Walter concerts with the Philharmonic Orchestra. The State Opera with its performances of Alban Berg's *Wozzeck* and Leoš Janáček's *Jenůfa*. The Municipal Opera. The Kroll Opera under Otto Klemperer, which he had heard others talk about.

It all reminded me of the days when we were children, when we would head out to a nearby slope and see the gleam of Skansin lighthouse compete with the swirl and sweep of the Northern Lights above these islands.

'Lie down beside me,' he would say. 'Stay still.'

We would compare the quality of beams and light. One minute, we would watch the lighthouse. Its light would be constant and persistent, a solitary shade among the bright and distinctive colours of the Aurora Borealis. They seemed to jostle against one another, competing for space and room among the darkness, their shapes shifting again and again. One moment, they might resemble circles. The next, it was as if they were tear-drops cascading on the Earth. We'd look up, too, at the Milky Way, and the constellation that some called the Cygnus, with its wide and spreading wings glimmering in the darkness. Someone whispered it resembled Jesus on the cross, a comparison another person described as close to blasphemy. We stretched out hands below it, imitating its sweep.

Father also told us some believed that the Northern Lights were the ghostly spirits of men who had died. Others thought they were falling flames, heavenly dancers, the souls of children loose and at play. Karl had looked up and given his own view, how our planet –with all its cities, lighthouses and houselights – sent out its own gleam into the darkness, not matched by the size or scale of the firmament that stretched around us.

'We're all only star-dwellers, you know. Perhaps these lights are sending out a warning – about what might happen if the heavens ever turned against us. They could wash us away in a moment.'

'Perhaps,' I said, laughing. 'Perhaps, however, we need their cleansing.'

And then he shut his eyes, imagining, he said, the lighthouse rising from its place to join the array of lights that spread above its tower, adding its twinkle to the night sky, uprooting itself to become one with its competitors in the sky.

He drew that later, sketching the scene he had pictured in his head out on a sheet of paper.

It had been at that moment I began to recognise the strange and disturbing talent my brother possessed. It was one that was mimicked by my youngest daughter, Malvina. I saw the intensity of my brother's vision in her face from time to time, especially when she lifted a pencil to draw. She had strange-coloured eyes – the right one possessing two shades, mingling blue and brown. They would become fixed and penetrating every time she looked at our occasional visitors, largely fishermen but occasional preachers or fish-buyers. Especially if they were unable to speak Faroese or

Danish, she would measure them with her gaze, wondering what part of the world's existence he might have come from.

'Bergen? Hjaltland? Suðereyar?'

I became nervous when I saw her act like that, conscious that I was imitating my own mother when I behaved in that way, watching her own son, all too aware that her husband's restlessness was being passed to the next generation – as it so often did. Sometimes I thought of talking to my husband about this, conscious that she was inheriting some of our family traits, but I was all too aware that he would have no answers.

'We have to accept God's will,' he would declare, reacting in the same manner as he did when some of his fellow fishermen were lost on a boat.

But then there would be Malvina's response to his words.

'We have to do our best sometimes to challenge and change it,' she declared on a few occasions. 'It isn't good to just endure and suffer. Sometimes you have to do much more than that.'

He didn't say anything, turning his gaze away. I was conscious that he was reacting to her words in much the same way as he did when I lingered too long in the pastor's company, revelling at his words. Heðin's eyes would fix hard on me for a moment or two before he would shake his head and look aside, conscious of my every move and expression but saying nothing, seeking to put all his doubts and concerns aside, trusting that God would keep me close and faithful, for all my behaviour might somehow suggest otherwise.

Hitler's Germany
1933–1939

Karl

JUST LIKE EGON, I was aware change might be coming. Unlike some of the more intelligent Germans that I met on occasions, that day in the Romanisches had made me conscious for quite some time that Hitler would find his way to power. My more sensitive, left-wing acquaintances all dismissed this possibility. 'There's no chance,' they would say. 'People aren't as crazy as that. You can rely on the ordinary person's common sense.' Even after the Reichstag fire took place in the early months of 1933, they continued with that state of mind. 'He's just a failed painter. It won't be long till things get back to normal,' they'd say, laughing. 'Just wait and see. People like me and you will just have to howl like wolves for a time, pretend to join in the chorus. It won't be long till their own friends will turn on them. Won't be long at all.'

I didn't share their confidence that this was the case. Instead, I saw these clever individuals as trapped in their own ideas and abstractions, unable to see what lay directly ahead. Either that or failing to take the Nazis and their odd notions seriously, not being aware that they were true and sincere about the aims they espoused.

Perhaps this was because I had inherited a powerful nose from my father, one equipped to smell and scent all sorts of objects that were well outside the nasal range of the average German. Before anyone else was even aware, I was able to capture the whiff of peat wafting from a chimney. The stench of fish rotting on a quay. The whiff of *skerpikjøt*, the dried mutton enjoyed by my fellow Faroese. The head-reeling fragrance of seabirds like gannets and puffins. The intense, overpowering aroma of fulmar oil and seagull shit. The reek of seaweed decomposing on the shore. It was, perhaps, because of this I had a sense of the lack of humanity of those with whom I shared these streets, how hopeless and lost they felt politically, how they saw Hitler and the Nazis as some sort of national equivalent of the lighthouse at Skansin I had seen so often in my childhood, pointing out a clear route ahead. They were not aware of the stink that came from their surroundings and their view of the world.

Perhaps, because I was a foreigner, I was aware of how the smell permeated everywhere, fouling all it came into contact with. I was conscious that some of those I met from other countries had a similar sense of the changes that the Nazis would bring about, putting their noses to the test. I heard similar warnings to the ones that echoed in my head from the mouths of several of my friends. There was Martin, a Jewish acquaintance of mine whose family had some connection with Heitinger's department store. 'I won't be long here,' he announced. 'Neither will any of my people.' Another French associate I came across declared, 'Don't people here see how poisonous all this is, how it will destroy us and them?' An Englishman I met told me how putrid he found the country these days. 'They've thrown all human decency away.'

I felt the same, but unlike them, I was not keen to travel back to my home country to escape what might be about to happen here. There was so much about Berlin that fascinated me. Especially its cinema. In contrast, even Denmark was dull. The Faroes were a place where it would be impossible for me to exist. But I could not stay the way I was either. I was all too visible in my present existence. The lighthouse at Skansin once again, isolated and far too distinctive and different from others. Even the fact that some of the Nazis I knew slapped my back and spoke words of comfort and cheer was of little consolation to me.

'You're an Aryan like us. Icelandic. Faroese. Pure Nordic blood.'

I knew the day might come when they might turn against me too for these very reasons, that being Icelandic or Faroese might be enough to perceive me as an imperfect Aryan, possessing some defect or fissure in my Nordic blood. Even my claim to be the Count of St Kilda could count against me, suggesting I had a hint of Celt or Gael in my ancestry, enough for Hitler's forces to find an excuse to castigate and punish me if ever they quarrelled with the Irish or some other race. I noted all this in my guide on *How to be a Mountebank and a Charlatan* guide, scribbling it down on a page.

- Always pretend to be the same as everyone else. The day may come when being different is dangerous.
- Variety is not always the spice of life, as the English claim. Sometimes it can bring about the end of it.

And then came the moment when I realised it was not safe to continue my customary detachment from the world. That occurred one night when there was a political meeting in Mrs Lindgren's room below mine in the Bahnhofstrasse. I heard the uproar as I sat at my desk trying to draw a film poster for which I had been commissioned. It was for one of these *Bergfilms* that were popular at that time. I drew the peaks, snowscapes and even glaciers with which I had been familiar as a young child, summoning up recollections of Skaftafell, which my father had so often spoken about, talking about the quiet whisper of its water-falls, the black sands that could be seen at times, its green birch forest, the creeping, slithering tongues of the glacier, men, too, with ice-picks in their hands. Suddenly I could hear the uproar in the room below. It began first with the stamping of jackboots, a chorus of loud male voices coming together.

'Heil Hitler,' they cried, clicking their heels.

A moment later I could hear the shrillness of female voices, including that of my neighbour, Mrs Lindgren. The Swedish lady's cries were louder than anyone else's, each word penetrating the floor of my attic room, shaking its walls. It was as if she was the source of the dramatic skills of her actress daughter, Anna, whom I had seen on stage and screen, one of the many Nordic goddesses – like her fellow Swedes, Zarah Leander, Karin Albihn and KristinaSöderbaum, as well as Renate Müller – who had appeared, glittering, in the country's theatres and cinemas, the perfection of their form flickering like a persistent temptation before us.

'Heil Hitler! Heil Hitler! Heil Hitler!' I heard from below.

An instant's silence and the Horst Wessel song started, its triumphant beat pounding through the building.

Die Fahne hoch! Die Reihen fest geschlossen!
SA marschiert mit ruhig festem Schritt.
Kam'raden, die Rotfront und Reaktion erschossen,
Marschier'n im Geist in unser'n Reihen mit.

Raise the flag! The ranks tightly closed!
The SA marches with calm, steady step.
Comrades shot by the Red Front and reactionaries
March in spirit within our ranks.

No sooner had the music stilled than I heard the knock at the door.

'Yes?'

Mrs Lindgren was standing there, red-faced, wearing a black cloche and coat, a fox-fur draped around her shoulders. Her nose was crinkled in a smile, her cheeks dimpled. From the scent of her breath and the sparkle in her blue eyes, it was clear she had been drinking.

'Herr Einarsson?'

My stomach curdled. I knew there were Brownshirts downstairs, and I wondered for an instant if they were coming for me.

'Yes?'

She clicked her high heels together. For a moment, I braced myself for the uplifting of her arm, the repetition of a particular phrase. Fortunately, it didn't happen.

'I was wondering if you might come down and join us, raise a toast or two to the Führer. Would you like to do that?'

'I've got work to do,' I stammered, nodding towards the papers stretched out on the table.

'Oh, I know. Beautiful work it is, too. I've seen it around the place,' she said, smiling in its direction. 'But I'm sure you could take a little time away from it. Might do you good. Might help to restore your' – she paused for a moment or two, smiling knowingly – 'creativity.'

'Oh.'

I must confess I shook, thinking of what happened to Egon that day, the conversation, too, I had already gone through with members of the SA, in which I had been dismissed as an 'innocent' and an 'islander'. Perhaps this was the moment I had to alter, put on a new guise and shake off the old.

'All right. I'll come.'

And then Mrs Lindgren did something she would often do during the months and years ahead: she stretched out her arms to embrace me.

'Great!' she cried. 'That's just wonderful. Wonderful! I knew I could persuade you.'

Karl

AMONG ALL THE SCHNAPPS and spirits that were being doled out, they quizzed me about my opinions.

'Do you hate Jews?'

I confessed that I disliked Brandes, who had been in charge while I was working in Copenhagen, recalling how he had dismissed me when I was young.

'Any others?'

I mentioned a few names, exaggerating my feelings about them.

'Good. Good. Do you consider yourself an Aryan?'

'Yes ... yes.' I nodded. 'I certainly do.'

'Why?'

I talked about my people, mentioning how they came from Seyðisfjörður on the east coast of Iceland, how I had been brought up in Havn; how, too, my father had been obsessed with the idea of Atlantis, a notion that had been passed onto me.

'I believe that ancient civilisation was the home of the Aryans, that some escaped when the continent was destroyed. That included those who made their way to Germany, Iceland, most of Scandinavia, Hjaltland, my own home islands.'

'The superior races,' my interrogator said, nodding and squinting at me through his right eye. The other wore an eyepatch, a scar on his cheek indicating he had been wounded in some way. Perhaps in the war. The rest of his face looked not Aryan in the slightest – swarthy, shave-headed, possessing a stocky frame. 'What do you think of the Führer?'

'I think he's the salvation of Germany. More than that – he's the saviour of Europe.'

'Good, good.'

Mrs Lindgren clapped her hands together when I said this. 'I knew that. I knew that,' she declared. 'He has the face and form of one of us.'

'Yes … quite,' the man with the eyepatch said. 'Why haven't you joined the party, Mr Einarsson?'

I shrugged my shoulders. 'I keep meaning to. I just haven't got round to it yet.'

'Well, do so,' he said. 'If you help us, we will look after you. It is safer to depend on us at a time of great change.'

'Of course.'

The man stood up from the table, pushing his chair underneath. 'And look after Freja too, Mrs Lindgren here. She's been a great promoter of your work. An enthusiast for your art. A wonderful disciple for our cause.'

I smiled. She had come to my doorway many times in the past few months. The first time, she was carrying a letter that had been sent to me but delivered to the wrong address.

'I think this is yours,' she'd declared, her gaze swirling round me to take in every last detail of my apartment.

And then there were the occasions when it was clear she knew exactly in what activities I was involved. She would ask me for some coffee.

'I hear you know exactly how to get your hands on some,' she said, her eyelids fluttering at me.

On another evening, just after I obtained a few cases of wine from a contact in Bordeaux, she was greeting me again, this time wearing a loose and low-cut dress, bowing down to allow me to take in the fullness of her figure.

'Rumour has it that you have obtained some wonderful supplies, a desirable source of intoxication.'

She hitched her skirt up, too, as she was talking, allowing me to glimpse the bareness of her skin, permitting me to imagine what it would be like to close my eyes and touch her with my fingers, bring her body into close contact with my own flesh. The possibility of this sparked a quick and sudden surge through my being in a way – apart from these moments I would struggle to resist the attraction and appeal of Ásla – it had done so rarely in my life. I might imagine my own lips and tongue in contact with her, no longer the solitary individual I had chosen to be for much of my life but preferring instead to have the opportunity to share a bed with her, lying between her thighs, kissing her in all the secret places her body contained, all that had been hidden to me in my years of isolation revealed and exposed.

And then there would be the countless occasions when her conversation would seem simple and innocent at first, only to reveal itself to be more complex and manipulative a moment later. She would talk perhaps about the acting achievements of her daughter, Anna.

'People say she acquired her good looks from me,' she might say, smiling, her eyelashes fluttering. 'And her deep voice. What do you think, Mr Einarsson?'

I would grin and agree with her, declaring that it was obvious where the young lady gained much of her appeal. Once I even went so far as to declare, 'She's just like her mother. Wonderful charm. Exotic Swedish allure. Warmth from a chilly climate. Both beautiful and smart. Women like that are rare individuals indeed.'

Mrs Lindgren blushed and tittered in response to this – just as she did when the man with the eyepatch made those remarks about her.

'I know Karl appreciates me. I can see it in his eyes,' she said.

Christianna

FROM THE MOMENT the Reichstag went on fire, Karl wrote nothing about what was going on in Germany. He kept his pen still about the Night of the Long Knives, when Ernst Röhm and his friends tucked up in their brown shirts were killed. He didn't mention how Jews had to wear yellow badges to allow them to be identified by their faith. Or how their shop and house windows were smashed and broken by thugs. How men against the government were sent to camps to be punished for thinking differently from others. Instead, I found about these matters from Bedda, who had discovered them from some relatives of Kasper, the young man whose family Karl had stayed with all those years earlier.

'They say it's a terrible place. People are in fear of even saying a wrong word. All around Berlin, there's people being beaten for being unusual in some way. Goodness knows the time may come when they will turn on Karl.'

But there was none of that in Karl's letters. Just strange and different things. He mentioned how he had been asked to create a poster for a film called *The Blue Light*. On it, there was a drawing of a mountain, the halo of the sun circling its peak, a young fair-haired woman called Leni Riefenstahl looking outwards, the backs of three muscular men dressed in short sleeves, one of them gripping a piece of wood in his hand. Karl folded up a copy in the envelope for the girls to admire – Malvina imagined it was one of the mountains that could be seen from the window of our home.

'What a life he must have,' she declared with an excitement that reminded me of Karl when he was young. 'I can't wait to get away from here and see all these things. Do you think he'll have room in his home?'

I nodded and smiled as I did when either of my daughters – especially Malvina – came out with a remark like that. 'Just be patient. Your time will come.'

But Heðin was different. Settled in the place where he'd lived all his days, he loved his existence in Faroe. Sometimes he'd raise an eyebrow when Malvina spoke like that.

'It's not that magical,' he'd mutter. 'I've sailed to quite a few ports in my time. Norway. Denmark. Latvia. Germany. You're better off here. Not as dark or as dangerous. Sometimes I feel my life is more at risk strolling around a harbour on a quiet, calm night than it is in a storm at sea.'

'Tell me more about that,' Malvina would ask, the mixed shades of her eyes vivid and bright with curiosity. 'I'd love to know more about the places you go to see.'

More at ease with fish than women, Heðin would become flustered at her questions. He flapped the *Dimmaletting* in his hands, focusing on headlines he had studied a thousand times before.

'Time may bring you some understanding of that. In the meantime, just be glad you're in a place like Vágar. Lots of people in Copenhagen or Berlin would be desperate to live in a peaceful island like this.'

'Really?' Malvina snorted with laughter. 'I imagine it would be thrilling for them!'

'There are more important things in life than thrills.'

'Really?' Malvina smiled again.

I grinned, admiring my youngest daughter's spirit.

'Really,' Heðin said.

It was one of the next letters that arrived from Karl that made me begin to suspect – for once – that Heðin might be right. Along with a shorter note than usual, there were a few pictures advertising *Hitlerjunge Quex – Ein Film vom Opfergeist der deutschen Jugend*. He sent us a copy of the poster that was to be displayed outside cinemas, showing a young fair-haired man, who was wearing a short-sleeved shirt and a Nazi armband and looking nervous and anxious. In the background, there was the chaos of a city street with a young woman being chased along the road by a horde of men. There were also a few scenes from the film. That rarest of sights to us – a forest – standing rigid and straight as a troop of men bearing a Nazi flag marched down a track, bringing form and order even to the natural world that surrounded them. A white-shirted young man wearing a cap was stretched out on a bed being smiled at by four of his friends wearing Nazi uniforms. I trembled when I saw it, hiding the poster in the dung heap behind our home, using a spade to conceal it.

Another time he sent a programme he had created for a film called *Flüchtlinge*, which was about Germans living near the Volga fleeing the Bolshveiks. This displayed a strong, muscular man with thick blonde hair wrapping his arms around a terrified young woman, clearly seeking to protect her. Printed on it was a succession of slogans describing the film. One proclaimed, *They had imprisoned and persecuted him because he loved the Fatherland*. Another declared, *Out of the flaming inferno, home to a German haven*.

I remember thinking that maybe Karl had got it wrong. Perhaps he was the one living in the inferno. Perhaps he should be thinking of a return to Havn in these troubling times.

He would, at least, be much safer here.

Karl

AT THAT TIME, I was the only person not wearing a disguise. All around me there were legions of people who never stepped out without one. They included Freja, the lady with whom I now lived as man and wife, and her actress daughter, Anna, who occasionally came to visit us. Every morning before she stepped out, Freja would apply her make-up, puffing up and painting herself. Her eyes looked wide and white, her pupils bright and shining – as if they had been transformed into fried eggs served on a plate. Her lips were a red slit on her face, emerging from the layer of white powder that cloaked her cheeks and forehead. And then there was her wavy fair hair, the great waft of perfume she carried around everywhere with her. When she finished creating this person, she would rise to her feet on strong arrogant legs, turning to me with her eyelashes fluttering.

'What do you think?'

'You're beautiful. Beautiful,' I'd gasp, grasping this woman who was a few short years older than me and holding her tightly. 'I cannot bear to let you go.'

She'd laugh, pressing my nose with a finger. 'Tonight, Karl. You'll have to wait until tonight.'

'That's a pleasure to anticipate,' I'd say, grinning. 'I can hardly hold my breath till then.'

'Oh, Karl.'

There was more than a little truth in my assertions. As someone who had always tried to keep isolated and distant from others, I had discovered the joys of being with someone during the last few months. I felt safer, especially during a time when someone seen as unusual was vulnerable and exposed to the attentions of those in authority. It was a situation I had seen for so many – Jews, homosexuals, Gypsies, those on the left in politics. The old guidelines I had written in *How to be a Mountebank* no longer applied. People could no longer afford to be isolated and alone. It left them exposed, like a seal swimming in the waters around my home when a school of whales were nearby.

But there was more to it than this. I was all too aware that Freja had a great deal of knowledge of what I had done during my years as her neighbour, all revealed during the times she had come to my home asking for coffee, drugs or wine.

And then in her presence, I had discovered something else about myself, a need I had never recognised or acknowledged in myself before. I thirsted for sex, craved for her nakedness. Her body resembled the seas that swept into Havn when I was a youngster. Her breasts were like waves that surrounded me, her thighs possessing the clasp and clutch of deep water as our bodies thrilled and shuddered together. There was in her kisses, and much of the rest of the anatomy, too, the salt and sharpness of the ocean, the thrill of being carried away by rollers and breakers that were so much more powerful – in many ways – than the weakness of my own male flesh. I rejoiced in all this, especially as I was aware that there were also many differences from the seas I had known as a child. There was warmth instead of chill, pleasure instead of danger.

'A kiss before you go,' I'd ask.

'Yes. Yes. Yes,' she'd declare, and I feel once more her round-ness of her flesh, the glory of her body.

And then she'd be off, heading off to her work in a jewellery shop on the Kurfürstendamm, where she had worked since her husband had left her a decade or so before.

There were many similar-looking women there, sporting the same faces and coats of moleskin fur; none looking like those I had grown up among in Havn, where they dressed far more for warmth and comfort than style. Back there, the fingers of the women often bruised and wounded. None carried the red-tipped fingernails their equivalents sported here. Their faces, too, were often flushed and coloured by wind and salt. Not like those in the street in Berlin, with their skin pale and powdered white.

The same was true of many of the men. They dressed in smart, well-pressed suits and white shirts, as if they were either foreign diplomats or salesmen, their tongues as glib and sharp as their clothing. Or there were those in uniform – either soldiers, policemen or men from the Waffen-SS, much more forceful and brutal in appearance. I was aware how some of them behaved in the streets. Freja told me once about how the SS had acted towards a Jewish man one afternoon.

'Hell. They made a mess of the poor soul. He was lying on the road, and they were kicking him again and again. There was blood running from his face. Vomit spilling. Some of his bones were clearly broken.'

She was sobbing as she said all this, clinging to my shoulder as she spoke.

'I've never seen the likes of that. Who are these people? How can anyone behave like that?'

I said as little as I could, knowing that there might come a time when the two of us might part. I had heard her speak about her own husband in the past, the wrongs he had apparently done to her, and I was nervous that she might say similar about me one day. Her mind clearly whirled and spun in terms of her devotion both to a political cause and the men in her life.

'Shhh, shhh … There may be a reason. We don't know.'

'Do you think the Führer knows that his men act like that?'

'No,' I lied. 'I don't think so.'

'No. I didn't think so either. But the way they're behaving …'

I tried not to think of them. Instead, I bowed my head and worked on various projects that had been allotted to me. Sometimes, these were arranged through the Reich Press Chamber, which often put work my way, publishing my artwork in such outlets as *Volkischer Beobachter*, the weekly *Illustrierter Beobachter* and the *Nationalsozialistische Monatshefte*. At other times, it came through my contacts in the movie industries, especially Anna, who was in a relationship with a film producer.

Some of these were works of propaganda, but one or two appealed to me. There was one called *Der verlorene Sohn* – 'The Prodigal Son' – which matched my own life, about a young man who grew up in a rural location and moved to a city, swapping the soil for the street, before returning once again to his quiet and timeless home. Another was a film about Münchhausen, the boastful baron who was as much of a fiction as the members of the nobility I had sometimes conjured up in my existence. I grinned as I drew him, seeing my own face, recalling the likes of the Count of St Kilda, Earl Dunganon, Emperor Cormorant XII of Atlantis, all these men I no longer pretended to be. There was no audience for them. No nobility. No foreign royalty. No aristocratic visitors in the streets of Berlin anymore.

And then came the day I changed my mind. A hammering on the door of our home when Freja and I were drinking some coffee that had been smuggled out of Utrecht, swilling it down before we were caught.

'Yes?' I grabbed the walking stick I used to employ when impersonating Charlie Chaplin years before, clutching it before opening the door.

'Herr Einarsson? We need to speak to you.'

It was the man with the black eye-patch who was there, surrounded by others in their dark uniforms.

'We need to speak to you,' he said again.

I opened the door, noting how he briefly nodded in Freja's direction, uttering her name. I had suspected that they had been lovers, but she'd denied this, claiming that he had been Anna's instead. 'Sometimes, young women need older men to teach them about life. The heads of younger men are too screwed up and clouded to do that,' she claimed.

'Heil Hitler!' he declared.

'Heil …' I responded, dropping the walking stick that was in my grip. 'Yes?'

'Herr Einarsson. Someone very important requires your company.'

'Really?'

'Really.'

My stomach curdled. I had pretended not to hear a thousand stories about what these people did to those whom they captured and took away with them. Each half-forgotten tale filled me with terror and fear. Even the thought that I was not a German national came into my thoughts. I knew the SS and all their kind did not like Jews, Slavs, Poles and Gypsies. Perhaps the moment had come when they turned on those who were Danes or from far-flung islands. One could never anticipate the twists and turns of their minds, more unpredictable even than the sea in a storm.

'You need not worry,' he said, smiling. 'It will be good news for you.'

'You sure?'

'Yes.'

I nodded, unable to say anything else.

'Just pack a case to bring with you. You'll need it for staying over for a few nights.'

'Fine.' I nodded my head. 'I'll just go to the bedroom and pack.'

'Good.'

I left the room, watching as the man with the dark eye-patch stretched out his hand towards Freja, noting the ease of his smile, his friendly demeanour, the way she called him by his first name, Heinz. For once in my existence, I wanted to be back in Havn, to be far away from men who acted as these ones sometimes did.

THE FOLLOWING DAY, I felt my wish had been half-fulfilled and I had gone back to Havn. There was the pitch and tilt of roads. The depth of valleys. Height of slopes. The swoop of wings as an occasional bird veered over our heads on the way from Munich to Tegernsee. It was a place I had heard of before, where many of the most important Nazis stayed. Hitler sometimes visited there. Ernst Röhm had been arrested in the town, just before he was taken out and killed. The Norwegian cartoonist Olaf Gulbransson, the SS leader Heinrich Himmler and Max Amann, the one in charge of the Reich Press Chamber, all had homes there. I had met the last named – a one-armed man – on a few occasions, his scribbled notes summoning me to some place or another. I thought it was him who wanted to see me, that I had made some mistake or another in my work, and I was about to get punished for it. I could already see his face twisting in anger.

'Herr Einarsson. What did you mean by this?'

Or there might be questions about my past life.

'Herr Einarsson. Did you ever pretend to be the Count of St Kilda? What about Emperor Cormorant?'

But I did not dare ask Heinz Ullermann any of this. Not on the train journey to Munich where he had talked of Hitler's plans to make Austria part of the Fatherland, bring Czechoslovakia under German control. 'It isn't far away,' he announced. 'The French and the English are too weak to resist.'

Not during the time I spent in the Hotel Königshof on Stachus Square either, unable either to eat or sleep while I was there. All night I had heard the noises on the street outside the window – car horns, the stamp of voices speaking in accents that were unfamiliar to me. I fretted and was unable to sleep, even sitting at a table for a while and writing a letter in which I told my sister Christianna that I was living with Freja, the mother of a well-known Swedish actress. I also told her that, over the last few years, I had begun to regret ever leaving Havn.

It's safe there, I noted. *You don't have to worry about things. Not in the same way. I wish I had never left.*

Not in the way I had to worry in the way I did when I sat in the train beside Heinz. Not in the way I had to concern myself either when the two of us were perched in the back seat of the car to Tegernsee, swung this way and that by every snake and swirl of a road that threatened to send us downwards to the lakes and valleys below. I wondered why I was travelling there, having all sorts of theories in my head. The most likely was to be scolded by Max Amann for something I had done wrong, a mistake in one of his many publications. Or to work together with Olaf Gulbransonn, an artist who was much more well-known than me. To speak to Heinrich Himmler for some unknown reason. Each of these possibilities made my stomach churn with fear.

It was the last of these that happened. When we drove through a forest perched on a hillside, we came across a black Maybach Zeppelin DS 7 parked in front of another car at the side of the road.

'That's where he is,' Ullermann muttered. 'Stop the car as near as you can.'

We walked down a path from there, hearing the crack of a rifle-shot a short distance away. The scale of the slope reminded me of how far I had travelled from my days in Havn. I stumbled once, clearly too familiar with the roads and pavements of Berlin. At the end of this winding track, there was a large hunting box made of black wood.

'In there …' Heinz declared.

He knocked on the door. A moment or two later and an SS officer – wearing a Death's Head ring, embossed with a skull – opened it. I noticed, too, it bore the date '30/6/34' on it. It was familiar to me. The Night of Long Knives.

'Herr Einarsson,' Ullermann declared.

The officer nodded, allowing us into the box. Together with Heinrich Himmler, two other SS officers were in there. They looked at me with suspicion.

'Herr Einarsson,' Ullermann said again.

'Oh,' – one of the SS officers smiled – 'the Faroese man. The man with many languages. The Count of St Kilda.'

I shuddered as I nodded, wondering if my use of that title was going to land me in trouble. It was why I had tried to distant myself from that identity in the recent past.

'A man, too, who shares my interests.' Himmler put down his rifle for a moment, staring at me through his spectacles. 'Tell me, how long have you been fascinated by stories of Atlantis?'

'All my life.'

'Go on.'

'My father used to talk about it all the time. Part of his endless stories.'

'And he was from?'

'The east of Iceland. Though he spent years in the Faroe Islands.'

'Yes, yes.' Himmler nodded, his muffled Bavarian accent coming to the fore. 'All places that might be part of ancient Thule.'

'Yes.'

'As in the map by Karl Georg Zschaetzsch in his work called *Atlantis, the Original Homeland of the Aryans*. You are familiar with this map?'

'Yes. I have seen it.'

'And are you impressed by it?'

'Very much so. "Without Aryan principles no state can exist,"' I said, quoting from the work.

'Good, good.' He nodded his head in the direction of a book that lay on a bench. I glanced at its title. *The Last Queen of Atlantis*, by the writer Edmund Kiss. 'As for this one, you've read it too, I presume?'

'Yes.'

'Your opinion?'

'It's a novel but it's very good,' I said, recalling how it was all about Baldur Wieborg, a native of Thule, leading the inhabitants of Northern Atlantis, who settled throughout the world. 'It showed me how the origins of civilisation came from a part of the globe I know well.'

'Even St Kilda?'

'I believe its high cliffs were the edge of that lost world,' I said, blushing.

Himmler looked at me intensely. I glanced at his face for a moment – the neat dark moustache, not unlike Adolf Hitler's, the cropped grey hair – but quickly turned my head away again. It probably wasn't a good idea to stare in his direction.

'An interesting idea,' he declared. 'Might even be a correct one.'

'I have believed it a long time,' I said.

He turned away from me, raising his rifle once again. 'You're a fascinating man, Herr Einarsson. Just like some of my officers claim you are. Different. Eccentric. Exceptional in many ways. I understand you are a master of many languages too.'

'Yes.'

'Excellent.' He swirled his rifle round, bringing it to the open window. 'We shall be calling for you soon. I have no doubt there will be a thousand uses for your talents.'

'Thank you. Thank you,' I declared.

A moment later, there was the blast of the gun, Himmler firing at some bird or deer he had seen among the trees.

'WEAR YOUR COUNT OF ST KILDA SUIT,' Freja urged me. 'Or your Dunganon one. Just this once. Just for the occasion.'

She smiled, giving me that look that resembled the gleam of a star, one reflecting its sheen and glow on my body.

'You sure?' I thought of the green velvet cloak edged with leather that had hung for so long in the wardrobe, the tartan trousers that were draped alongside. 'It'll make me stand out.'

'Yes.' Her smile glinted once more. 'On this occasion you

should also wear your medallion and chain.'

'Really?'

'Yes. You've never worn it. All the time you've been with me. Time to do it.' She stroked my chest with her fingers to underline her words, tapping my shirt buttons with her fingers. 'Time to see if you can outshine me for once.'

I kissed her. It was hard to resist doing this when she was wearing one of her more slight and insubstantial nightgowns with a georgette-adorned bosom and a revealing cleavage, the scent of Paris clinging to her skin as I held onto her, a glassful of brandy tight in my other hand. Even her voice was as bright and shining as her smile. She pulled away from me.

'No,' she said.

'No?'

'Not unless you promise to wear your medallion and chain.'

'In bed?'

She laughed and slapped me gently. 'No. At the celebration tonight.'

'All right then. I'll do it.' I grinned.

'Fine, then. Fine,' she said, surrendering to me, allowing me to slip her nightgown off her shoulders. At the same time, though, I was worried. There were a few notes that I had added to *How to be a Mountebank and Charlatan* recently. Some of them related to my relationship with Freja:

- Never tell the lady in your life exactly what you're thinking.
- Always listen intently when Freja is talking about her work.
  It's as important to her as sex.

There were others, too, that I underlined, ones that I had written over the last few years as well as some of my earlier notes:

- If the conversation turns to Jews or Romany people, make sure your lips are transformed into a sneer.
- Always pretend to be the same as everyone else. The day may come when being different is dangerous.
- Variety is not always the spice of life, as the English claim. Sometimes it can bring about the end of it.

Here I was, however, disobeying them, drawing attention to myself, attending Hitler's birthday celebrations wearing a cloak, tartan trousers and a medallion glinting on my chest. Occasionally people stopped me on my way to my seat in the grandstand and asked me what the words inscribed on it were.

''*S Rioghal Mo Dhream*,' I would declare. 'Or, "Aryan is my race."'

They smiled and applauded my mistranslation, admiring too the peaks and troughs of the cliffs displayed on the medallion, showing once again how much Germans longed for the heights of mountains.

'Amazing to come from a place like that.'

There was no end to the incredible sights we witnessed that day. There were the bowls of flame on top of white columns that lit up the East-West Axis stretching to the Siegessäule and beyond. The scores of red swastika flags flapping in the vicinity of a chariot pulled along by four horses. The cheers that greeted a motorcade carrying Hitler to the scene, where he was welcomed by Albert Speer, who declared into a microphone, '*Mein* Führer, I herewith report the completion of the East-West Axis. May the work speak for itself.'

Freja squeezed my hand as he said this. 'Isn't this wonderful? Isn't this the perfect world?' And then she called me by that name she occasionally used during our private life, one I later adopted for myself. 'You have taught me a great deal, Professor

Valentinus. You have taught me how to be happy.'

I nodded, blushing as I spoke. 'That's mutual,' I declared.

Moments later, she settled back into the routine she had displayed much of that day, pointing out those she recognised in the vicinity. Goebbels. Göring. Himmler. The numerous artists and actors who had done such fine work for the regime. Lord Haw-Haw, William Joyce. Edmund Veesenmayer. Von Ribbentrop. All gathered as the huge number of troops – twelve companies of the Army, Navy, Luftwaffe and SS – marched by, taking hours to do so. Two hundred warplanes. Tanks and artillery guns. A chorus of 'Deutschland Uber Alles' boomed out by a thousand voices.

Amid all this, disturbed by the noise, hundreds of swans rose from the Tiergarten, terrified and deserting the lakes and nests that are to be found there. I found myself staring at them, remembering tales like the Children of Lir – how the children of that Celtic king were forced into exile, cursed and changed into swans by their father's new wife, compelled to leave their homeland and not return for hundreds of years. I recalled, too, the seabirds that thronged the cliffs near Havn, the way they fluttered when anyone approached; the gannets, too, that rose up into the greyness of the sky before plunging into the waves. I felt tears fill my eyes as I thought of them that moment, smaller, more compact versions of the birds unsettled by all this uproar and noise.

I longed for them at that moment, half-aware even then I was betraying myself, becoming like Faust, the character who had sold his soul to the demon Mephistopheles in Goethe's German drama. I was dimly conscious, too, of the horrors we were about to face, how this frenzy was going to come to a bloody and unfortunate end.

The Second World War

1939–1945

Christianna

A STORM WAS COMING.

And even Heðin could sense it every time he listened to our new wireless or lifted the latest issue of the *Dimmaletting*. He would sit and squirm. Pages would rustle in his fingers. It was a way of behaving that I had only seen in him once before, when the newspaper featured the story of St Kildans having to leave their native island.

'How long before that happens here?' he said, becoming agitated. 'Before the people of Mykines or some other places are forced to leave their homes.'

'We can only wait and see on that one,' I said.

'The way the Danes neglect us in these parts, it can only be a matter of a few years.'

This time, though, his behaviour was more consistent. It carried on for months. He trembled each time he read about what the Germans were doing on the continent, mumbling words like Poland, Czechoslovakia and Austria, which would have been foreign to his tongue a few years before. Before then he mainly used to read short pieces about the price that various kinds of fish were reaching in the market, how the odd new boat was being built or another was being scrapped.

'Your brother, Karl, is still there. In Germany. What does he think of all this?'

I shrugged. 'I don't know. He doesn't mention anything about things like that in his letters,' I lied.

'It must be a desperate place to stay.'

I nodded and lied once again. It didn't seem to be all that uncomfortable for him, judging by the success he was achieving. There were all the programmes and posters he sent the children and me. They showed the titles of films with names like *Jud Süß*, *The Eternal Jew* and *The Rothschilds*, tales that were advertised with dark portraits of men with long jagged noses, beaked like seabirds, sneering as they looked at passers-by.

'Something seems to be happening to him,' my daughter Malvina said. 'Why does he hate Jews so much?'

And I couldn't answer her. I had no idea. He certainly hadn't got this trait from my father. He liked Jews – though he had only met one or two of them. 'It would help Havn if a few settled here,' I remembered him once saying. 'Bring a little enterprise and new thinking to the place. Too many cut from the same cloth here. Only gives us one way of seeing things.' And then he'd laugh. 'But what would they do for food? Puffin and *skerpikjøt* aren't exactly kosher.'

And then I'd hear my sister's quiet sardonic laugh.

'As if you'd know something like that. As if you'd know ...'

And, too, there was the time when Karl told us how he had been present at a meeting hosted by a man called Albert Speer, who was one of those responsible for the creation of a new Berlin, destroying forever the many old neighbourhoods that lacked any sense of order or beauty, sweeping aside all that was disordered and unplanned.

'Imagine a city,' Speer had said to the architects, designers and artists before him. 'Imagine a capital greater than Paris and Rome, a metropolis that will eclipse Babylon and Karnak. Imagine a new Berlin, one that will possess a new name and identity, Germania – the greatest city in the world.'

Imagine I've got a place in all of that, Karl had written. *Imagine! Who knows? There might come a time I have the chance to redesign Tórshavn, create a new place for it on the map, when the Führer takes over my native land.*

I trembled, reading these words, hiding them away from my husband and daughters. For all that my father had sometimes been silly and delusional, it was clear he was now being outmatched by his son. Instead, I could only see the judgement and good sense of Heðin and Pastor Lukas, men who shook their heads every time they heard names like Mussolini, Hitler and Stalin, who believed that the madness of mankind would one day be swept away by the Lord, that Christ would soon restore His kingdom and grind away the dreams of Speer and my brother, reducing them to rubble and ruin. I would hear, too, the urgency of their prayers, especially the day we heard that Denmark and Norway had been invaded. They would talk about how the Nazi government was a danger to those who held their beliefs, as well as the Jews.

'Oh, Lord, protect us from the evil that threatens us, washing all around our shores, that may even soar through the skies around us. Protect, too, those we know and love in Denmark and Norway from the wickedness that has swept across our lives. We feel for them and know how much they must be suffering.'

This was the day, too, when Heðin turned to me after the family prayers were over and spoke in a bitter voice that I had never heard before.

'Oh, Christianna. When will that brother of yours leave Berlin and come home? He's disgracing this family the way he's behaving.'

It was all he ever said about it, but his words hurt. So much so that were times when I would prefer the presence of poultry around me to his company, going out to feed them or clean the shit of hens and ducks that sometimes fouled the pathway to our home.

The worst thing of all about it was that I knew he was right.

Karl

I TRIED NOT TO THINK about what was happening when German troops invaded Denmark. I tried instead to let Freja divert me, the touch of her body, the way her fingers left a trail of excitement when they travelled up and down my flesh. There was the presence of her daughter Anna, too, when she and her friends came into our apartment, wearing their white fox-fur coats and light and flimsy dresses, talking about the eccentricities of the various people they met in the movie industry, gossiping about the strangeness of their ways.

'Oh, that Luis Trenker,' she might say. 'He's such an odd figure. I can't make him out.'

'Karl Heuser,' another might add. 'A wonderful writer!'

But I would do my best to stay silent in all of this, doing my best to keep at a distance from all their discussion. It was a role I had played with increasing success since Hitler had come to power, doing my best to ignore the injustices I could see daily, the moments of madness and cruelty that were displayed on the street. Ignore that, I kept telling myself. Pretend you never noticed a thing. I even did this when the SS hammered at the door of a neighbour's apartment, taking out the mild, quiet old man who lived there, abusing him for the crime of being a trade unionist a decade or more before.

'You bloody traitor,' they shouted. 'You betrayed your homeland, the people that you came from!'

'You brought misery to them, made them feel ashamed of themselves.'

'You bloody turncoat, crook, deceiver. You deserve to be killed for all you've done.'

And then the force of fists, the pounding and pummelling of boots as they threw him to the ground, kicking and hammering him with boots and batons, a lash and stick or two before they hauled him away from the door of his apartment.

'You damn traitor. You bloody turncoat,' they yelled again, their voices echoing in my head.

Despite all my attempts to suppress them, when the invasion of Denmark took place, a thousand thoughts tumbled into my mind. All the places I knew and recognised being filled with men in uniform, milling through its streets, some even on cycles they had stolen from houses they had passed on their way. In my imagination, I could see the Tivoli Gardens filled with tanks and lorries, occupying every space found there. I could see, too, the Rosenborg Castle Gardens, but instead of the members of the aristocracy I used to glimpse through the wrought iron grill that surrounded the grounds, there would be armed men, twirling rifles in the way either the nobility or me in my younger days once twirled sticks. They placed them, too, on their shoulders, in the same way as women once carried umbrellas.

In my dreams, I could see Ásla being hassled by soldiers as she walked around Copenhagen, pushed and harried by them all. I had visions, too, of Kasper being questioned as he made his way to his office, asking him for his ID papers, wondering who he was and what he was doing, probing him with the Lugers in their hands. Or his own mother, too, ageing and crippled, her face looking troubled and tortured as she was approached.

But it was my old boss, Brandes, whom I felt most sorry for. I could picture him being bundled away by men in SS uniforms from the lithographer's office in Kronprinsessegade where he had worked for so many years. They would be forcing him to stumble and fall, calling him out as a 'Jew', using my words, perhaps, as a testimony and excuse for being unpleasant to him.

'You were a cruel, harsh boss. You deserve all that's going to happen to you.'

'We've heard about you, you rat!'

They might round up his wife and family, too, taking them to one of these camps I knew existed within the German borders, all possessing names I did not want to know or recognise.

There were moments when I felt myself adopting the habits of Pastor Anders, the man whom I had seen my father mock all those years before, knitting my fingers into prayer, calling out to a God I scarcely believed in. There were instances, too, when I felt I had been transformed into a different member of the nobility from the one I had thought of myself as before. No longer the Count of Monte Cristo, I was now Count Dracula, prospering because of the blood of others, aware at all times of the brutality of those I had chosen to side with.

'How blessed are some people,' I would recite in my head, recalling the words of that book, 'whose lives have no fears, no dreads; to whom sleep is a blessing that comes nightly, and brings nothing but sweet dreams.'

Neil MacCusbic

UNCLE IAIN, IF ONLY I could tell you where I am going now, send a note to your home on Scalpay, all those miles and waves away – for I am on my way to the Faroes, that place which you told my brother about, where your fishing boat was blown by the fiercest wind you've ever seen stirring and shaking sail, flesh and bone, forcing you away from the destination where your boat was bound, no longer fishing in the waters to which you were accustomed but sailing further north and east than you had ever been before.

And I feel much the strangeness you must have experienced way back then, never having thought anything like this would happen when I volunteered for the Lovat Scouts all those years ago. I believed that I was only going there to raise a little bit of money every month or two to help build a new house of my own, a clinking of small change each time I trained at the shooting range at the Sunset Lodge on the Committee Road – that track which my mother's ancestors built all those years ago across my home island of North Uist, when the people here were hungry and starving from want and famine, where even to this day birds of prey, like the short-eared owl and the buzzard, scan the skies to find food for their chicks, where swans and ducks could be seen swimming on nearby lochs.

Like the others who are with me, I only saw it as a little a break for myself from my house and family, a time to grow and alter before I settled down in marriage with my true love, Mairi, an escape from the croftwork at our home in Sollas, the lines and nets we threaded over rock and sand there, and a chance to learn how to fire a rifle in case it were ever required. I was more than prepared to pay the price of marching up and down, wearing a uniform and the possibility of going to war, fighting for some cause or other – a possibility I never really considered likely, for all that I knew the words that Dòmhnall Ruadh Chorùna wrote when he was fighting in the Great War, ones that my friends and I had sung for many years.

> *Gur duilich leam mar tha mi*
> *'S mo chridhe 'n sas aig bron*
> *Bhon an uair a dh'fhag mi*
> *Beanntan ard a'cheo*
> *Gleanntannan a'mhanrain*
> *Nan loch, nam bagh 's nan srom*
> *'S an eala bhan tha tamh ann*
> *Gach la air 'm bheil mi 'n toir.*

> Sad I consider my fate,
> my heart weighed down by sadness
> From the very hour I left
> These high hills veiled with mist,
> The glens in which I wandered,
> The lochs, too, the foreshore, and the bays
> And the white swan resting there
> Which my eyes would follow, chase.

Then came the day the call-up papers came, arriving in the house, before I exchanged a few words of farewell with my family, a hurried kiss with Mairi, and then my friends and I made our way along the Committee Road to the Drill Hall in Lochmaddy, where there were men who had travelled all the way from Carinish, Benbecula, Iochdar, all wearing the same uncreased uniforms and polished boots as we did, aware that we were repeating the same actions as Dòmhnall Ruadh Chorùna and our uncles and fathers had done, going to war against Germany for some reason we only half-understood.

'Hitler's a much worse man than the Kaiser,' one fellow, a teacher's son, told us. 'A much more dangerous sort.'

We nodded as if we believed him, listening to some fellow from Griminish playing on the bagpipes he had brought along in his kitbag, while we occasionally sang, a verse or two from the 'Eala Bhan', pondering on their meaning in a way we never had done before.

A Mhagaidh na bi tursach
A ruin, ged gheibhinn bas
Co am fear am measg an t-sluaigh
A mhaireas buan gu brath?
Chan eil sinn uile ach air chuairt
Mar dhithein buaile fas
Bheir siantannan na blianna sios
'S nach tog a'ghrian an aird

Maggie, don't be mournful,
Love, if I encounter death,
For who among humanity
Possesses eternal breath?
We are all upon a journey
Like flowers where cattle graze.
The wind and rain will bear us down
And the sun will never raise.

After that, there was the clambering up the gangway on the steamer to Kyle, the journey to Fort George together with those from Skye and the West Highlands who joined us on the train to Inverness. It was within the walls of the garrison that we were told that we were sailing north to the same place my Uncle Iain had gone on his boat from Scalpay all those years before. Sent to occupy the Faroe Islands to try and save those who lived there from the threat of Hitler and win over their hearts and minds, in what they called 'Operation Valentine'. Hoping that – like Dòmhnall Ruadh Chorùna – I would make it through the conflict and come home.

Tha 'n talamh leir mun cuairt dhiom
'N mheallan suas 's na neoil
Aig na 'shells' a'bualadh
Cha leir dhomh bhuam le ceo
Gun chlaisneachd aig mo chluasan
Le fuaim a'ghunna mhoir
Ach ged tha 'n uair seo cruaidh orm
Tha mo smuaintean air NicLeoid

All the ground around me,
It's as if the heavens pour
Hail from shells exploding,
How they both fall and soar.
My ears too are deafened
By bombs and bullets, clear and loud.
Despite them, throughout war's savagery,
My thoughts are on the girl Macleod.

Karl

THE WAR CAME TO ME in May 1940. Before that, it had all been talk and whispers, the rustle of a newspaper, a quick scan of headlines – 'Germany Invades France', 'Norway Now Under German Rule' – before I would shove the pages away, reluctant to read any further. Like all the stories I had heard about Jews being attacked, their windows being smashed and broken, I preferred not to know much about it, only muttering that it meant I would not be able to hear news from my family while the war went on. 'I feel far enough away from them already,' I'd muttered. Freja would shake her head when I refused to talk about the conflict, despairing at what she thought was my wilful ignorance.

'Our troops are doing really well,' she kept saying. 'You have to know these things, be able to share the good news with others.'

'I know that,' I would mutter. 'I just don't want to know the details.'

'You have to know these things. If you don't, they'll think you're on the other side. You don't want them to believe you're one of their enemies. Especially as some of them think of you as a Dane.'

'I know that,' I said again. I was aware from a Danish friend of mine that the people of Copenhagen and elsewhere were not exactly friendly to the German troops in their midst. There was little actual resistance – at least not so far. Only a sullen resentment against the intruders who marched up and down their streets. Or the Danish fishing fleet making their way towards England rather than being under the dominance of Germany, fishing in the Irish Sea rather than the waters off their own coast, their home ports now in the Isle of Man or Whitehaven. There were rumours, too, that some Danes were sheltering a few of the Jews who lived in their cities, hiding them away from the eyes of the Gestapo. Shivering at the thought, I wondered if one of them was my old boss.

'I'll catch up with it,' I would say. 'I promise.'

It was just as well I did. At a reception in Berlin, I met the Icelandic writer Gunnar Gunnarsson, who was in Germany around that time, mingling with the Nazi leadership among others. He had a home in Skriðuklaustur on the east coast of Iceland, not far from Seyðisfjörður where I had spent my early days.

'I know the place well,' he declared. 'You'll have to come back and visit us when this war is won.'

'I'll certainly do that,' I said, bowing my head.

'Or when the Germans take over our native land. That might happen sometime.'

'Perhaps.' I nodded again, pretending I welcomed the prospect. 'The sooner the better.'

But then came the time, a few days later, when I heard that the Allies had invaded Iceland. Placenames that had been long forgotten – like Akureyri, Hvalfjörður, Sandskeið and Kaldaðarnes – came into my head once more as I pictured Canadians in their uniforms standing beside fishing harbours, moving through small towns and villages that my parents might have been familiar with years before. I was aware that they would be as uncomfortable as those in Aarhus or Copenhagen at the sight of tanks and lorries churning through their open landscape, planes taking off from strips of land that had been cleared and flattened. I could see my father reacting to their presence, lowering his head and pretending to have a set of horns, making a loud, lowing noise as he had done that day the Hebrideans were in our home.

'*Tarvur, tarvur.*'

The solders would not respond, any more than their counterparts in Denmark would, apart from late at night when they were sure that no one was looking. There would be the thunder of boots then, a chorus of blows and cries, a whoop of triumph afterwards that might resemble the call of a bull. Afterwards, men like my father would lie buckled and broken on the kitchen floor, his body cut and bruised by their assault on him.

'That'll teach you,' they'd mutter as they walked away.

It was a day or two after the Icelandic invasion that Heinz Ullermann came to see me again. He arrived around midday with a couple of companions dressed in Gestapo uniforms, disturbing me when I was bowed over my desk, working on posters and programmes for another film. There was a clamour of knocks, the yelling of my name. I reached for my walking stick again, glad that it was there for my fingers.

'Herr Einarsson?'

'Yes?'

I shivered when I saw who was at the door, reluctant – for an instant – to let him through.

'We need to speak to you. We need your assistance.'

'Of course,' I replied. 'If I can, I will.'

He sat down. 'You have heard the news?'

'No. What news?'

'The English have invaded your home islands.'

'No.'

'It happened yesterday. A way of preventing our troops in Norway taking over the Faroes. Of keeping an eye, too, on our shipping. Perhaps of even taking over the shipyard that's there. You know they've built a new steel ship, the *Vónin*, there? Made the place more valuable to them.'

'No. I didn't know that. I'm losing touch a bit with the place.'

'How do you think the people there will feel about the British coming to the place?'

I shrugged my shoulders. 'I don't know. They might prefer them to the Danes.'

'Really?'

'Yes. Some of them truly hate the Danes. They think they've been neglecting them for years. If the English spend a little money on the place, improve the roads and harbours, they might just win them over.'

'That's interesting.'

'It's also the case that some think they have more in common with those who live in islands like Hjaltland, Orkneyjar and the Outer Hebrides than they have with those in Denmark. They see most Danes as farmers rather than fishermen, city-dwellers rather than those who live in small places like themselves, distant from each other. All flat-landers, too. Not a mountain or a slope in the place.' I paused for a moment before I went on. 'A very different world. The two peoples don't really understand each other.'

His forehead creased. 'But you do?'

'Me?'

'Yes. You speak and understand both languages. Icelandic and Faroese. Other tongues too. That might prove very useful to us.'

'How?'

'You have heard of the RRG? The German Broadcasting corporation. The Reichs-Rundfunk-Gesellschaft. Parts of the station broadcast to other countries – England, Ireland, the United States.'

I nodded. I had even occasionally listened to it on my People's Receiver in the evening, the words and nasal tone of Lord Haw-Haw filling the room. 'Where else in Europe will you find a privileged class comparable with the upper nation of England? Look around anywhere in Britain and you will understand what I mean. Go to the slums and there you will find the lowest stratum of the lower nation huddled together in indescribable filth and poverty. Here will you find the permanent underdogs of the capitalist system: recruits for Borstal, Barnardo's hospitals, jails and brothels.' And then there would be the words in contrast, describing the German nation. 'There are no unemployed outcasts here as in England,' he announced, forgetting the other kind of outcasts that were found throughout the streets of Germany, those wearing badges of different shapes and shades – Jews, communists, Slavs, Gypsies. Even places like Faroe had their own variety – I thought of Ásla and all she had suffered during her early years there.

'Would you consider working for them? Your presence might be very helpful to our cause.'

My face turned pale. I knew there was only one possible answer to the question. Another might lead to my imprisonment, the police or the Gestapo raiding our home. Despite this, it was a reply that felt uncomfortable on my lips.

'Yes,' I declared. 'I'll do that.'

Christianna

So, THE PRINCES of Suðereyar have gathered here in Vágar. The Counts of St Kilda. Dukes of Skye. The Earls of Benbecula. The Royal Highnesses of South Uist. Scouts of Lovat. All working here among us, helping in the creation of the airfield here on the flattest land in the Faroes, constructing air-raid shelters and Nissen huts, building a road or two. Sometimes, too, I would see them walking towards the island's edge, manning the anti-aircraft gun to ward off the German planes that sometimes flew in our direction, or winching up some of the heavy equipment brought to assist them in their labours, the harbour at Sørvágar considered too narrow and slight for that purpose. A few of them were singing as they made their way to these places, the sounds of their language bringing them both to my attention and that of my daughters, disturbing them in their sleep.

Chan eil mo leannan ann an-seo,
Cha robh e 'raoir, 's cha bhi e nochd;
Chan eil mo leannan ann an-seo,
Neo duine a thogas m'inntinn.

My love is not here just now.
Not yesterday or even tonight.
My love is not here just now.
To keep my spirits high in flight.

They stayed sometimes in island houses – some of them empty because the women and children who lived there had been sent elsewhere, their homes considered too close to the airfield for safety. They slept, too, in attics or a nearby *hjallur*, the drying sheds where fish and *skerpikjøt* hung. Two of them stayed each night in the one near our home.

'So how do you find it?' I asked them. 'Disgusting?'

'No,' one called Hugh answered. 'It reminds me of home. The smell of peat and smoke there.'

'And where is home?'

'North Uist in the Hebrides. A little place called Sollas.'

'Oh, I came across two men from the Hebrides once when I was younger. They were washed up on a fishing boat near my old home in Tórshavn. I remember them so clearly.'

'Can you recall their names?'

'Yes. One of them was called MacCusbic.'

'From Scalpay? Harris?'

'Yes … Some place like that.'

'I've heard the story. His nephew Neil told me it. He's here with us just now. Working away building one of the Nissen huts.'

'Really? Really? Really?' I laughed so loud that my daughter Malvina came racing from the house, clasping my arm.

So, I stammered out the tale, telling her of the day the two men from Suðereyar had been washed up in the harbour, their boat smashed and broken by the weight of wind and waves; how my father had talked with them, seeking to speak in their language; how Karl, too, had watched and imitated them, taking on their identity for the first time. I even recalled his first drawings of the Count of St Kilda, his toes large enough to grasp and grip rocks. Alongside there was the Emperor Cormorant of Atlantis, surrounded by dark-winged courtiers, a caption written in what Karl said was the Atlantean tongue alongside. There was also my own favourite, the Prince of Suðereyar, with his tartan and sheepskin clothes. I felt my heart drum once again, as it had done so often years before.

But it was not me but Malvina who spoke after this, turning to the Hebridean who had told us of MacCusbic's existence.

'Invite him up here. I'd love to meet him.'

Karl

I HAD SEEN JACK TREVOR a few times before, his face bright and aristocratic, looking down on me from the cinema screen.

Sometimes he played the role of the British Consul in an African court. At other times he was either a British officer or the president in an Irish courtroom, working in films like *Ohm Krüger*, *Carl Peters* or *My Life for Ireland*. There were times when I used to model my face on his expressions, looking at people with a similar disdain and disparagement, twirling my stick between my fingers, measuring out my vowels in accurate mimicry of his voice.

It was not, however, the way I saw him as I wheeled my bicycle towards the door of the Rundfunk radio building. It had been a mistake to take it that day, the road too slippery for its wheels to master. Snow veered and dipped around the Masurenallee while Trevor berated an SS guard who was standing and shivering there.

'We need to liquidate all the Jews,' he was declaring. 'And do it as quickly as possible.'

'Ja. Ja Ja.'

'It is a matter of urgency. Something we must do as soon as we can. Otherwise, the bastards will bite us back.'

'Ja. Ja. Ja.'

'The SS is being a bit slow about all of this. They should be killing the Jews in greater numbers. They are a plague upon our planet.'

'Ja. Ja. Ja.' The guard stamped his feet again and bit his lip, no doubt wondering how long both these flakes and words would whirl around him, desperate to escape from the chill of this man's company and the power of the blizzard; surely wondering, too, if all Englishmen were as mad and fevered as this one.

I avoided him, aware that if he spoke to me, I would also be subjected to a tirade. They were an odd bunch, the ones I saw within the Rundfunk. There was the likes of Norman Baillie-Stewart, who greeted me loudly when I first stepped into a room near the studio.

'I hear you're the man some call the Count of St Kilda.'

I gulped, nodded and dodged his words. 'Some call me that.'

'Oh, I was in the army with a number of men from the Hebrides. In India with the Seaforth Highlanders. Fine people, most of them. I learned a few words of Gaelic when I was in their company. *Ciamar a tha sibh?* What do you think?'

'Very good. *Tha mi gle mhath.*'

He ignored my attempt to speak in Gaelic, remorseless in the continuation of his own tale. 'That was in the days before I became the Officer in the Tower. Arrested for passing on information to the government here. A big occasion, that. I had decided I couldn't work for the British anymore. A weak crowd. Their days are coming to an end.'

I passed him by, too, aware he had been replaced in this form of work, broadcasting to the British, by William Joyce, the man they called Lord Haw-Haw. I never met him during my first months there. Instead, there were the odd Scandinavians, John Reilly and the other Irishmen, Scots like Donald Grant, Welshmen like Raymond Hughes, who used to broadcast to the Welsh in his native language, condemning the Jews that were both in his own country and in London: 'They are the real enemies of us all, these Jews, dribbling their poison all over London, destroying all that is good and noble that is in the Welsh people.'

I shrugged when I heard this, aware that there was little point in mentioning Jews in my broadcasts to my fellow island dwellers in Iceland and the Faroe Islands. I was aware that – apart from a few who saw the Jewish people as an enemy of their Christian faith, missionaries for communism and Marxism – most of my people would be indifferent to that message. Best instead to find my own way of communicating, layering my message like the volcanic rock that formed the outline of the islands. I scribbled down what I knew of the locations where the Lovat Scouts were based. Near the lighthouse in Suðuroy, where I knew some RAF men lived, occupying the Nissen hut between the three dwellings there. Skansin lighthouse near Havn, where the old fort was now transformed into a kind of garrison for the British troops based there. And then there was Vágar, where my sister stayed. There were many soldiers there – either Royal Engineers or Lovat Scouts – building the airfield within its shores. Some of the local men and women worked for them, being trained as plumbers or electricians or helping to prepare food. A plane touched down almost daily there, touching down on Lake Leitisvatn, the largest stretch of water within those shores, bringing supplies. Those men stood on guard near lighthouses, haunted cliffs, marched round the edges of the islands, keeping their gaze fixed on the horizon where planes, ships or U-boats might appear.

'My fellow Faroese,' I said on my first broadcast, 'this is Germany calling. It is good to be speaking to you again. I have much missed hearing your voices, the language that we all share, even to be walking near your homes, on your slopes and valleys. It is truly a magical, wonderful place and one I have much missed since leaving it all those years ago. My heart aches at the absence. I understand that much has changed since I have gone. You have the presence of many soldiers among you. Many from the Scottish Highlands. Many, too, from our nearest neighbours, such as Suðereyar. Do not hate or dislike these men. Many of them will be people just like you, having spent much of their lives working on poor, bare soil or fishing in the sea, sometimes even capturing an occasional whale or even seal to eat. They will even know how to clip a sheep or prepare its meat to eat.

'Like us, too, when we were forced to fight for the Danes, their uniforms will be a tight and uncomfortable fit on their bodies. Some of them will feel exactly the same as we do about the government we have over us, all too aware that there have been times when it persecuted and misused them. They will know that – just like us – they have been prevented from speaking and hearing their own language at various times in their history. Like us, they have not been allowed to sing their version of the *kvæði*, that right taken away from them in their schools. So much. So similar.

'And that is what you should whisper to them, asking why they are wearing British uniforms and parading under the Union Jack. Like the white-on-red flag of Denmark, it has done so much to devalue and dishonour the people of the Suðereyar. Tell them they should not be wearing these clothes, that they should not be saluting that flag. They are – like us – part of the Aryan race, remnants of the ancient population of Atlantis. They should not be fighting for the British nation, one that – like the Danes have done to the people of our islands – has kept them poor and humiliated. Instead, they should be standing alongside those in Germany, those who want to return to the purity and dignity of our former lives. They have not been treated well. Remind them of that. Continually. Your words will strengthen and enlighten them, showing them the error and stupidity of their ways. Heil Hitler! I will be back to speak you again soon.'

And then there would be the singing of a *kvæði*, one of the Faroese ballads, the words uplifting the mood of the listeners, reminding them that they were not Danish, as they had for years been told, but Faroese.

Christianna

I RECOGNISED THE VOICE on the wireless right away. More than a little, it resembled the speeches of my father, all the pontificating and preaching he had done all those years before; how he had stood behind his counter and lectured his customers about the ideas of some mad American called Ignatius Donnelly who claimed there were connections between the island of St Kilda and the edge of Atlantis, that our islands too were likely to have been part of that lost world.

Or else he might say that many of the Faroese were the descendants of those who had settled here after falling out with the likes of Harald Fairhair, the first king of Norway in the late ninth century.

'The people here are the children of rebels. What makes them such a timid lot today?'

I switched it off as soon almost as Karl started, gripping the table edge as I did so, not wanting to give Dagrún and Malvina the chance to be aware that this was their uncle speaking on the wireless.

'What a load of nonsense!' I proclaimed.

As usual, it was Malvina who quarrelled with me. With her tangle of dark hair and the mix of colours sparkling in her eyes, even the dimple she had inherited from me on her cheeks, there were signs of persistent rebellion in her gaze, as if she was always looking for an opportunity to defy our will and – indeed – the rules of the community she always chafed and quarrelled against. In this, she was so unlike her elder sister, who resembled her father – quiet, shy and conservative, her hair a blurred and cloudy form of fair, her lips rarely revealing what she thought, keeping all that concerned her hidden deep in her thoughts.

'We've got a right to listen to it,' Malvina protested. 'We need to know what both sides are saying.'

'No. Not in this house. Not in these times when we have British soldiers all around us, listening, perhaps, to every word that's broadcast to our homes. We've got to stay clear of all of that.'

'Well–'

'Besides, we've got Neil MacCusbic and his friend coming in an hour or so,' I said. 'We don't want these types of words to foul the air. Just in case he arrives in the midst of it.'

'That's ridiculous,' she said. 'Words don't have that kind of effect in people's houses.'

'Oh, I don't know. Sometimes they can poison the atmosphere of a home. I've seen it a few times in my life.'

'It must have been rough living in Havn,' she said, laughing. 'All these foul clouds drifting around from one neighbour to the next.'

'Yes,' I said, grinning. 'It must have been the cause of all the rain that pours down there.'

Again, the giggle, so unlike Dagrún's reaction. My older daughter reminded me of my sister Bedda, constantly unimpressed by my father's endless ramblings. She would frown and purse her lips each time he spoke, ignoring his talk of history and Atlantis. 'He's like some kind of pastor,' she told me once, 'with his own strange theology and doctrines. They make a lot less sense than those you hear in church.' It was a thought that had come into my own head when I met the occasional islander who believed that the Nazis were right in all their talk of Aryans and the master race, believing too that the Jews were the anti-Christ.

'Anyway, let's get ready,' I said.

We had finally got a message through to Neil, inviting him to dinner in our home. He arrived an hour or so later, a friend called Hugh Macdonald by his side. A spasm passed through me when I saw Neil. For all that he was taller and broader than the man who had sailed from Scalpay all those years before, his hair was, like his uncle's, dark and curly. His voice possessed a similar lilt to the one I recalled whispering to me one night in Havn. He even mispronounced my name the same way his uncle had done.

'It's lovely to meet you, Cairstiona. My uncle has mentioned your name, Cairstiona.'

I didn't correct him. It was – in so many ways – wonderful to recall the nights we had spent together in my home. I found myself recalling a thousand moments that were part of that evening. My family singing a *kvæði* and other Faroese songs which rarely came to our lips when we were sitting in our homes at other times. Talk of Uspak Hákon and his descendants. My father sprouting horns and calling out, '*Tarvur, tarvur!*' Laughter resounding through the household.

Hugh and Neil spoke of their island life in North Uist, how similar it was in many ways to an existence in Faroe. 'We've got nicer beaches,' Hugh said, grinning and puffing out his chest. 'And the hills aren't quite so steep.' And Neil mentioned what had happened the other day to both him and some of the other Lovat Scouts. Their commanding officer had complained that without any real military action – except the occasional visit to the anti-aircraft guns to fire at a German plane winging towards them from the Norwegian coast – the soldiers were getting unfit.

'Go for a march around the island,' the officer had declared.

'It's pouring,' someone muttered.

'Is it ever anything else? Go. March round as quickly as you can.'

And they had done so, tramping round the shores of the island in a downpour of rain, feet slipping on slopes and in pools of mud. They even walked round the edge of Lake Leitisvatn with its depths almost tipping over the edge of a cliff towards the sea, circling the borders of Lake Fjallavatn too.

'A wee diversion,' the officer had said.

'Aye.' Neil shook his head, the song on his lips faltering.

And then there was the arrival back at base.

'How did you get on?' the officer asked.

'Fine, sir,' one of the men from Skye had answered. 'We could do it all again.'

'Then go and do it,' the officer had commanded.

'Really, sir?'

'Yes. Really.'

And so they had done as they were instructed, marching once more. This time, though, the song Neil had been singing completely faded from his lips. He felt far too weary and exhausted for even the Gaelic melodies that had strengthened and nurtured him since childhood to urge him onwards.

'What song did you sing?' Malvina asked.

'This one. It's from Uist.'

He started to sing then, revealing a finer voice than his uncle had ever possessed.

Thugainn leam, thugainn leam, o hi rì 's o ho rò,
Thugainn leam, thugainn leam, o hi rì 's o ho rò,
Thugainn leam-sa thar na mara null
do dh'Uibhist bheag nam beannaibh,
'S gheibh sibh mil ann agus bainne, thugainn leam, thugainn
leam ...

Come along, come along, let us foot it out together.
Come along, come along, be it fair or stormy weather,
With the hills of Uist before us and the purple of the heather,
Let us sing a happy chorus, come along, come along ...

'That would have kept your spirits up,' Malvina said when he finished the song, laughing and clapping her hands like the rest of us. 'I can see how it would have done that.'

'Yes. Yes,' my husband Heðin grinned, speaking for once. 'It's a very cheerful song.'

'It is indeed,' I said, nodding.

And then I looked across at my daughter, seeing her in a new and different light. Her dark brown hair spilling over her shoulders. The shock of blue eyes. The dimples on her cheeks. I had never imagined her as beautiful before. Yet I saw her in a new and brilliant guise that day. All dressed up, eyes sparkling, the two young Hebridean men watching her every movement as she made her way around the kitchen, bringing food to the table in order that they all could eat. She served out mutton, kale and potatoes we had prepared for the occasion, talking to them all the time in the English she had learned from the local pastor, aware that they were drawn to her every word and gesture. She listened to them talk, too, as they spoke about the differences between their islands and the ones they had come to know here.

'What do I miss most?' Neil asked himself. 'I suppose it's the flowers on the machair, not far from the sand upon the shore. They're beautiful. Like a carpet set in place for a king. Yellow. Red. White. Purple. A thousand different shades. And then there are the birds that nest in it. Oystercatchers, like those you find here. Lapwings. Curlews. Sandpipers. Corncrakes. Every time you walk along the shore, it's as if a hundred creatures are breaking out in song.'

'That's wonderful,' Malvina declared. 'And is it warmer there?'

'A bit,' Neil said, laughing. 'Though we complain about the cold there too. It's only a little bit closer to the equator.'

'A few miles might make a lot of difference,' Malvina said.

'Perhaps,' Hugh said. 'I must confess, it's the stories I miss. My grandfather was great at telling them.'

'Tell me one then,' my daughter asked.

'All right. I will ...'

He began to speak of a cairn of stones that stood on the nearby isle of Benbecula.

'It marks a shieling that once stood there, a place where three men stayed when they worked together on the moor. One of them had a useless dog, which the others wanted to put down. Its owner shook his head at that. "It's been put on earth for a purpose," he said. In the middle of the night, these three women turned up. A pair of them went with two of the men to a backroom. Only the dog's owner didn't go. Why? He noticed that the animal kept sniffing and growling at the women. At the last moment, he became aware that the remaining one had hooves instead of feet. He fled then, with the woman – a witch – chasing him. He was saved by his useless dog, which turned on his attacker, allowing him to escape to his home in Nunton. The next day, he went out with a bowl of cream to reward the animal. It was lying there dead without a scrap of hair on its body. The two men were also found dead. The shieling was never used again.'

'Wow,' – Malvina shivered – 'that's a great story. Our grandfather told loads like that. Didn't he, Mother?'

'Yes. No end to them.'

'There's one I can remember. About how a young farmer on the isle of Kalsoy went to the beach to watch the selkies – the seal-women – dance. He hid the skin of a beautiful selkie maid, so she could not return to sea. He forced her, too, to marry him. He kept the skin in a chest. The key came with him both day and night. One day when he was out fishing, he discovered that he had forgotten it. When he returned home, his wife had escaped back to sea, leaving their children behind. Later, when the farmer was out on a hunt, she killed both her husband and two selkie sons. She promised, too, to take revenge on the men of Mikladalur, where her man had come from. "Some will be drowned," she declared. "Some will fall from cliffs and slopes, and this shall continue until so many men have been lost that they will be able to link arms around the whole island of Kalsoy."'

'And did this happen?'

'Oh yes. There are still deaths that occur in this way on the island. Ask any fisherman in the Faroes about it. And there's stories about the descendants of the selkie. How you can tell them by certain traits, such as the way they have very short fingers.'

Neil nodded. 'There's stories on North Uist that are very similar to that. About the MacCodrum family – how they're descended from seals.'

'Tell me it,' Malvina said.

She reminded me of someone that day – my younger self and how I, too, had listened intently to my father's stories; how I had also watched and followed that young man's uncle all those years before. He had been my Prince of Suðereyar. Lord of the Hebrides. The distant neighbour I had always imagined from a great distance. The offspring of Uspak Hákon. Fine people living there. Decent and honest. No danger of contamination by all the evils of the modern world. So much so that I anticipated the moment coming at the end of the evening when she would slip a note into his fingers, arranging a time and place to meet.

But that didn't happen.

Instead, I overheard Neil's voice in the stillness outside, Malvina standing close to him.

'We've finished building a new entertainment block for the men. How would you like to come and see a picture next week?

It's not something I've been to see myself.'

'Yes. Yes. It would be great to do that.'

I gripped the table in much the same way as I had done when I heard my brother speaking on the wireless for the Nazi cause. After years when I had only experienced stillness and predictability, life was beginning to swirl and twist once more.

Karl

THE DAY AFTER I MET HERMANN GÖRING, I became aware that Freja's attitude to the war had shifted and changed. The Reichsmarschall had come along to visit Jack Trevor, one of his friends and allies, and spent ten minutes or so listening to him complaining about William Joyce or how the Nazis weren't killing the Jews off quickly enough.

'Very slow. Very, very slow. They could be doing it much more quickly.'

Fat Hermann nodded his head a few times, clearly paying little attention, before turning to me. I had come across his wife, Emmy, before. Both actresses, she and Freja had spent time together. This, however, was the first occasion he had ever spoken to me directly. I tried to avoid looking at his rounded face, the belly that swelled behind his thick coat, his bottle-green uniform weighed down in a different way, by the array of medals on his chest. Something was both monstrous and ridiculous about the appearance of the man, generating both laughter and fear. I had little choice but to concentrate on his words. Who knows what the slightest glance in his direction might cause me to do?

'You're the Faroese man?'

'Yes.'

'Tell me, how are your fellow islanders responding to Operation Valentine? Reports tell me they are being wooed.'

'I'm afraid that's true,' I said, nodding. 'Some of the men there are even getting work from the British – being trained as electricians and other trades. They're being well looked after. Lifted from the poverty they've known for years.'

'And the women?'

'The British are being very generous with them. Even giving them some of their food supplies.'

Göring nodded. 'Yes. I've heard that. And the Icelanders. How are they responding?'

'Some of them hate the Americans and British, for all sorts of reasons. Many of them are much more inclined to follow our cause.'

'Well, they are all Aryans.'

'Exactly that. The British have also been fishing near their shores for years.'

His brow furrowed. 'Tell me. You're one of the few people we have who are familiar with these islands. Most of our people come from miles away from the sea. Would you have any advice for us?'

'Yes.' I nodded. And then an idea came to my lips. It was one that had stormed through my head on many occasions but never came out of my mouth. 'I think you should invade St Kilda on the west coast of Scotland.'

'I've never heard of St Kilda,' he confessed.

'It's far out from the mainland. But it would allow you to attack the country from way out west. It would also have huge symbolic value. Some people believe that the island's cliffs are the far edge of the lost world of Atlantis, the place where the Aryan race lived for centuries.'

'Oh? Who are these people?'

'Those like Himmler and others in the SS. Those who read the work of an American politician called Ignatius Donnelly. Some people, too, who live in Norway, Sweden, Iceland. It might help to win them over to the cause.'

He pondered my words for a moment. 'Let me think about that,' he declared. 'I'll speak about it to a few others.' He nodded his head once again, his coat swaying back and forth, his jackboots echoing on the building's floor as he wandered away with his bodyguards.

'Thank you,' I heard myself saying. 'Thank you.'

I was still sweating uncomfortably at the thought of my meeting with him when I came home that evening, wondering if I had said the right thing. I spoke to Freja about it, relaying the details of our conversation.

'That's what you mentioned?' she said, laughing.

'Yes.'

'Nothing about your poor wife having to queue for hours today to buy potatoes and getting none? Only a single cauliflower head. And I only got that because I lied and told them it was for my daughter, that she had four children to feed. Every day I only manage to get pasta and bread for us to eat. And look at the effect it's having on me' – she prodded her waistline – 'I'm beginning to look like the Reichsmarschall. I have the same swollen guts as him.' She laughed contemptuously. 'I thought you were meant to get slimmer the less you ate. Some fairytale that is.'

'You're not that bad,' I said, ignoring how she often claimed these days that she was my 'wife'. 'Loads to do if you're going to catch up with Hermann.'

She ignored me, launching into one of the theatrical performances that increasingly marked our years together as time passed. Her every gesture was florid and flamboyant, her words carrying her away with all the force of the waves I had seen during my time in Havn.

'Did you ask him any more questions, my dear husband? What about the way that we were told that Berlin was one of the safest cities in the world with the best anti-aircraft defences, and yet every day an RAF bomber breaks through and drops its load down upon us? Wouldn't that have been a more interesting question to ask?'

I shrugged. 'I don't know how well he'd have taken that one. I'd probably have been sent to a death camp somewhere if I dared to ask it.'

'Perhaps. But that may be where we're all heading anyway, the way things are going.' She paused for a moment, her flood of words abating. She was like so many people I knew, her optimism a thing of the past since news had come of the German invasion of the Soviet Union and the United States entering the war. The dark end – which at one time seemed so unlikely – now appeared to be on its way. We sat there looking at that ending. In my head, I was flicking through the pages of *How to be a Mountebank and Charlatan*, which I had written before I met Freja, before I decided that I would be safer with her as part of my life. The wisdom of my old rules was beginning to influence my judgement once again. *Trust nobody else*, one sentence had read. *Do not live with anyone. The day will come when their presence might undermine your pretence.* I had been right when I decided that. Despite the comfort that both warmth and food had given me over the last few years, I had been a fool to change my mind.

'You're a fortunate man,' she said to break the silence.

'How?'

'You still have a Danish passport. The day may come when that will prove very convenient indeed.'

I shrugged my shoulders, barely aware of what she was talking about. Since the beginning of the war, I had almost forgotten where my passport was – lying in a drawer full of socks and underwear. A few handfuls of US dollars were in there, too, hidden away where not even Freja would notice it.

'It will give you the opportunity to escape from the disaster that is about to befall us. You can at least argue that none of this has anything to do with you.'

'Uh?'

'Don't you see, Karl, that the wheel is turning? The moment is arriving when it will be us Germans who will be the victims. There will be no mercy given because we never gave it to others. The Russians, the Poles, the Czechs, the British – they will do their best to kill us.'

And then she gave me that look I remembered from the beginning of our relationship, one that had faded from her face as the years went on. Her pupils were bright and shining, her lips a red slit on her face, emerging brightly from the white powder that cloaked her cheeks and forehead. And then there was her wavy hair, turned grey, too, with the years, the great waft of perfume she carried around everywhere with her. She stretched out her arm towards me, clutching my shoulders and bringing me towards her, offering me her mouth, the softness of her body.

'Oh, Karl,' she said, 'I sometimes forget what a blessing you are to me. Do you think you could do me a favour?'

'Of course. Of course,' I whispered in her ear.

'Do you think you could manage to get me a Danish passport? I could then escape with you if things went wrong?'

'Of course. Of course,' I repeated.

'Oh, you're such a good man. So, so satisfying to have you around.'

As I undressed her, unclipping her dress, poorer and more threadbare than the ones she had worn before the conflict, I kept thinking to myself that her plan would never work. She couldn't speak Faroese, Icelandic or Danish. Never shown the slightest interest in any of those tongues for all she had occasionally heard them spoken. A few questions from a Danish border guard who had been handed her passport and he could only reach one conclusion: that she was one of these Swedes who had collaborated with the Nazi cause.

His rifle would be turned on her and she would be turned back once again towards the nation from which she had come.

Christianna

I HEARD KARL ON THE WIRELESS AGAIN some months later. This time he was talking about how much the Christian people of Suðereyar and the Faroes had in common.

'They all go to church, whether Catholics from South Uist or Protestants from farther north. They are decent, God-fearing people who have respect for the Bible. Fine people living there. Pure and isolated. Decent and honest. No danger of contamination from the evils of the modern world. What are they doing then fighting on the side of Stalin and the Soviet Union, a state that has no faith or time for the Lord? What are they doing standing alongside those atheists and Jews – like Leon Trotsky and others – who dug the foundations of that Godless regime? Do they not know what they stand for? The destruction of churches. The destruction of the cross. The burning of the holy book. When I was a child, I used to know and recognise the words of the Faroese anthem, how it called upon us to kneel to God in prayer so that He could cleanse our souls and bless us. Today, we in Germany are fighting those who would destroy that faith. And yet what do the faithful believers of Suðereyar and the Faroes do? They stand with those who oppose us ...'

I switched it off, becoming agitated the moment I heard my brother's voice. It was happening to me a great deal recently. It occurred when Heðin told me of a fishing boat from Havn sinking after it was struck by a mine. I did something I rarely did, stretching out an arm to comfort him, aware that this might even happen to him on his boat one day.

'Oh, Christianna.' He laughed and blushed, fending me off.

It took place, too, when my sister Bedda sent me a note that made it clear she, too, recognised the Faroese voice echoing on the wireless. *Some people around here all know who he is. 'It's that fool of a brother of yours, isn't it?' someone asked me the other day. I am terrified that someone will tell our mother, that she will discover exactly the truth about the son she raised.* So I crumpled her letter and put it in the fire, terrified that even the smoke would give away its contents, that both neighbours and British soldiers would be able to spot the content of the message from the layers of dark cloud wafting from our chimney, somehow succeeding in putting its words together once more. I visited Pastor Lukas to speak about it, gaining some comfort from his response.

'How many years since you last saw him, Christianna? No one's going to blame you for his folly. At least, no one with a scintilla of sense.'

But mostly it was Malvina and Neil that troubled me. One day when I went out to feed the birds, I saw them working in the fields together; Neil helping to build a few more hayricks to allow the grass to dry more quickly. He did this by using wood left over from the buildings the British army had constructed near the airfield, fixing them deep into the ground. Malvina helped by gathering grass, stacking this on Neil's creations. I saw how closely they moved together when they worked, her fingers brushing against his jacket, the heft of his shoulders. I heard him singing too, the softness of a Gaelic melody. I was aware that such singing was coming to an end soon – one of my neighbours told me that there were rumours going around that the Lovat Scouts were going to be sent elsewhere, returning to their base in Scotland before travelling to some other part of the world.

'Operation Valentine is nearly at an end,' she said, using the term by which their time in the islands was known. 'There will be some hearts broken when it's over.'

I knew that. I could see that in my daughter's every look and expression. I had tried to talk to her about it, the inevitability of Neil going, how it might affect her, but she brushed my concerns away.

'Don't worry. We will work it out. We'll find a way.'

'That might be hard,' I muttered.

'Even if it is, it's not your concern.'

So, I said nothing else, watching them instead when they walked to the entertainment block together, attending the occasional concert, going to watch films that neither of them had ever seen before.

'You couldn't go and see any films in North Uist,' Neil said. 'Some of the fishermen from Lochmaddy used to go and watch them in the picture house in Stornoway a few years before the war, but I never had the chance.'

'Neither did we,' Malvina said. 'Though Uncle Karl used to send us posters from the films he worked on.'

'Malvina …' I muttered.

'I'm sure we still have some of them around somewhere. We

used to have some tacked up in our bedroom, but Mother took them down some time ago.'

'Malvina …'

She blushed, acknowledging my look this time. 'Oh, I'm sorry, Mother,' she stammered before telling a lie as fluently and well as my father and brother used to relate one of their stories. 'I'm sorry, Neil. I forgot. Mother took down those pictures after she fell out with Uncle Karl. She went and burned them soon afterwards.'

Neil smiled. 'Oh, that's not unusual with families. Even in North Uist, some households fall out with one another all the time.'

'Happens here too,' Malvina added.

'Not that it isn't sad when it occurs,' Neil muttered. 'It breaks some people's hearts.' He paused for a moment then looked at me. 'Would it be all right to take Malvina to the pictures tonight? There's a Charlie Chaplin film on. One called *The Great Dictator*.'

I clenched the back of the chair, my brother returning to my mind once more. I was aware Karl often used to impersonate him, twirling a stick or a rifle between his fingers as he meandered down the road in Havn. The other children would snigger at him, seeing his actions as a mixture of oddness and arrogance.

'That's fine,' I muttered. 'That's fine.'

'You can come with us if you want,' Malvina said.

'No, no. I won't bother.'

'You sure?' Neil said, smiling. 'You might enjoy it.'

'No. That's fine.'

He nodded, giving in.

I watched them wander together down the slope from the house, the gush of a stream concealing the sound of their voices on their way to watch a film in which – I heard later – Chaplin impersonated the very man my brother had chosen to serve.

Karl

LOOKING FOR MOMENTS OF CHEER in Berlin during these years was like snatching for air in the smoke of a witch's cauldron. Each day brought more bad news. Buildings being bombed. Tales of Hamburg's destruction, a firestorm raging through that city, with so many – some forty thousand – of its inhabitants being killed. We heard stories from those who had survived and fled, arriving in Berlin on their way east. They spoke of people drowning in asphalt, choking in flames, all the sights they had witnessed. The tales preyed on the minds of many. Freja told me of one woman she knew who said that she could see the red glow of Hamburg still burning night after night from the window of her apartment.

'But that's not possible, is it?' she asked. 'There's no chance that she could see it from there.'

'No. There's none,' I said. 'No chance at all.'

'But it still could be true.' She shook her head. 'What if the fire's still spreading? What if it's coming in this direction and nobody's told us yet?'

'That's unlikely,' I said, shrugging my shoulders, though I was tempted to add that a blaze like that might almost be welcome, given the lack of coal or any other fuel that could be found in Berlin. Every night brought its shivers, the tenacity of cold.

And then there was the November night the raids started increasing. Crammed inside a U-Bahn station, I could hear the planes overheard, the bombs dropping, the sound of people screaming as walls toppled and fell all around us. Voices and cries of alarm seemed to tumble down the stairs towards us, echoed by the length and height of steps. By my side, I could feel Freja trembling, repeating the same point again and again.

'You'll have to get me a Danish passport, you hear me? You'll have to get me one.'

'I will,' I said once again.

'You'll have to.'

Though I knew there was no chance of this ever happening, I nodded. I was even aware that there was the possibility the Danish government would not even allow the likes of me across their border, far less my 'wife'. They were likely to see me as a traitor. At a time when thousands of Danes had helped to shelter and protect Jews who lived in their community, I was guilty of having assisted the German cause, broadcasting to the Faroese and Icelandic people in their midst, calling upon them to join the Nazi cause. They would not forgive these actions. Not unless I acted to protect myself in the months and years ahead, before Hitler's inevitable defeat.

My old self was with me the following morning, the one that had written the words of *How to be a Mountebank and Charlatan*. I kept my thoughts secret. I trusted nobody else. I maintained a distance from others. Each time I looked at Freja and others around me, I kept thinking of the words I had written in my notebook many years before: *Pity softens and debases. Do not succumb to it.*

As I took out my bicycle that morning, I ignored the sound of children screaming, the sight of broken, injured people everywhere in the city streets, the rumble of buildings falling down. I pretended not to see how the cathedral of St Hedwig had been destroyed, its dome collapsing into the ruin, how the old American embassy on Parisier Platz was now wrecked and almost levelled. My sense of smell had gone too. The aroma of smoke. The stink of piss and shit as men and woman emptied their bowels and bladders wherever I passed. I had become oblivious to them. They were no concern of mine.

I even felt the same distance from others when I sat in the studio buildings. There were the sounds of explosions not far away, the rattle of guns, the call of sirens, but I just ignored them all. Instead, I sat and drew – not the film posters and programmes on which I had worked for years, but the start of drawings I called 'Oracles', work that resembled much of what I had done years before. I sketched monsters with sly, snide smiles either attacking one another or groups of human beings lying sprawled on the street, like some I had passed a short time before. One was of an Icelandic volcano with clouds and fire erupting from its peak like those that had shrouded Hamburg, a man and a horse standing nearby, looking at the explosion in a puzzled manner. Another was of a man wearing a pixie hat observing a wide-mouthed whale thrashing about in water. It was as if they were asking themselves the question:

'What kind of weird world do we inhabit?'

And when the broadcast began, I did not speak of war and conflict to those few who listened. I knew that even those who ran the Rundfunk were no longer interested in that. Instead, I began to read aloud the poems I had written in twenty languages for the *Corda Atlantica,* the collection I planned to publish after peace had once more settled among us. For all they included tongues as varied and distinct as Icelandic, Faroese, Russian, Finnish, French, even some of the dialects and languages found among the Maori population of New Zealand and the lost people of Atlantis, many were in that of the land I had turned my back upon many decades before – the Faroe Islands. I started the reading in English.

> Man! do remember: of life and death,
> deeply, the intervals are stringed.
> But little birds—if duly winged—
> can sway the ocean's breath.

As I did this, something strange happened – a reaction to my own words I had never experienced during all the hours I had broadcast propaganda to the Faroese and Icelandic people before.

Tears began to dampen my cheeks.

I was only diverted from my self-pity by the sound of a bomb going off a short distance away, somewhere between the studio and the Brandenburg Gate.

Christianna

I COULD HEAR THE SNATCHES of song on Malvina's lips. It was the same one he had often sung. Each syllable was just about exact and right, but it was all pronounced in a deep and sonorous manner, so unlike the way it had been on his lips. Back then, there had been a lilt and lift to it. Now it only sounded dark and gloomy, as if she was scraping out her heart and soul with every sound and word.

Chan eil mo leannan ann an-seo,
Cha robh e 'raoir, 's cha bhi e nochd;
Chan eil mo leannan ann an-seo,
Neo duine a thogas m'inntinn.

My love is not here just now.
Not yesterday or even tonight.
My love is not here just now.
To keep my spirits high in flight.

Si o a-lo a-laidh ti um
Si o a-lo a-laidh ti um

Si o a-lo a-laidh ti um
'Si o a leam 'si haodh rum.

Caolas eadar mi 's mo luaidh
Caolas eadar mi 's mo luaidh
Caolas eadar mi 's mo luaidh.
Is cuan eadar mi 's m'annsachd.

A strait between me and my love,
A strait between me and my love,
A strait between me and my love
Ocean between me and my favourite one.

She had been acting like that for days, ever since the men of the
Lovat Scouts had left these islands. She walked gloomily in their
absence, as if part of her had disappeared with them on the boat.
Not only I but her sister Dagrún tried to talk to her, probing away
at her silence.

'You'll hear from him again soon,' I said.

'Don't worry,' Dagrún declared, 'you'll have a letter from him
soon. As soon as he gets to land, there will be one in the post for
you. Wait and see.'

'You're not the only one in this situation,' I reassured her.
'There's women the length and breadth of the Faroes who are
thinking and feeling the same way as you, waiting for word from
their own Princes of Suðereyar. Their wait will soon be over.
News will soon arrive.'

A few days later and she broke down. Trembling, tears misting
her face, she turned towards us, her body shaking as she spoke.

'No. I won't hear from him again.'

'Really. And why not?'

Her fingers let loose a note she carried in her fingers. Short and crumpled, it looked not unlike the one I had passed to Neil's uncle all those years before. It lay in her palm for a while.

'What's that?' Dagrún asked.

'It's a note Neil gave the officer in charge of the entertainment block to hand to me. He passed it to him the day he was leaving. It says …' She paused as she tried to squeeze the words out. 'It says …'

'What does it say?'

She cast an irritated look at Dagrún. 'It says he has a girlfriend back in North Uist. That he promised to marry her years ago. He's sorry for any hurt and harm he's causing me. But it'll all work out in the end.'

'Really?'

'Yes. Really.'

Once again, my fingers gripped at a chair or table to keep me upright. For some reason, I remembered my father's words, how he believed there were fine people living in the world's islands. 'Pure and isolated. Decent and honest. No danger of contamination by the evil that existed elsewhere.' How untrue that was. They were no different from those who lived elsewhere.

'Bastard,' I said.

My two daughters looked at me. They had never heard me use a word like that before.

'Bastard. Bastard. Bastard.'

Dagrún shook her head in disapproval. It was not a word that either she or her father would ever use. She was far too pure and isolated, decent and honest, to ever employ language like that.

'It's not just that,' Malvina muttered.

'What else?'

'I think I'm expecting his baby.'

I reeled once more, this time recalling how unmarried mothers were treated in Havn when I was young. Girls like Ásla who had been around Karl's age, ostracized and ignored because she was born out of wedlock. Her mother, too, subjected to whispers and rumours because no one quite knew the father's name, whether he had been from Hjaltland, Denmark or Norway; the constant questioning about his identity and why she had behaved that way in the confines of a fishing boat or somewhere in the shelter of the harbour.

And then I recalled something about myself that night I had been with my own Prince of Suðereyar, Neil MacCusbic's uncle, the times I had walked with him through the harbour at Havn – how he awakened forces in me that my own husband with his decency and diligence, his piety and prayers, had never quite stirred; how my skin had been warm with gratitude at the clasp of his arms, the closeness of his chest; how my eyes sparkled like stars or diamonds at his presence; how I felt there was nothing ugly about him – like most men I knew – which I would have to try my best to ignore; how the very distance of the islands which he had come from made him somewhat exceptional and glamorous, as far from the realities of my life as the splendour of the Milky Way or the spread of the Northern Lights.

And I wondered, too, how things might have been if I had been in his company over months, like my own daughter had been in the presence of her own prince – how long might have passed before I could no longer resist the opportunity to see him lying naked beside me, to feel part of him within me? I could not imagine I would have resisted the temptation for very long.

It was with this in mind that I stretched out my arms to hold my daughter, providing her with comfort. I could not condemn her. Like my brother and me, we had all been victims of my father's legacy of words.

Karl

'The Russians will be here soon … The Russians are coming.'

Every night I heard Freja sobbing, trembling as she sat there in her coat, fearing the arrival of soldiers from the east. I tried to reassure her, saying again and again that the Americans and British were just as likely to arrive in Berlin before the Red Army, but she dismissed my words, asking once more about the matter she had raised so many times before.

'Did you get my passport yet? Did you speak to your people about it?'

'I've tried,' I lied.

'And?'

'I've had no success.'

'Well, try again. Try again. We've got to get out of here before the Russians arrive.'

'I will … I will.'

'As soon as possible,' she declared. 'We're not going to last for much longer. And you're one of the fortunate ones. You can help others escape.'

But I knew there was no point. Already some of my fellow countrymen had tried slipping through the doors of the Danish embassy, only to be turned away. Mainly members of the SS Division Wiking, they were looking for shelter in its bunker, a place where they could hide from the Russian attack when it came. One of them I recognised had even spoke to me one day.

'We were fools, Karl. Fools. I volunteered in good faith years ago, but I don't want to die for that act of folly.'

I said nothing, passing him by. I didn't want to be seen with anyone who was thinking of deserting. I wanted once again to be the man I had sought to become many years before.

- Be guarded with your opinions. Others may be listening.
- Trust nobody else.

I was also aware that if Freja accompanied me to the Danish border, she would only endanger me, making the authorities there question my loyalty to their cause. I knew they weren't the only ones doing that now. Some of those working at the Rundfunk were already asking questions about that. The grim and humourless figure of Ludwig Mühlhausen – a gaunt, bespectacled man who had been sending the Irish to sleep for years because of his tedious broadcasts – would look at me with contempt.

'When are you going to use that Danish passport of yours and slink off over the border home?'

'Never,' I declared. 'I am going to stay loyal to the cause till the end.'

'Really?' he sneered. 'The only one your kind is ever loyal to is yourself.'

Finally, I decided to prove him right. I filled up my haversack with food and clothes and took my bicycle to work one morning. After I had finished my usual broadcast, reading aloud my verse in the dialect of Atlantis I often employed these days, I walked to the store where all the records of our broadcasts were kept, slipping them into a pocket of my haversack, leaving only accounts of the times I had read out verse or spoken in the language of Atlantis behind. There were many fires these days in the streets of Berlin, where any evidence of my time in the Rundfunk could be destroyed. If I was ever put on trial, I knew what my defence would be.

'I never spoke to the people of the Faroe Islands or Iceland in their own tongues. I only ever addressed them in the language of Atlantis or read poetry to them. What harm might be caused by that?'

The prosecution would be forced to shrug their shoulders. Apart from hearsay, they would be unable to find proof of the evil I had undoubtedly done.

After that, I was on my way.

I decided to head in the direction of the Danevirke, which my father had told me had been built by Queen Thyra way back in the ninth century.

'The work of the Aryan race,' he had proclaimed. 'A wall that has marked off the Danish race for centuries.'

It was still standing, even though the Wehrmacht, fearing an invasion from the Danish coast, had wanted to destroy it. Himmler had persuaded them otherwise, saying it was part of the ancestral heritage of the Nordic race and must not be damaged in any way.

I headed towards it, following a route I had scratched out on a map for months before, avoiding all the towns and villages that were on the way.

Christianna

'IN THE NAME OF THE FATHER, the Son and the Holy Ghost ...'

I watched the aged, wrinkled fingers of Pastor Lukas trickle water on the head of Malvina's son, the child's face creasing and becoming twisted as the baptism took place.

We called the child Magnus.

We told people it was out of respect for his grandfather, who had died many years before.

The truth was a little vaguer and more uncertain than that.

Karl

FOR ALL ITS STREETS WERE FAMILIAR, Copenhagen seemed hostile to me the day I returned. Though there was not the bedlam and destruction I could see in Berlin, there were signs throughout of all that had happened over the last few years. The damage that had been done to the Forum Arena where the walls had been blasted. The effects of the attack on the shipyard at Burmeister & Wain. Works of sabotage done by the resistance movement. I had heard that such things had happened during the last few years. Now I could bear witness to them all.

It wasn't all that easy even to walk through its streets. Sometimes police or soldiers would stop me on my way, asking for my passport. Mainly I would hand over my official one, but, on rare occasions, if I thought there were relaxed and cheerful expressions on the faces of those who had halted me on my way, I would sometimes provide the one I had fashioned for myself years before, with my face on its cover, the following words printed below:

> Our countryman ambassador and Bard, Charles Dunganon Count of St Kilda, author of the famous Oracles, is voyaging throughout the length and breadth of the world as our special envoy representing the old Atlantic dynasty Cormorant, doing astro-psychic business everywhere as he goes along. Port Nirvana, St Kilda, Commonwealth of Atlantis, the 20th century. Valid on all dates. Our hand and seal.

For all that they would allow me to pass with a smile, it was not a stunt I tried with everyone. I could see members of the resistance group called Holger Danske all over the place, the country's flags on their armbands. They pushed women around with their rifles, insulting and calling them names – my former neighbours, perhaps, in Vesterbro, or those who had filled the atmosphere of the railway station in Helgolandsgade with the stink of perfume and powder.

'You whores,' they'd say. 'Sleeping with the enemy.'

As if they had much choice. I thought of Ásla and wondered how she had got through these years, where she was now. Outside my own family, she was the one person who had touched the core of my existence, an outsider like me because of her upbringing in Tórshavn, someone who never quite belonged. Looking back at my life, she was the one person I should have married, if I hadn't been so determined to fashion a shield around my heart.

I also saw members of Holger Danske taking out a group of Waffen-SS men they had discovered in hiding, rattling them along with their guns. On this occasion I had a little sympathy with those Danes who shouted and yelled in their direction, until I thought that some of those who called out insults at them were people like me, those who until a few years ago – or perhaps recently – thought there was some deep and inner righteousness in the cause we followed.

The wind had turned since then.

I thought of a thousand options – going, perhaps, to Kasper's home to see if they would shelter me for a while. The thought didn't stay in my head for long. Kasper had never liked me, not since he used to go to Havn with me when I was young. 'A conceited fool,' I had overheard him tell others once. 'Too many ideas that feed his own self-importance.' The years since then would not have helped matters. He would probably have told his parents – if they were still alive – about how I had broadcast to the Faroes and Iceland on behalf of the Nazis: 'The Lord Haw-Haw of

Tórshavn. The Count of St Kilda has become the Reichsmarschall of Reykjavik.' They would have shaken their heads when they were told of this, their Faroese fool transformed into a traitor. Perhaps they had even listened to my broadcasts once or twice. If they had then it would not be long before the likes of Holger Danske would turn up, prodding me out the door of their home with their rifles.

'You quisling,' they would mutter. 'You bloody traitor.'

I could envisage a bullet being fired, my body dumped in either Assistens or Vestre cemetery in Copenhagen for others to bury or burn. And, too, the words of approval when they discovered how I had behaved in the war years and before.

'If anyone bloody deserved it ...'

There was also the option of returning to my past life. Haunting the zoo to obtain raw meat. Being lifted by the police and thrown into a cell to be fed. Going, perhaps, to Kronprinsessegade to see if I could get my old job back. For different reasons, none of these were real possibilities. I was too old and unfit now to sleep for long on park-benches. I would soon rot in the cold and damp or starve. Neither could I return to my old workplace. They would ask questions there, questions I was not inclined to answer.

'What have you been doing since you left us all these years ago?'

Copenhagen was not a safe place to be. Neither was any other part of Denmark. I cycled west, heading past countless acres of farmland, the odd haystack, herd of cattle and pigs, the occasional house. When my bicycle suffered a puncture, I threw it away in a drain beside the road. It was no use to me anymore. One night I even slept by the side of a lake. I was woken up by the hiss of a swan standing in front of me, its feathers puffed up, the sharpness of its beak pointing in my direction. Clearly, I had slept too close to the bird's nest, disturbing its peace and stillness. I ran away from it, apologising again and again as if it could speak and understand.

'Sorry … sorry … sorry.'

I continued walking, heading to the only place I knew where there might be the possibility of escape from the turmoil which I, along with so many others, had helped to create. Back to my homeland. Back to Faroe.

Eventually I arrived in Esbjerg, that port which reeked of sour milk, rotten fish and smoked eel. The scents that I had hated for much of my life still percolated the harbour in much the same way as they had done when I landed there years before. This time, however, the concoction did not make my stomach swirl and throat gag. Instead, it had a different kind of reek, offering the possibility of a new beginning for my existence, albeit one in the place where my life had first started. I sucked in the smell as if it were perfume, an exotic blend of smells I had never experienced before but made me feel at ease and at home. Even in my exhaustion, it strengthened and emboldened me, allowing me to approach a couple of fishermen I saw nearby who were working on a boat that came from Havn.

'You been in these parts often since the beginning of the war?' I said in Faroese.

'No. This is the first time since the whole thing started.' The fisherman looked at me, his eyes half-closed in suspicion. 'Don't know if we'll be back any time soon. Things haven't settled down yet.'

'You're right. I suspect they won't be good for a while. Loads of rebuilding to do after years of destruction. It'll take a while.'

'Ages.' He glanced at me again. 'Where are you from, my friend?'

'The same place as you. The Faroes. My sister stays in Vágar.'

'And you have another sister in Tórshavn,' he said. 'I know exactly who you are.'

My legs wobbled. I was aware at that moment I could be reported to the Danish police or even the army, my identity made known to them. Trembling, I dipped my hand into my pocket, bringing out a few crumpled dollar notes. They hung in my fingers for a while.

'I've got lots of these I can give you,' I said. 'Take me back to Vágar. I'll pay you well for the ride.'

Christianna

'YOU BASTARD. YOU BASTARD,' I said when Heðin's friends brought him from their boat to our door. 'What are you doing here?'

'I had nowhere else to go,' he said. 'Anywhere else and I might get killed.'

'Nothing more than you deserved for your behaviour. Mingling with those thugs.'

'I didn't know they were like that in the beginning.'

'Well, you should have soon learned. The signs were all there.'

'You're right, sister. I was just blind to them.'

I was unable to say anything more. I gripped the table as I nodded in the direction of the chair where Malvina had been sitting with her infant a short time before, watching as he heaved himself down into it. My brother looked tired and old, his thick and wavy hair now grey and receding, features tired and pale, his body having been pitched and swirled for hours as he lay in the cabin on the boat. 'He's not much of a sailor,' one of the fishermen had told me as they half-carried him to the house. 'Was sick much of the way.' I had shaken my head in response. 'He's got a lot to be sick about,' I declared. 'Must be his conscience.' But I said nothing about why it might be troubling him. I assumed they knew. Just like my two daughters had recently found out what he had been doing. Before that, I had hidden my knowledge of his behaviour from them, assuming it could be kept secret. I had been wrong. One of those in the base asked Dagrún a question when she had gone to the entertainment block to watch a film.

'Is it true you have a relative working for the Nazis?'

'I don't think so,' she said.

'Well, I'd check if I were you. We've heard otherwise.'

So, she questioned me about it afterwards, becoming angry when it turned out I already knew.

'Why didn't you tell us?' she asked. 'How long have you known?'

I only answered the last question, telling them of the night I recognised his voice on the wireless and turned to switch it off.

And now Karl was back with us, asking for our help and support.

'It won't be for long,' I told him. 'A month or two, that's all.'

'That'll be fine.'

'After that, you'll have to make your own way in the world. We can't protect you forever from the cost of your follies.'

'That's fine,' he said again, nodding. 'It doesn't take people long to forget these things. I'll go back to Denmark. Start a new life there.'

'You're a bit old for that,' I muttered.

'So is the rest of the continent. We'll all have to do it nonetheless.' He laughed to himself as a thought passed through his head. 'I even know by what name I'll do it. I'll call myself Professor Valentinus. It's what a certain lady used to call me. It'll also remind me of how life has changed here.'

It was a week or so later that I became convinced he might manage it. He was standing outside in the chill of daylight, sketching the mountains he had glimpsed when he had stepped outside our home for the first time a few days before. There was the flat ridge on the top of Heinanøva with Árnafjall alongside, its peak concealed by mist as it so often was at any time of year, a serpent slithering towards it, twisting and turning as it writhed towards its top.

'I've been thinking of stories,' Karl said, smiling. 'Some of those our father used to tell us. Like about how Trøllanes on Kalsoy gained its name.

'I can't remember that one,' I confessed.

'Oh, I do. Very well.' He laughed. 'How that village was visited by trolls from the surrounding mountains every twelfth night of Christmas, and how the villagers had to flee and seek shelter for the night in the neighbouring village of Mikladur. How it was this that gave the village its name. One year, though, there was this old woman who wasn't able to escape from her home because of sickness and infirmity. She hid under the table in the living room when the trolls came. They danced and partied and made such a racket that the old woman, in fear, called out the name of Christ. When the trolls heard that holy name, they stopped partying and cursed the old woman. They left the village, never going back there again. When the villagers returned, they expected to find the old lady dead. She was alive, though, and able to tell them about what happened that particular night.'

I shook my head. 'I can't remember that story,' I said again.

'No? Perhaps it's come to mind because I've spent too long with trolls. Too many of the past years. It's time to escape them. Time to break their hold.' He shook his head. 'I only hope they're not coming to get me, that they won't come back and haunt me anymore.'

Karl

WHEN THEY ARRIVED I was in the middle of painting a picture, a creation based on a poem by the writer William Heinesen about how winter sometimes lights a flame on these islands, transforming the 'opal grey' of the daylight with the 'new moon's red knife-edge on the horizon'; how it sometimes brought, too, the sparkling of ice-crystals on the roads and the 'stately constellations of the Northern lights'. I was sketching, too, how my 'dead friends' were congregating at a table, warming their hands at the fire, thinking of those who had died at the hands of the Nazis.

And then the hammering at the door began, a loud hollow sound that echoed throughout the house.

'Karl Kjerúlf Einarsson! Are you in there?'

'Get out here now!'

I did as they asked, performing my old Charlie Chaplin walk as I stepped into the brisk, cold wind that was blowing outside, hoping it might amuse and divert them. It failed to do so. I recognised some who were standing there. There was Arno with his red and florid face who had been around my age in school. A number who were clearly related to Hørður and Árni, the two fishermen neighbours to whom my father had told his stories. Their faces – despite the generations – told their own tales of where they had come from. All that had really altered were the expressions on their faces, much harsher and more brutal than they had been all those years before.

'Bedda sent us,' Árni's descendant declared.

'She's bloody embarrassed that you're back here after all the things you've done. Especially since your mother is on her deathbed. She doesn't need the likes of you around. It would all just add to the poor woman's agony.'

'She said we should take you away with us.'

'Really?' I muttered, aware that my other sister was not here. She was away at some meeting that was taking place in the church. Half of me wondered if she knew this was about to happen and had gone there for her own safety.

Árni' grabbed my shoulder. 'Really,' he said.

And then the rest of them were upon me, clutching my shoulder, my jacket and neck.

'You bloody traitor,' they shouted. 'You betrayed your home-land, the people that you came from!'

'You brought misery to them, made them feel ashamed of themselves.'

'You damn disgrace!'

'You bloody turncoat, crook, deceiver. You deserve to be killed for all you've done.'

There was then the force of fists, the pounding and pummel-ling of boots as they threw me on a stretch of ground covered with hen-shit, kicking and hammering me with boots and rods, lashing me with a stick or two. It all reminded me of that incident I had witnessed in Berlin a few years before, when a man was beaten near the door of his apartment.

'You damn traitor. You bloody turncoat,' they yelled again, their voices echoing in my head.

Among all the blows and bruises, I heard a litany of other reasons why they were treating me this way. They mentioned the names of dead sons and brothers who had been killed in the conflict, lost on fishing boats and Merchant Navy vessels, killed by German attacks.

'That's for Alexandur ...'

'Regin ...'

'Karsten ...'

'All for one and one for all,' I heard Árni' declare, echoing the words of the Three Musketeers as he tore into me like a seabird cutting through the flesh of some creature lying on the shoreline.

'For Christian ...' another yelled, naming some lost relative.

I felt as if I was being punished for every person who had died in these islands during the years of conflict, that I was beached beside that doorway as if I were a whale – and the human equivalent of a *grindadráp* was taking place, boot, fist and hand tearing my skin as I lay there. Blood trickled from my lips. Bruises and the shit of ducks and hens adorned the rest of my body. And yet the ritual still continued. One blow after another after another ...

Finally, they stopped. I lay there moaning in the same way as I had heard so many others do after they had suffered the attentions of the Waffen-SS. One reached down to lift me.

'Right. That's enough,' he declared. 'We'll take him on the boat to Havn. They'll sort him out there.'

Christianna

IT WAS THE DUCKS AND HENS that let me know something was going on. I saw a fluster of feathers, the birds leaping to the roof of my home and squawking. I was walking back from the church when this occurred. Pastor Lukas was accompanying me up the track. It was the first time he had ever done that, explaining his actions by saying I was going through so much just now.

'There's your mother ill and unlikely to get well again. Your daughter with her baby. And, of course, your brother too, his situation.'

He left the last part of all that without an explanation, aware that in this community Karl was seen as a disgrace, one who was said to have betrayed his native islands. Over the last hour or so, we had talked about these matters, the pastor listening patiently as I came back to Karl's behaviour again and again. 'I can't understand why he didn't keep his head down and mouth shut. It would have been the safest and most sensible thing to do.'

I was grateful when he offered to walk me home, but I didn't tell him the reason for this – how I felt blessed and comforted each time I was in his company, even after all these years of knowing one another. There wasn't the same excitement I had experienced and suppressed when I was younger. My physical longing for him had long since waned and gone. Instead, there was an ease at being in his presence, a feeling that this was where I should have been all along. It was with this in mind that I walked alongside him up one of the new roads the British army had been built around the airfield, one of the few advantages anyone had gained through the war. It was little wonder that there were some people in the community who argued that we should join Hjaltland, Orkneyjar and Suðereyar in becoming part of the group of islands to the south. More had been done for us since the British had come than the Danes had managed for generations.

And then we saw the ducks and hens spinning and circling around my home, creating pandemonium with their calls and cries. There were men out there too. Some of them were shouting and yelling. I could glimpse their shapes and shadows near the doorway, all grouped together there, bustling back and forth.

'What's going on?'

I quickened my pace, heading home to find out what was occurring. It was then that Pastor Lukas stretched out his arm, reaching for me.

'Christianna ...'

I tried to wriggle free from him and then looked in his direction again, my mind filling with alarm at his calm features, how quiet and controlled he looked.

'Christianna,' he said again. 'You know this has to be done.'

'What?'

'Karl has to be taken back to Copenhagen. He betrayed his country, spoke up for Hitler and the Nazis. Justice has to be done.'

'No.'

'Christianna …'

'No. Leave him alone. Give him the chance to set things right.'

'Christianna. You know that's impossible.'

And then Lukas acted in a way he had never done before, enclosing my body in his arms, clasping me tight and close.

'Christianna, you know how much I care for you, more than any other member of my congregation, more than any person on God's earth. But you know, too, that this must happen. Humans must have their own form of justice carried out. These things are important too.'

'Lukas, I feel much the same way. Not about Karl, but about you.'

'You do?'

He thrust me away from him then, more than a little embarrassed at his own indiscretion, blushing at the words he had just said and heard.

'Christianna …' he stammered.

'Yes?'

'I should have left these words unspoken. In a small place like this, they should never have come to my lips.'

'You sure of that?' I muttered, shaking with the shock of all that was happening.

'Yes. I'm sure.'

'Lukas. Surely God would never compel us to deny ourselves.'

'Yes. He would. For the sake of our souls. For the sake of all eternity.'

He clasped his hands and began to pray, each phrase and expression delivered in a frenzied manner I had never seen before when he stood in his pulpit or visited a home in the community. His voice was almost an echo of the uproar from the hens and ducks, their clucks and cackling resembling the stammering of his tongue. However, I recognised some of it – the words of Psalm 91, which I had heard before when the people of these islands went out to hunt for seabirds. But Lukas spoke with an unusual strength and urgency, each word bearing a different weight of meaning from the occasions I had heard them before.

'Deliver us both from the snare of the fowler, and from the noisome pestilence that troubles our lives. Cover us both with His feathers, and trust in the shelter of His wings. Let His truth be our shield and protection, allowing us to be protected against the terrors of the night, the temptations that sweep and trouble us by day. Let us be strong in His service, for all that our weaknesses and frailty let Him down ...'

I trembled and shook before deciding to stand where I was for a while, waiting for him to say, 'Amen'; waiting, too, for the drama and uproar that surrounded my home to come to an end, allowing me to return to its shelter, the safety I could find there.

Karl

THEY DID THEIR BEST to sort me out, allowing me a few moments of freedom to go and visit my mother, who was lying in her bed in my sister's home. Cheeks scooped and hollowed, skin ravaged by illness, she looked at me while I stood by her bedside.

'Who are you?' she asked.

'Your son, Karl,' I answered, reaching for her hand. 'You remember me, don't you?'

She tore her fingers away from me, refusing my grasp.

'I don't recognise you,' she said. 'You're an imposter. A fake. A fraud.'

I tried again, but with the same result, her rejection bringing tears to my eyes.

'I am your son,' I insisted. 'I promise that.'

'No,' she maintained. 'I lost my son years ago. He's gone long ago.'

'You sure about that?'

'Yes. Yes. Yes. He's gone long ago,' she repeated.

'No. I'm here. I promise I'm here.'

'No.'

I was guided away from her side by Bedda, who led me out of the door.

'There's no point,' she said. 'You're only causing her distress. Just like you've caused for the rest of us.'

'I know, I know, I know,' I repeated, shaking and trembling, barely able to stand.

It wasn't the end of my humiliation. That only increased the following day, sitting in a cell in Havn, hearing the voices of Hørður and Árni's descendants as they went past, calling out in my direction.

'You bloody count. You bloody traitor.'

'I hope they kill you, Karl.'

'I trust you'll get exactly what you deserve.'

'*Ssssiiiiizzzz*,' they shouted, imitating the sound of an electric current, one that someone outside predicted would soon be passing through my bones. '*Sssssiiizzz, sssiiizzz, sssssiiiizzz.*'

Eventually, I was taken by chain and boat all the way back to Copenhagen, to the police station where I had been years before. At least it was silent there. No yells or shouts disturbing my peace. Its musty smell was also familiar to me. So, too, was the flaking paint on its walls. The conditions there had not improved. There were other things on which they could spend money – more important people and places which might benefit from any spare cash.

Once again, I became the Count of Monte Cristo I had read about in my childhood.

'Take off your clothes,' one of the policemen said when I arrived. 'Give me your watch. Your wallet.' He handed me the prison uniform I would wear. 'Put that on.'

I nodded, doing as he asked.

'The place is familiar to you,' he said. 'You've been here before.'

'Yes. A few years ago.'

'Well, you're in much bigger shit this time. But I guess you know that.'

'I do.'

'Well, don't you forget it. Any time you dare to misbehave, and we'll remind you of the wrongs you've committed. Some of us might take pleasure in that.'

'I'll remember that,' I muttered, my body still bruised and wounded by the blows I had suffered some weeks before.

'Make sure you do.'

A month later and the interrogation began. The same questions endlessly repeated. Spoken by a variety of mouths. Underlined by a range of voices. All seeking to make a similar point continually, relentlessly, constantly.

'What is your real name?'

'Where did you come from?'

'Have you been known by any false names or pseudonyms?'

'If so, which ones?'

'Did you broadcast on behalf of the German government to the people of the Faroe Islands and Iceland?'

'What did you say to them?'

It was that last question that formed the substance of my defence.

'I spoke to them in the language of Atlantis.'

'Really? How did you do that?'

I then began to recount the stories I had first heard from my father years before – how Atlantis was a lost continent that had once stretched from beyond the edge of the British Isles to Gibraltar at the mouth of the Mediterranean. 'That was before it was destroyed in the Great Flood, the survivors taking to their boats and ending up in places like Ireland, Iceland, the Faroe Islands, Hebrides, Orkneyjar, Hjaltland. It is the tongue of these places that I used in my broadcasts to the Faroes and Iceland, one that I explored, discovered and wrote in myself.'

And once again, as I spoke, I was back there, returning to St Kilda in my mind and imagination, noting the cliffs that had once marked the edge of Atlantis, the boulders at their base, the turf that occasionally clung to spaces where the rocks jutted out, the tide and surf that sometimes licked, curled and ground against their heights, the slopes below on which a handful of houses stood, the only remnants of a continent lost centuries before. I tried to describe them as they had been in times when they marked the boundaries of a world that once included within its borders the Garden of Eden, the Gardens of the Hesperides, the Elysian Fields, the Gardens of Alcinous, the Mesomphalos, the Olympos …

'This is the foundation of our civilisation, one that has been lost to us. When I spoke in the language of that ancient world, I was seeking to bring it back once again. We still have need of it.'

They shook their heads when I spoke like that.

'You're mad,' they said before they let me go. 'Completely bloody mad.'

I nodded when they said this, conscious that they might be right.

Author's Note

The 'Facts' of Karl Einarsson's Life

Sources are few and far between about Karl Kjerúlf Einarsson, but he was born on May 6, 1897, in Seyðisfjörður, Iceland. His life came to an end in Copenhagen, Denmark, on February 24, 1972. An Icelandic writer, artist and adventurer, he referred to himself mainly as Cormorant XII, Emperor of Atlantis, and the Count or Duke of St Kilda. Further pseudonyms were Carolus Africanus Dunganon, Professor Dr Emarsson, Professor Valentinus and Lord of Hekla – the last clearly a tribute to his homeland in Iceland. The name Professor Valentinus may have a different explanation. One of the sources I recently came across alleged that he also worked for a time as a sex therapist.

According to an article in the Icelandic newspaper *Alþýðublaðið*, the house in which the family lived was called Dunga, which sounds 'a little Gaelic' and which inspired Karl to use the Dunganon pseudonym. The Reykjavík Grapevine website tells another variant – that the Faroe Islands were a 'dung heap' for Karl, which he said goodbye to when he left the archipelago for Europe, with the exclamation 'Dunga – *non!*'

The Icelandic Nobel Prize-winner Halldór Laxness wrote about Karl Einarsson. His short story 'Corda Atlantica' concerns Count Dunganon, Duke of St Kilda, a man who has his own 'country'. In Dunganon's mind, this small island off the coast of Scotland is reputed to be the last remaining part of Atlantis. The Count 'differed in no way from the rest of a class that has been more harshly treated than any other group in the world, not excluding the Jews: the so-called petit bourgeoisie, consisting, as everyone

knows, of university professors, linen drapers, roadworks super-
visors, assistant managers of breweries, and violin-makers'.

Dunganon spent the last years of his life in the Danish city of
Frederiksberg, where his funeral also took place after his death
in Copenhagen. He left his artwork to the people of Iceland. The
National Gallery of Iceland in Reykjavik holds a collection of
the artwork, which is sometimes on display. It was there I first
encountered it. The images can be viewed on the gallery's website
at sarpur.is (using 'Dunganon' as the search term).

Karl Einarsson's St Kilda passport reads:
'Our countryman ambassador and Bard, Charles Dunganon
duke of St Kilda, author of the famous Oracles, is voyaging
throughout the length and breadth of the world as our special
envoy representing the old Atlantic dynasty Cormorant, doing
astro-psychic business everywhere as he goes along.
Port Nirvana, St Kilda, Commonwealth of Atlantis, the 20th
century. Valid on all dates. Our hand and seal.'

Bibliography

Barth, Rudiger and Friederichs, Hauke, *The Grave Diggers*, Profile Books, 2019.

Bru, Heðin, *The Old Man and His Sons*, Telegram, 2011.

Ditlevsen, Tove, *Childhood, Youth, Dependency*, Penguin, 2019.

Ecott, Tim, *The Land of Maybe*, Short Books, 2020.

Ferguson, Robert, *Scandinavians: In Search of The Soul of the North*, Head of Zeus, 2016.

Francis, Gavin, *True North*, Polygon, 2008.

Friel, Brian, *Translations*, Faber and Faber, 1995.

Gay, Peter, *Weimar Culture: The Outsider as Insider*, W.W. Norton, 2001.

Heinesen, William, *The Tower at the Edge of the World*, Dedalus, 2018.

Hett, Benjamin Carter, *The Death of Democracy: Hitler's Rise to Power*, Windmill, 2018.

Hutchinson, Roger, *The Silent Weaver*, Birlinn, 2011.

Jacobsen, Jorgen-Frantz, *Barbara*, Dedalus, 2013.

Johnston, George, *Rocky Shores: An Anthology of Faroese Poetry*, Wilfion Books, 1981.

Kershaw, Stephen P., *A Brief History of Atlantis*, Robinson, 2017.

Lampe, David and Riis-Jørgensen, Birger, *Hitler's Savage Canary: A History of Danish Resistance in World War Two*, Arcade, 2014.

Linklater, Eric, *The Dark of Summer*, Bloomsbury, 2012.

—*The Northern Garrison*, HMSO 10941.

Bibliography

Maclean, Rory, *Berlin: Imagine a City*, W&N, 2015.

McDonough, Frank, *The Hitler Years Triumph 1933–39*, Head of Zeus, 2019.

Millman, Lawrence, 'The Last Emperor of Atlantis Was An Icelander', *The Reykjavík Grapevine*, 2014.

Moorhouse, Roger, *Berlin At War*, Vintage, 2011.

Roth, Joseph, *The Hotel Years*, Granta, 2015.

Serner, Walter, *Last Loosening: A Handbook for the Con Artist and Those Aspiring to Become One*, Twisted Spoon Press, 2020.

Shirer, William L., *Berlin Diary*, Rosetta Books, 2011.

Toksvig, Sandi, *Hitler's Canary*, Yearling, 2006.

Weidermann, Volker, *Dreamers – When the Writers Took Power, Germany 1919*, Pushkin, 2018.

Acknowledgements

Thanks to Iain Mackinnon and Hanna Lísa Ólafsdóttir, who unwittingly gave me the idea for a certain Hebridean prince (apparently, he was a character in various Icelandic children's books). My thanks also to Aðalsteinn Ásberg Sigurðsson and Gyrðir Elíasson, who gave me such a warm welcome during the three occasions I have been in Iceland. I was also accompanied both there and to the Faroe Islands by the late and much missed Lise Sinclair, from Fair Isle in Shetland, along with Jen Hadfield and Matthew Wright. That trip was organised by another individual who I miss very much, the late Alex Cluness, who worked at that time in Shetland Arts. I would also like to express my gratitude to Yvonne Malcolmson who, together with two pupils from Sandwick school, accompanied me on another occasion. My friend Donald Farmer also helped me with the costs for yet another trip to Iceland. It was there I met Orlygur, Gudny, Anita and Steinnin at the Herring Era Museum in Sigludfjorður in the north of Iceland. The first two also gave me information about the character known as the Duke of St Kilda, even possessing photographs of his passport.

There were others who also assisted. My fellow writer Lorn MacIntyre, Douglas Macleod and Kenneth Fraser helped provide me with information on those who broadcast from Berlin during World War Two. Lawrence Millman has written a number of articles about the central figure in the book and provided much of the inspiration for the work. However, it should be noted that I also employed a great deal of imagination in his creation. The account should not be considered a reliable and accurate story of

even the islands where he came from. In this, it reflects
of the reality of Karl's life. It remains as unclear and nebu-
s as his existence.

Others, too, helped. These include John MacMillan, who read
this book at an early stage, and Lynn Bennett-Mackenzie, who saw
the potential of the book in terms of its artistic inspiration. Others
have assisted me in various ways, including Rob Dunbar; Alasdair
Maceachen; Iain Mackenzie; Angus and Eileen; Arthur Cormack;
Ryno Morrison; Tormod Macleod (Scalpay); Cailean Maclean,
who provided me with a valuable piece of information used in the
book; Liza Mulholland; Roddy Walker, who I taught but now lives
in Denmark; William MacDonald; John and Alasdair Morrison,
formerly of North Uist, and Maggie Priest. Many assisted me by just
allowing me to talk about the tale while I was working on it. Others
– largely in North Uist, Benbecula and South Uist – informed me
privately about their family connections to both the Lovat Scouts
and the Faroe Islands. This was especially valuable during periods
of lockdown. In an ideal world, I would have travelled to the Faroe
Islands, Denmark and Berlin to assist me in the venture.

I am also grateful for the help of MacTV, based in Stornoway,
who provided additional enlightment by producing a programme
entitled 'Ealtainn: Faroe Dance' for BBC Alba a number of years
ago. A special thanks to my fellow Niseach Jayne Macleod, who
took part in a special Faroese ballad and dance on that occasion.
She also provided a CD of the programme while I was in the midst
of researching this book. *Tapadh leat,* Jayne!

From my teenage years, I have met various people from the
Faroe Islands. Mostly fishermen, they aroused my curiosity about
the islands to our north from an early age. (I recall working with
my friend Tom Maciver at a fish factory in Stornoway where we
met a few. On another occasion, I came across some others while

Acknowledgements

still a schoolboy in the town.) I also encountered a large number while speaking in Tórshavn some time ago – too many to mention here. I have met others since, including the extremely talented Kristina Sørensen Ougaard whom I came across in Jersey at the Inter Island Games a few years ago.

Finally, I want to thank those connected to Saraband, my publisher. These include the wonderfully encouraging Sara Hunt, Rosie Hilton, proofreader Megan Whitlock, and – especially for his work on this book – Craig Hillsley. He has family connections to Denmark, which were extremely valuable. *Tapadh leibh*, as they say in Lochmaddy and Bayhead, I am truly grateful you were there.

Donald S Murray

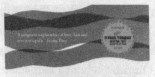

As the Women Lay Dreaming

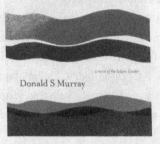

Donald S Murray

In the small hours of January 1st, 1919, the cruellest twist of fate changed at a stroke the lives of an entire community.

A deeply moving novel about passion constrained, coping with loss and a changing world, *As the Women Lay Dreaming* explores how a single event can so dramatically impact communities, individuals and, indeed, our very souls.

WINNER OF THE PAUL TORDAY MEMORIAL PRIZE

"A classic Bildungsroman." *Allan Massie, Scotsman*

"Flawlessly written and cleverly structured … destined to be read for many generations to come." *Graeme Macrae Burnet*

"A book that's big with beauty, poetry and heart … full of memorable images and singing lines of prose." *Sarah Waters*

"A searing, poetic meditation on stoicism and loss." Mariella Frostrup, *Open Book*